GHOULS' NIGHT OUT

THE JUNIPER JUNCTION HOLIDAY MYSTERY SERIES: BOOK FOUR

AMY M. READE

PAU HANA PUBLISHING

BOOKS BY AMY M. READE

THE JUNIPER JUNCTION HOLIDAY MYSTERY SERIES

The Worst Noel

Dead, White, and Blue

Be My Valencrime

Ghouls' Night Out

THE CAPE MAY HISTORICAL MYSTERY COLLECTION

Cape Menace

THE LIBRARIES OF THE WORLD MYSTERY SERIES

Trudy's Diary

Dutch Treat (coming soon!)

THE MALICE SERIES

The House on Candlewick Lane

Highland Peril

Murder in Thistlecross

STANDALONE BOOKS

Secrets of Hallstead House

The Ghosts of Peppernell Manor

House of the Hanging Jade

PRAISE FOR AMY M. READE

The Worst Noel: "This is such a light and fun holiday mystery that I just could not put down! I am hooked and can't wait for the next one! It reminds me of the books they made into movies on the Hallmark movies and mystery channel." From Amazon reviewer

Dead, White, and Blue: "I really enjoyed this book and how the characters evolved. As a mother of two boys, I could relate to the teenage characters in the book and the story line kept me interested in turning the next page. A fun read and would highly recommend!" From Amazon reviewer

Be My Valencrime: "Reade goes beyond these cozy attributes and gives real-life problems to her main character, Lilly, a single mom of teenagers as well as the daughter of an aging mom who is showing signs of dementia. Lilly is, essentially, part of the sandwich generation, taking care of her children and a parent, running a business (a jewelry store), sharing sibling worries with her brother, and working on a new relationship that makes love seem possible despite all of her life's challenges." From Goodreads reviewer

Cape Menace: "It isn't easy to write a novel set in a time period so different from your own. Reade has provided sufficient detail to transport us to another time without engaging in those information dumps so often employed and which take us out of the story rather than getting us involved. If you like historical mysteries, this is one I highly recommend." From Goodreads reviewer

Trudy's Diary: "The narrative of present-day Daisy alternates with nineteenth-century Trudy after she starts reading Trudy's diary, and it kept me reading late into the night. The plot, full of twists and turns, and the memorable characters made for a fascinating read. I love mysteries and loved this one! I highly recommend it." From Amazon reviewer

Secrets of Hallstead House: "Thank you, Amy, for taking me to a new place and allowing me to imagine." From Phyllis H. Moore, reviewer

The Ghosts of Peppernell Manor: "If you're a fan of ... novels by Phyllis A. Whitney, Victoria Holt, and Barbara Michaels, you're going to love *The Ghosts of Peppernell Manor* by Amy M. Reade." From Jane Reads.

House of the Hanging Jade: "House of the Hanging Jade is a suspenseful tale of murder and obsession, all taking place against a beautiful Hawaiian backdrop. Lush descriptions of both the scenery and the food prepared by the protagonist leave you wanting more." From The Book's the Thing

House of the Hanging Jade: "I definitely see more Reade books in my future." From Back Porchervations.

The House on Candlewick Lane: "As in most gothic novels, the actual house on Candlewick Lane is creepy and filled with dark passages and rooms. You feel the evil emanate from the structure and from the people who live there ... I loved the rich descriptions of Edinburgh. You definitely feel like you are walking the streets next to Greer, searching for Ellie. You can feel the rain and the cold, and a couple times, I swear I could smell the scents of the local cuisine." From Colleen Chesebro, reviewer

Highland Peril: "This is escapism at its best, as it is a compelling mystery that whisks readers away to a land as beautiful as it is rich with intrigue." From Cynthia Chow, Kings River Life

Murder in Thistlecross: "Amy Reade's series has a touch of gothic suspense, always fun, and this particular entry has the extra added attraction of the old Clue board game (later a movie that was equally delightful) wherein the various suspects move around the castle and the sleuth has to figure out who killed who, how and where." From Buried Under Books

Pau Hana Publishing

Print ISBN: 978-1-7355221-1-1

Ebook ISBN: 978-1-7355221-0-4

Printed in the United States of America

For Mary Ann and Ken

ACKNOWLEDGMENTS

There are several people who have been instrumental in the production of this book. I would first like to thank my editor, Anneli Purchase. Anneli does great work and has helped me improve my writing, so I'm grateful for her participation in the process. I would also like to thank Holly Bolicki and Patti Linder, both of whom caught errors in the book and whose suggestions made the book a better read.

And, as always, thanks to my husband, John, for his support and encouragement.

CHAPTER 1

It was the week before Halloween and Lilly Carlsen had bedecked her jewelry shop in swaths of burnt orange and black. It was a look she liked to call "rustic elegant" and she achieved it by using yards of tulle, witch silhouettes, art deco pumpkins, and a small wooden black cat named Whiskers. He sat sentry in the front window of the shop, an orange gingham ribbon tied in a bow around his neck.

Though Halloween afforded Juniper Junction merchants a bonanza of marketing opportunities, Lilly didn't love the unofficial holiday that fell every October thirty-first. For one thing, it reminded her that her kids, Tighe and Laurel, were growing up. Now that they were both in college, it had been many years since they had held her hands to go trick-or-treating or begged to wear their Halloween costumes everywhere they went. And second, she didn't like masks. She knew a psychiatrist would have a field day with that, but it didn't matter because she didn't have a psychiatrist.

Maybe I should get one, she thought. *I've got loads of things we could talk about.*

She stood back to survey her decorative handiwork and turned around when she heard a knock on the front window. Her boyfriend of almost two years, Hassan Ashraf, stood on the sidewalk carrying a cardboard tray with three coffees and wearing a scowl.

She hurried to unlock the front door and stood aside to let him in. She leaned over to kiss his cheek and he kissed the side of her head in return. He set the coffees on the display case and gestured toward them for Lilly and Harry, Lilly's assistant, to help themselves.

"What's wrong?" she asked.

He shook his head, his lips a thin line. "It's Michelle. She started in on me early this morning."

Lilly groaned. "What's the matter this time?"

"She said that she can't possibly work in her house while the landscapers are working at my house. The leaf blowers give her migraines, she says." Hassan puffed his cheeks and let out a long sigh.

"You know if you didn't take care of the leaves, she'd be complaining about them. There is no pleasing her."

Harry was watching the exchange and Lilly turned to him. "Michelle Conover is Hassan's next-door neighbor and she's awful."

"Yesterday it was the smell of the wood smoke from the fireplace outdoors. I built a fire out there last night and she came over and said the smell from the smoke was giving her bronchitis." Hassan shook his head. "She's been like that since I moved in, but lately it's gotten much worse."

Lilly smirked. "I wish she would find another place to live."

"She'll live next door to me for the rest of her life." Hassan reached for a cup of coffee and took a long sip. "I've got to get back home because I'm expecting a call from New York, but I wanted to stop by and vent. And bring coffee for you two."

"Thanks for the coffee, Hassan," Harry said. "It's too bad about your neighbor. Isn't she married to the guy who's going to open that tearoom across the street?"

"She was," Hassan said. "Their divorce was final a couple months ago."

"I haven't seen him around too much," Harry said.

"He's probably spending all his time in therapy after being married to her," Hassan replied.

"I hope your day gets better," Lilly said. She checked her watch and moved to the front door to unlock it. Hassan took his coffee and followed her.

"I'm sorry to be such a downer first thing in the morning." He pulled her to him and kissed her forehead.

"And I'm sorry you have to deal with Michelle," she said. "I'll call you tonight. Ignore her if she comes to the door today."

"I will."

Hassan left and Lilly finished setting up the display she had been working on.

"Having a lousy neighbor is the worst," Harry said.

"I know. Michelle makes Mrs. Laforge look like Mother Teresa." Mrs. Laforge, Lilly's neighbor, had been a thorn in Lilly's side for years. She criticized Lilly's parenting skills, complained about Tighe and Laurel, and didn't like Barney, the Carlsens' dog. Those were three big strikes against Mrs. Laforge.

"What is Hassan having done at his house that's making Michelle so mad?"

"He's having a fence put in—you know, because good fences make good neighbors—and a lot of landscaping done. Since he's been spending more and more time in Juniper Junction, he's got the time to oversee things like that."

"Do you know Michelle well?"

Lilly shook her head. "No. I've been around when she's lodged some silly complaint with Hassan, but I barely know her."

"Do you know her husband? Her ex-husband, I mean."

"Ted? I've met him once or twice, but I don't really know him."

"The tearoom looks like it's going to be nice."

"That reminds me, yesterday we got an invitation to the soft opening of the tearoom next week," Lilly said, turning to go back to the office.

"You and me?" Harry called after her.

Lilly disappeared into the office and came back again just a couple seconds later holding a piece of card stock.

"That's what it says here," she said. She glanced at the card and handed it to Harry. "It looks like we're both invited and we can each bring a guest."

He looked at the invitation. "Tranquilitea. Cool name. I'll see if Alice is busy that afternoon. Are you taking Hassan?"

"I don't know. From what I've heard, Ted and Michelle's divorce was pretty acrimonious, so I don't expect Michelle to be there. But if there's even a small chance she'll show up, Hassan won't want to go. The trouble is, I don't know if there's a polite way to find out. I'll ask Noley if she wants to be my plus-one. Or maybe Mom."

"I hope there'll be food at the opening," Harry said.

Lilly laughed. "I'm sure there will be. Ted's going to want to serve food so we can tell prospective customers how good it is."

"I suppose that's the point of the soft opening?"

"Probably. Ted wants the Main Street merchants to help him spread the word about the tearoom."

After work that evening Lilly stopped at her mother's

house on her way home from work. Her mother, Bev, had been on a slow, steady decline from dementia for a couple years, but she was lucky enough to still be living in her own home. She had two nurses who stayed with her. Nikki, the day nurse, opened the door when Lilly knocked.

"Hi, Nikki. How did today go?" Lilly asked.

Nikki shrugged. "Not bad."

"Did you take her shopping today?"

Nikki nodded. "I asked her if she wanted to go shopping, to the park, to visit Mildred next door, everything I could think of. She didn't want to go. That's normal, Lilly. People with this type of dementia often turn inward and don't want to go anywhere."

"I was invited to a tearoom opening tomorrow. Maybe I'll see if she wants to be my plus-one. Do you think she'd be interested?"

Nikki's eyes lit up. "You know, that might just get her out of the house. Let's go ask her."

CHAPTER 2

*T*he two women walked into Bev's living room, where she was sitting in her favorite chair, watching television.

"Hi, Mom," Lilly said.

"Hello, Lilly. How was work today, dear?" Bev asked with a gentle smile.

"Good. We were busy, so that makes the time go fast."

"Is Billy with you?" Bev asked, craning her neck to see around Lilly. Lilly suppressed a sigh. Though Bev called on Lilly whenever she was upset about something or needed help, it was Bill, Lilly's brother and a member of the Juniper Junction police force, whom she often longed to see.

"No, Bill is not with me." Lilly hoped her annoyance wasn't obvious in her voice. "He's probably working."

"That boy works too hard." Bev shook her head sadly.

"'That boy,' as you call him, is perfectly capable of handling his workload. Don't worry about him," Lilly said. She turned so only Nikki could see her and rolled her eyes. Nikki gave Lilly a knowing smile.

Lilly sat down on the sofa facing Bev. "Mom, yesterday I got an invitation to the opening of a new tearoom on Main Street. I get to bring a guest. Would you like to come with me?"

Bev looked up, confusion flickering across her face. "What tearoom? I don't care for tea. I like coffee."

"The name of the shop is Tranquilitea and you don't have to drink any tea or even like it to go to the opening. It's just to have a look at the place and maybe try some of the food they make there."

"I don't know, Lilly. I think I'd rather stay home. But thank you for inviting me. Maybe Beau would like to go with you."

Lilly leaned forward and spoke in a quiet voice. "Mom, Beau and I aren't married anymore, remember?"

"Who is the man that comes here with you sometimes?"

"That's Hassan."

"Hassan who?"

"Hassan Ashraf. His parents bought a house near you last year, remember?"

She nodded slowly, but her eyes belied her confusion. She didn't remember.

"How about this, Mom? How about you decide later about going to the tearoom? I won't invite anyone else and that way if you change your mind, you can still go."

"Okay." Lilly knew Bev wouldn't change her mind.

"Would you like to play cards?" Lilly asked.

"I suppose so," Bev said. Nikki reached into a drawer in the end table next to Bev and pulled out a deck of cards.

"What should we play?" Lilly asked. "Nikki, are you going to play with us?"

"Sure," Nikki said with a smile.

The three of them played poker, Bev's favorite game, for

the next hour, then Lilly stood up to go home. She kissed her mother's cheek and Nikki walked her to the front door.

"I'm sorry she keeps referring to Beau as my husband," Lilly said in a low voice. She had been married to Beau years earlier, but he had left her and Tighe and Laurel when the kids were toddlers. He had returned to Juniper Junction almost two years previously and Lilly was still trying to get used to having him back in their lives. And to make matters more complicated, Beau had been dating Nikki for over a year.

"That's okay," Nikki said. "Don't let it bother you."

"I'll see you tomorrow." Lilly turned and left.

When she got home, she poured herself a bowl of cereal for dinner and called Noley Appleton, her best friend, while she ate.

"What's up?" Noley asked.

"Just eating dinner. Probably not as good as whatever you had for dinner." Noley laughed. She was a nationally renowned chef who was always whipping up something fabulous; Lilly wished her own cooking were half as good as her friend's.

"For your information, I had a peanut butter and grape jelly sandwich for dinner," Noley said.

"Still, I'll bet it was better than the Yummy-Os I'm having."

Noley laughed again. "There's nothing wrong with cereal for dinner. I do it all the time."

"Listen, I have an idea. I'm planning to visit Laurel this weekend at school. I think she's having a hard time. Want to go with me?"

"Sure. I'm always up for a road trip. Isn't Hassan going?"

"He has to be home on Saturday. He's got a call with someone in Afghanistan and he needs to be on a landline. The connection is better than with a cell phone."

"Hasn't Hassan had enough of Afghanistan for a while?"

"You'd think so, wouldn't you? After all he went through on his last trip, being shot at and having to escape tribal violence disguised as a woman in a burka, you'd think he'd never want anything to do with that part of the planet again. But the people he deals with aren't the ones who were shooting at him. He still loves it there and he loves the people. The non-violent ones, anyway."

"I'm sure Laurel would love to see him, but I'll happily take his place this weekend," Noley said. "When do we leave?"

"First thing Saturday morning."

"I'll whip up some treats to take to her," Noley offered.

"She would love that."

"Is this visit a surprise?"

"I'll tell her we're coming. She's been so down that this will give her something to look forward to."

"College is a tough adjustment."

"She's having a much harder time than Tighe did, and to be honest, I expected it to be the other way around."

When Lilly hung up with Noley, she phoned Laurel.

"Hi, Mom." Laurel's voice was flat.

"What's wrong?"

"Just a bad day, I guess."

"Anything in particular? How are your classes going?"

"Okay, I guess."

"What are you doing this weekend?"

"I don't know."

"Would you like some company?"

"Definitely! Who's coming?" Lilly could hear the lift in Laurel's voice and she smiled.

"I thought I'd come up and bring Noley with me. How does that sound?"

"That's great! When will you be here?"

"We'll leave first thing Saturday morning."

"I can't wait!"

By the end of the call, Laurel seemed in better spirits. Lilly hoped that would last. She had figured Laurel would have a hard time adjusting to college life, but she hadn't been prepared for the scope of Laurel's discontent.

CHAPTER 3

The next two days sped by in a flurry of activity at the jewelry shop. Lilly asked Harry if he would mind the shop while she visited Laurel on Saturday, and he was happy to do it.

Lilly woke up at dawn on Saturday morning. She gulped down a cup of coffee and opted to skip breakfast, hoping Noley would supply something homemade and delicious once they were in the car. She had intended to keep Barney indoors all day and hope he could hold his bladder, but she had a feeling Laurel would love to see him even more than her and Noley. So she opened one of the doors to the backseat of the car and Barney launched himself inside, his tail wagging furiously.

They swung into the driveway at Noley's house and Noley waved from her back steps, where she was ready and waiting for them. She picked up a cooler bag and a small paper bag from the back step and hurried to the car.

"Barney!" she exclaimed as she slid into the passenger seat.

The dog slobbered on the side of Noley's face while she laughed and scratched his ears.

"I thought Laurel would like to see him," Lilly explained. "I hope he's not going to bother you."

"Are you kidding? I love Barney," Noley said, turning in her seat to accept more dog kisses. "Are you hungry? I brought breakfast."

"I was hoping you'd say that." Lilly grinned. "I'm starving."

Noley rifled through the smaller bag and held up a muffin. "I've got cranberry-orange muffins and a little container of orange butter."

"I knew it was smart to ask you to go with me today."

Noley spread some butter on a muffin and handed it to Lilly, then fixed one for herself. Barney whined in the backseat, so Noley broke off a piece of muffin and fed it to him.

The trip was a noisy one, as Barney barked at every car they passed.

"Barney, it's a good thing I love you so much." Lilly glanced into the rear-view mirror and grimaced.

"Everyone loves Barney," Noley said.

"Wrong. Hassan's neighbor, Michelle, hates him."

"Why?"

"Because he's the reason Hassan put up the new fence. He wanted to have a place for Barney to play outside when we're over there. The pool has a fence around it, but Hassan wanted Barney to have a closed-in grassy space. And the fence is causing no end of problems for Michelle."

"What kinds of problems?"

"Noise. She works from home and goes nuts when there's any noise in the neighborhood."

"What does she do?"

Lilly shrugged. "Something in finance, but beyond that I

have no idea. She and her ex-husband, Ted, came from Wall Street a few years ago, apparently."

"I feel bad for Hassan. He's so mild-mannered. It must be awful to have a neighbor like that."

"She has the ability to drill right through his mild-mannered-ness and infuriate him."

"Hassan? I don't believe it."

"Maybe you'll be around for it someday. His eyes bulge and he clenches his fists, probably to keep himself from decking her. It's not pretty."

After a while Barney started barking and refused to let up. Lilly laughed. "You're right, Barn. We're here. How didyou know?"

She took a fork in the road that led down a leafy lane. Brick buildings on each side of the car announced their arrival on campus. A few kids milled around, but it was still early in the day. Most students were probably recovering from a late night.

Lilly drove slowly past Laurel's dorm while Barney went wild in the back.

"Do you see her, boy?" she asked.

"There she is!" Noley pointed toward a small group of young women standing in front of the dorm. Lilly smiled when she saw her daughter, whose back was to them. It took a few minutes to find a parking spot, and when they approached the front of the dorm, they found that the group had dispersed, leaving just Laurel standing there. Barney strained against his leash to get to her.

Laurel's eyes widened when she saw Lilly, Noley, and Barney coming, and she set off at a run toward them. She fell to her knees as Barney slammed into her in his excitement. She rubbed his back and head, hugging him to her chest. When she stood up, she was crying.

"I can't believe you brought Barney!" She laughed and a loud hiccup escaped from her throat.

"We thought you might like a visit from him, too." Lilly stepped forward to give her daughter a hug, then Noley followed suit.

"I've missed you!" Lilly hadn't seen Laurel since dropping her off on Incoming Freshmen Day in late August.

"I've missed you, too." Laurel turned and gestured toward the dorm. "Want to see how I've decorated my room?"

"Do you think we can bring Barney inside?" Lilly asked.

Laurel shrugged. "What are they going to do, kick me out? I wish."

Lilly frowned as Noley shot her a sidelong glance. "Let's go in, then. Come on, Barn." She led him to the front door of the dorm, then handed Laurel the leash. "You can be in charge of him."

Laurel grinned and ushered everyone inside. Lilly recalled move-in day, which had been a circus. Hallways teemed with nervous parents and their freshmen, boxes and bundles were strewn about, and uniform-clad resident advisors ran to and fro, consulting clipboards and leading bewildered families to the correct rooms.

Today was much different. The hallways were quiet, with only a few voices audible through closed doors. The small group passed just one young woman as they walked to Laurel's room, and she appeared to be half asleep.

Laurel opened the door and stood aside to let Lilly and Noley in, then she brought Barney into the room with her. Lilly stood looking around at the bright space, admiring the pictures on the walls and the little touches of home that Laurel and her roommate had chosen to display. Barney immediately started sniffing around, clearly intent on finding the source of the funky odor that permeated the room.

Laurel wrinkled her nose. "What you smell is Jasmine's rotting yogurt." She rolled her eyes. Laurel hadn't mentioned Jasmine to Lilly very often, but Lilly had the distinct feeling that Jasmine was not Laurel's favorite person.

After Lilly and Noley had admired the room and Laurel had shown them the rest of the common areas of the dorm, they all headed outside. It was a crisp day and the leaves on the trees all over campus were turning every shade of orange, yellow, and red. Barney was in his element, running through piles of leaves and sniffing all the new smells.

Laurel showed them where her classes were and took them on a tour of the library, which was beautiful.

It wasn't until lunchtime that she dropped her bomb.

CHAPTER 4

They had walked into the quaint town of Rocky Gulch, just off campus, for lunch. They found a table in a small, crowded dive that Laurel swore had great food. The restaurant welcomed dogs, so that was a plus. Noley observed the surroundings through narrowed eyelids.

"Are you sure this place has good food, Laur?"

Laurel smiled. "I promise. I've been here a couple times. It doesn't look like much, but it's delicious. The restaurants are practically the only things I like about Rocky Gulch."

"What do you mean?" asked Lilly.

Laurel shrugged. "I don't know. I just don't like too many things here."

"But you've made some friends. What about them?" Lilly thought back to their phone calls, when Laurel had mentioned meeting and going places with lots of nice people.

Laurel shrugged again. "Yeah, I guess."

Noley slid Lilly a concerned glance before picking up the menu, which was laminated and stained with a few crusty spots. She shuddered.

Lilly noticed and laughed. "You've got to be willing to take chances, Nol. This little restaurant might be the next big thing."

When their server arrived, she started with Noley. Lilly rolled her eyes and Laurel gave her a knowing smile.

"I'll have the open-faced steak sandwich, medium-rare, on Texas toast. And—"

"We cook all the steak to medium," the server said.

Noley pressed her lips together. "Okay, medium. And I'd like to substitute shaved Parmesan for the cheddar cheese. I'd like a green salad instead of the fries. Can I do that?"

The server nodded.

"Good. I'd like oil and vinegar on the side, no onions. Can I get an unsweetened iced tea to drink, please? With a slice of lemon on the side and only a few ice cubes."

The server blinked slowly at Noley before turning to Lilly.

Lilly smiled and inclined her head toward Noley. "That's what she does," she said by way of explanation. She could see Noley scowling out of the corner of her eye. "I'll have a cheeseburger and fries."

Laurel ordered last and they sat back to talk.

"Tell us about your classes, Laurel," Noley said.

"I take the usual. History, math, science, English."

"Are they hard?"

"Not really."

"Do you like them?"

"Not really."

"Why not? Do you like the professors?"

Laurel shrugged and took a sip of her water. "I just don't like the classes or the professors. They're boring."

"I'm sure it takes some adjustment, and once you start the classes in your major, things will get more interesting," Lilly said.

"Yeah, right," Laurel said.

"What's the matter, honey?" Lilly folded her hands on the table in front of her and gave Laurel a concerned look.

"I don't like it here," Laurel said in a small voice.

And then came the bombshell. "I want to quit."

Uh-oh. Lilly had been half-expecting something like this, but she was still dismayed to hear Laurel say it. She tried to hide her disappointment. "Maybe you need to give it some more time," she said. "Going away to college is a big adjustment."

"I know."

"You've made lots of friends," Lilly pointed out. "Have you talked to them? Everyone is in the same boat, so they're going through the same thing."

Laurel shook her head. "Everyone else loves it here. I'm the only one who doesn't. I'm the only one who doesn't like their roommate, too."

"I'm sure you're not the only one," Noley said. "Practically everyone has roommate problems at one time or another. I had a roommate in college who used to do yoga ... naked."

Laurel and Lilly laughed. "For real?" Laurel asked.

Noley nodded. "It was grotesque."

"Well, Jasmine doesn't do naked yoga, but she smells bad and I hate the music she listens to."

"Have you asked her to wear ear buds?" Lilly asked.

"Nah. That seems rude."

"Try asking her. You might be pleasantly surprised."

"Ear buds won't make her smell better."

Their food came a few minutes later and Noley gave her meal an approving glance.

"This doesn't look half bad," she said.

"I told you. It's delicious." Laurel picked up her fork and took a bit of her Greek salad. Then she put her fork down.

"Mom, do you think I could go home with you today and stay for a few days?"

Lilly saw Noley watching her and considered the question for a few moments.

"I'm not sure that's such a good idea. Coming home right now will only make it harder to come back here."

"But I hate it here." Laurel's shoulders drooped.

"I just don't think that's wise, Laur. You need to stay here if you want to adjust to being in school. You can't adjust to college if you're at home."

Laurel closed her eyes. When she opened them, they were wet and shiny. One tear escaped and rolled down her cheek.

Lilly reached out and placed her hand on Laurel's arm. "I'm sorry, honey. I wish there were something I could do. But I think you just need to give it some time. Ask some of your friends if they're having the same troubles. You might be surprised."

Laurel nodded and wiped her face with her napkin. "Okay."

Noley tried to keep the conversation light throughout the rest of the meal, telling Laurel about the goodies she had brought and about some of the funnier mishaps of her career in the food business. By the end of the meal, Laurel was finally smiling and the knot in Lilly's stomach had unclenched a little bit.

After lunch they returned to campus and piled into Lilly's car for a trip to a nearby state park that had some superb hiking trails. Lilly hoped Laurel would cheer up in the great outdoors, especially if she had Barney for company.

The trails were beautiful. Barney was in his element, running ahead, circling back, leaving the trail to chase whatever sounds he heard in the undergrowth, and racing back and forth between Laurel and the next bend in the trail. The leaves were in full color and the air and the view were clear and bright. Laurel seemed to enjoy herself and even laughed aloud at some of Barney's antics.

The time came, though, for them to return to campus and for Lilly and Noley to return to Juniper Junction. They walked Laurel to her dorm room and said their goodbyes after Noley had shown Laurel everything that was in her cooler bag: molasses cookies, chocolate chip cookies, homemade beef jerky, and trail mix. Laurel smiled her thanks, but her lips were trembling.

Lilly wrapped Laurel in a big hug, then held her at arms' length. "You're going to be just fine. No crying. Do you have someone to go to dinner with?"

Laurel nodded, sniffling. "Yeah. Mom, please let me come home. Please?"

Lilly wanted nothing more than to take Laurel home, to make the tears disappear, but she knew it would only be worse for Laurel if she did that.

"Just stay a little longer and see if it gets better. It definitely won't get better if I take you home, but it might get better if you stay here and spend some time with your friends."

Just then there was a knock at the door. "Laurel? You in there? Want to go to dinner?"

Lilly smiled at her daughter, who suddenly looked much younger than her eighteen years. "Who's that?"

"Cassidy. I'll go to dinner with her, I guess." She opened the door and a pretty young woman stood there, wearing a big smile. Laurel swallowed hard and introduced everyone, including Barney. The whole group walked to the front door of the dorm, then Lilly and Noley hugged Laurel one last time and walked toward the parking lot with Barney, whose head drooped. Laurel and Cassidy walked in the opposite direction, toward the dining hall.

The pit in Lilly's stomach was hot and growing. She didn't want to cry in front of Noley, but it was inevitable. She wiped her eyes with her sleeve as they approached the car.

"It's not easy. I think you did the right thing," Noley said quietly.

"I know." Lilly's voice sounded nasal. "It's hard, though. I hate to leave her here when she's not happy."

"Like you said, maybe things will get better with a little bit of time."

"I hope so."

The ride home was quiet. Even Barney seemed to be sad. He curled up on the back seat with his head on his paws and sighed.

CHAPTER 5

*M*onday evening after closing time Lilly was in the shop putting away the jewelry displays. She had just placed the last necklace in the vault when there was a knock at the front window. She peeked out of her office and saw Hassan standing there with a dark look on his face.

She unlocked the door and let him in, then locked it again behind him.

"What's wrong?"

Hassan's nostrils flared. "You will not believe what Michelle has done now."

"What?" Lilly's stomach tightened.

"She came to my door waving a property survey this afternoon. Now she claims I've had my fence built six inches onto her property and she's demanding that I take it down!"

"You're kidding. You had your property surveyed before having it installed, right? They couldn't have made a mistake."

"I called them and they're coming by tomorrow to re-check their measurements. They'll have to pay to have the fence taken down and moved if they were in the wrong. I can't believe this." He ran a hand across his face.

"What did you tell Michelle?"

He looked sheepish. "I lost my cool, Lilly. I yelled at her, I told her she's the neighborhood pariah, I told her never to set foot on my property again or I'll have her arrested for trespassing. You name it, I said it."

Lilly gave Hassan a sympathetic smile and placed her hand on his cheek. "She deserved it. It's a wonder no one has told her off before now. She's done nothing but badger you since you came back from Afghanistan and started the work on the house and yard."

"I know. But I shouldn't have lost my temper like that. She's got me so worked up I can't concentrate. Every time someone comes to the door I worry that I'm going to have another run-in with her."

"Would dinner at my house make you feel any better?"

"Much. The later I go back to my own house, the less likely I'll see her."

"Meet me at home and I'll see what I've got in the fridge. And you can't stop going home, you know. You can't let her get to you."

"Easy for you to say. She's not your neighbor."

"But I have Mrs. Laforge, remember? She's no peach."

"She's a lovable curmudgeon, though. There's nothing lovable about Michelle."

"Mrs. Laforge, lovable?"

"I know, I know. But what about the time she didn't press charges against Tighe and his friend? What about the time she brought Barney home in a blizzard? She's got a good heart underneath her gruffness. Michelle has a heart like a piece of coal."

"Okay, you win. Let's go. The sooner you get to my house,

the sooner you can have a glass of wine. Did you park out front? I'll be a minute behind you."

She unlocked the front door, let Hassan out, locked it again, and left through the back of the shop. She got in her own car, which she always parked in the alley, and pulled around to Main Street, where she hit her brakes suddenly.

There had been an accident at the intersection closest to Juniper Junction Jewels. Even in the dark with the only light coming from streetlamps, Lilly could see that one car had T-boned another in the middle of the intersection. One car's front fender was smashed, but the second car had fared much worse. Its entire middle section was crumpled. Lilly pulled over to the curb and jumped out of her car. She ran to the intersection, where other people were already starting to gather.

"Someone call 9-1-1," she shouted. Two people, both on their phones, gave her a thumbs-up. Several others had pulled out their phones and were recording the incident. Lilly glared at them and hurried over to where the two drivers were emerging from their vehicles.

Lilly stopped short and gasped.

Hassan was stepping gingerly out of the car with the smashed fender, trying to avoid stepping on the glass that was scattered on the pavement.

She recovered herself quickly. "Hassan! Are you all right? What happened?" She rushed over to him. He rubbed his forehead with his hand, then stared at his palm.

"Are you hurt?" she asked. Hassan just stared at her with a dazed look, nodding ever so slightly. An older man was approaching them.

"Is he all right?" the man asked.

"I don't know," Lilly said. "Can you take him over to the curb while I see about the other driver?" The man nodded.

Lilly took Hassan's elbow gently and steered him toward the man, who then put his hand on Hassan's upper arm and guided him to the curb. "Go with him, Hassan. I'll be right back."

Lilly wheeled around to face the T-boned car, where the other driver was trying unsuccessfully to push the driver's side door open. The impact must have jammed it shut.

Lilly ran around to the passenger side, where she yanked the door open and bent down to look inside.

Ivy Leachman, owner of the pottery painting studio on Main Street, was frowning as she pushed her weight against the driver's side door.

"Ivy, I think the door is jammed. Are you hurt? Can you get out through the passenger side?"

"I think so. I don't know what happened. I was just driving and BAM! I got hit. I didn't even see the other car."

"Let's get you out of there if you can manage it. Come on, I'll help."

Though Ivy was tall, she was also thin and wiry, so she was able to swing her legs over the car's center console and scooch into the passenger seat. From there she gripped Lilly's outstretched hand and Lilly was able to pull her carefully from the car. Ivy stood next to Lilly and surveyed the scene before saying anything.

"Are the police on their way?" she asked.

Lilly glanced at the people who had been talking on their phones earlier. "Yes. They should be here any minute. Can you walk to the curb?" She took Ivy by the elbow, as she had done with Hassan, and walked with her toward the spot where Hassan was sitting, his head in his hands.

"Is that the person who hit me?" Ivy asked.

"Yes."

"I don't want to be anywhere near him. Stupid fool was probably texting and driving."

Lilly said nothing, but turned around and steered Ivy toward the curb on the other side of the street.

A moment later she heard the first sirens, and seconds later a police car pulled into view. The officer stopped the car in the intersection behind Hassan's car and jumped out. The man who had accompanied Hassan to the curb called the officer over and he reached Hassan's side just as two ambulances arrived on the scene. The officer crouched next to Hassan and said something, then he straightened up and looked around. Lilly waved her arm so he would see her.

He came over to where Lilly was standing next to Ivy.

"Is this one of the drivers?" the officer asked.

Lilly nodded. "Her name is Ivy Leachman."

"I can talk to him myself," Ivy said.

"All right. I'll be over there." Lilly inclined her head toward Hassan. The older man was still standing next to him and she jogged over to them.

"How are you doing?" she asked Hassan.

"Not good."

"Are you hurt?"

"I don't know. My head hurts, but I don't think I hit it hard."

"Do you know him?" the man asked, gesturing toward Hassan.

"Yes."

"Can I leave him with you, then?" Lilly nodded and thanked the man, and he was on his way.

Lilly sat down next to Hassan and put her hand on his back. "What happened?" she asked in a low voice.

"I wasn't paying attention. Simple as that. I've got a lot on my mind. I'm not making excuses, just explaining what happened. I don't even remember seeing the stoplight before I entered the intersection."

"Is it possible she's the one who ran the red light?"

"No. I saw the red light the instant I hit her. It was all my fault, Lilly."

"What did you say to the police officer?"

"I told him my name, that's all. I told him I'm okay and that he should check the other driver first."

"The other driver is Ivy Leachman."

Hassan groaned. "Oh, no. Not her."

"I'm afraid so."

CHAPTER 6

A paramedic joined them and spent several minutes asking Hassan questions and examining him, then another police officer arrived to take more information from Hassan. Lilly stood several feet away and watched, noticing that another paramedic was examining Ivy. Before long, the other paramedic stood up and spoke to someone standing nearby, then headed in Lilly's direction.

"We need to take her to get checked out," he said to the paramedic tending to Hassan.

"All right." The paramedic spoke to Hassan. "It looks like you've got a big bump on your head. Could be a concussion, but I'm not sure. We can take you over to the hospital if you'd like, or you can have someone drive you home and you can go to your own doctor tomorrow."

"I'd like to go home."

"Okay, if you're sure. If you start feeling dizzy or sick to your stomach, go on over to the ER and they'll check you out." The paramedic looked up at Lilly "Can you drive him home?"

"Sure."

"What about my car?" Hassan asked.

"I can drive you home in your car if it's drivable, then No-ley or Bill can pick me up and bring me back here so I can get my car," Lilly said.

"Thank you."

The paramedic accompanied his partner over to Ivy, who was trying to stand up. After a brief consultation, the two paramedics headed to the ambulance. Lilly assumed they were retrieving a stretcher. She turned to Hassan. "Can you stand up?"

Hassan nodded and pushed himself up gingerly. Lilly grasped his arm lightly and helped him hobble to his car. She eased him into the passenger seat and was walking around to the driver's side when a shout got her attention. She glanced in the direction of the voice and saw Ivy struggling to stand up, a scowl on her face. She was yelling at Lilly.

"Hassan is the one who hit me?"

Lilly glanced around and saw that all eyes in the small crowd had turned toward her. Leave it to Ivy to make a bigger scene than it already was.

"I'm taking him home, Ivy," she called back.

"But he's the one who hit me?" Ivy had finally gotten to her feet and was swaying a bit. A person standing just a few feet away hurried to steady her.

"I've got to go, Ivy. I'll talk to you tomorrow."

"Wait!" Ivy cried. Lilly quickly slid behind the wheel, shut the door, and started the car.

"She's already at it?" Hassan asked weakly.

"Yeah. Don't worry. I'll talk to her." Ivy had taken over as president of the Juniper Junction Chamber of Commerce after Lilly's tenure had ended, and they had a relationship that could best be described as inharmonious. Ivy had often taken sides against Lilly whenever there was a tiff among the Main Street merchants, and Lilly hadn't forgotten one public and particularly unpleasant encounter with Ivy almost two years previously.

Hassan's car ran sufficiently well even with the smashed front end. By the time they reached his house his body had started to stiffen up from the accident and he had a hard time swinging his legs out of the car. Lilly helped him out and up the front steps of the house.

"Is that Hassan?" a querulous voice asked as they reached the front door.

"You have got to be kidding me," Hassan muttered.

Lilly spun around to see Hassan's neighbor, Michelle, coming up the driveway.

"I've been waiting for him to come home." Michelle waved a sheet of paper in the air.

"Not now, Michelle. He's had an accident," Lilly said. She fished in her purse for Hassan's house key and couldn't get her hands on it quickly enough. Hassan pulled his key out of his jacket pocket and handed it to her.

"What kind of accident?"

"A car accident. Now, if you'll excuse us…."

"Not so fast. You don't think I'm going to let him off the hook over his encroachment onto my property just because he has a boo-boo, do you?" Michelle had reached the bottom of the front steps and the light from the porch lamp gave her face an evil look despite her otherwise good looks. She tossed her raven tresses. She had a perfect figure and alabaster skin, but she was as ugly on the inside as she was pretty on the outside.

Hassan leaned his forehead against the door jamb and held his hand out to Lilly. She handed the house key back to him, then turned to face Michelle.

"Michelle, I said 'not now.' Perhaps you didn't hear me. Go home and bother him some other time."

"You can be sure I will!" Michelle shouted. "Don't think I'm going to forget this!" She turned on her heel and stalked across Hassan's front lawn.

Hassan had pushed the door open and stood in the foyer, waiting for Lilly. She turned to him and practically growled. "I can't stand her."

"My life would be so much easier if she dropped dead."

Lilly fussed over Hassan, making sure he had at least a little bit of food and an ice pack for his head. Then she helped him to bed.

"Thanks for everything, love," Hassan told her as he climbed under the comforter. "I'd be lost without you."

Lilly smiled and kissed his forehead. "Are you sure I can't take you to the emergency room, or at least urgent care? I'm worried that you might have a concussion."

"I'm not worried about it. If I feel worse, I'll go to the doctor, I promise."

"If you say so." Lilly wasn't convinced, but she sat down in an armchair in the corner of his bedroom to wait for him to fall asleep. She wanted to be sure he was okay before she left to get her car and go home.

When he was fast asleep and hadn't moved in over an hour, she checked on him one last time and crept downstairs. She texted Bill to let him know she was ready to be picked up. Bill, having heard about the accident earlier at the station, had texted to see if Hassan was all right. Lilly had asked him then if he minded picking her up and taking her back to her car.

When Bill arrived, Lilly locked the door behind her and slid into the police cruiser.

"How's he doing?" Bill asked.

"He got a bump on the head and he's sore from the sudden

hit. He'll probably hurt even more tomorrow, but by the next day he should be all right."

"I hear Ivy Leachman was in rare form when you left in Hassan's car."

"She was just being Ivy. You know, loud, obnoxious, rude. I'm sure I'll hear from her before long. She must have been furious that I shut the car door and drove off while she was shouting at me."

"She'll cool down."

"Don't be so sure. She's not one to let anything go." It occurred to Lilly how alike Michelle and Ivy were: stubborn, ill-mannered, and tenacious. She yawned. "Thanks for picking me up. I'm going to bed as soon as I get home. Have you talked to Mom today?"

"Only for a minute. She wasn't having a good day. She kept asking me why Noley and I are getting a divorce. I tried reminding her that we're not even married yet, but she didn't understand. Or maybe she wasn't listening. I talked to Nikki for a sec and she said that Mom tripped going up the stairs this afternoon. Nikki was right behind her, so she was able to grab Mom and keep her from hurting herself."

"Thank God we found Nikki. And thank God Meredith is staying with her at night. I worry about Mom almost constantly." Bev had started out with just a daytime nurse, but it had quickly become apparent that a night nurse would be good for her. Lilly and Bill had hired Meredith and were very happy with her.

"So do I. But having two nurses seems to be working out fine, so that's a relief. I don't even want to think about putting Mom in a home."

Lilly shuddered. "Don't jinx her. Hopefully with two nurses she'll never have to move out of her house."

Bill pulled up to the curb where Lilly's car was parked and

she got out, thanking him again for the ride. When she got home she found she was too tired to eat, and her mood was getting more melancholy by the minute. Between Hassan's troubles and Bev's troubles and Laurel's troubles, life was getting more stressful every day.

CHAPTER 7

The next morning Lilly and Harry were both waiting on customers when the bell jingled over the door. Lilly glanced up to see who had come in, turned back to her customer, then did a double take as Ivy, wearing a neck brace and sporting an orthopedic cast, shuffled up to the counter. Lilly excused herself from her customer and addressed Ivy.

"I'll be right with you, Ivy."

"Hmph."

Lilly continued talking to her customer while Ivy hemmed and hawed just a few feet away. The customer kept glancing at Ivy out of the corner of his eye.

"Ivy, would you mind standing over there?" Lilly asked, pointing to another display case. She could only imagine how angry and embarrassed she would be if the customer up and left because Ivy was making him uncomfortable.

What was Ivy there for, anyway? Lilly doubted she was actually shopping for a piece of jewelry.

The answer came soon enough, when Harry's customer left the shop and Harry offered to help Ivy.

"Thank you, but I will wait for Ms. Carlsen. She and I need to have a few words."

Lilly gave her customer a bright smile and pretended not to have heard Ivy. The man took several minutes selecting a watch for his wife. Lilly hoped her increasing anxiety didn't show, but she knew she wasn't fooling anyone when the man paid for the watch and leaned close to Lilly.

"I took my time hoping your friend over there would leave you alone. Sorry it didn't work," he whispered.

Lilly grinned at him and nodded her thanks. It was nice of him, but he couldn't have known that Ivy would stand there until the end of time if necessary.

The man left and Lilly turned to Ivy.

"How can I help you, Ivy?" She tried to sound professional.

"I want to talk to you about that boyfriend of yours. He's a menace to society."

"Would you care to explain that?"

"I mean, I'm just coming home from spending the night in the emergency room, as you can see, and I've had a lot of time to think about the accident while I was waiting to find out how badly I had been injured."

Lilly looked at her and blinked, saying nothing.

"And I've been badly injured." Ivy pointed to her neck brace and winced.

Obviously your mouth isn't injured, Lilly thought. Aloud she said, "I can see that you have a neck brace, yes."

"Hassan did this to me!"

"Accidents happen, Ivy. He certainly didn't mean for it to happen."

"There I was, driving along, minding my own business, when BAM! He comes out of nowhere and hits me. I'm lucky to be alive. The doctor implied as much."

"I don't know what you want me to do about it, Ivy. I

didn't witness the accident and I am not Hassan's keeper. Coming in here to complain about him isn't going to get you very far."

"You give him a message for me. Tell him his reckless behavior is going to land him in real trouble."

"Whatever you say, Ivy. Now if you'll excuse me, I have work to do."

Ivy glared at her for a moment, then turned on her good heel and hobbled out the door, looking over her shoulder and scowling at Lilly.

"She's a real piece of work," Harry said after the door had closed. "I didn't mean to eavesdrop, but she was kind of loud and it was impossible not to hear her."

"She ought to be ashamed of herself, coming in here like that." Lilly stopped, thought for a moment, and chuckled. "I sound just like my mother."

Harry grinned. "It's too bad she's the one Hassan hit."

"It sure is. I hope he calls soon. I left a note for him to call me when he wakes up."

As if on cue, Lilly's phone rang. She checked the caller ID —Hassan.

"How are you feeling?" she asked in greeting.

"Pretty lousy."

"What hurts?"

"Everything, but mostly my head and my shoulder."

"You should probably go see your doctor this morning. Are you going to call for an appointment?"

"I guess so. I had another look at the car now that it's light outside, and there's more damage there than I thought. The fender is dented pretty good, plus a headlight is out. I did a quick search online and there could be hidden damage, too. I'm going to have to take it in and have it looked at by a mechanic."

"Let's worry about your head and your shoulder first, shall we?"

"All right. I'll see if the doctor can fit me in today. Would you be able to give me a ride if I can get an appointment?"

"Sure. I'll have Harry watch the shop and I'll come get you whenever you need me to."

Hassan called back just a few minutes later with an appointment time just after lunch. At the appointed hour Lilly picked up lunch for him at Armand's bistro and drove to his house, then over to the doctor's office.

The doctor diagnosed Hassan with a sprained shoulder, a probable broken rib, and a nasty bump on the noggin. She advised Hassan to rest, though there wasn't much she could do to treat his specific injuries. As she said, Hassan would just have to wait to get better. She did prescribe some mild painkillers, so after the appointment Lilly drove Hassan to the drugstore to pick up his meds.

While Hassan sat in a hard plastic chair waiting for the pharmacist to finish preparing his prescriptions, Lilly did some quick shopping. She passed a display of Halloween candy and returned to Hassan.

"Do you have Halloween candy to pass out?" she asked. "I can pick up some for you if you don't."

"I forgot all about candy. Yeah, would you get some for me? I heard that about a million kids show up every year." This would be Hassan's first Halloween in Juniper Junction, since he had been out of town the previous year.

Lilly loaded up on bags of candy for him and grabbed a few for her house, too. Hassan lived in a fancy-schmancy neighborhood, so kids went to his cul-de-sac thinking they would hit the mother lode of good candy. Lilly's neighborhood was slightly more modest, so she never got more than about fifty kids on an average Halloween.

"Do you think that'll be enough?" Hassan asked, nodding toward her bags of candy. He was holding a small bag with his meds in it.

"Probably. You'll just have to limit the kids to one piece each."

"I heard something about a block party, too."

"That sounds like fun, if you're up to it."

Hassan nodded, wincing. Lilly took the bag from his hand and helped him to the car.

CHAPTER 8

*B*ack at his house, she made sure he took the first dose of each medicine and got him into bed. Then she returned to the shop. Harry looked up from a watch he was examining when she came in.

"You missed some excitement down the block at the new tearoom."

"What happened?" Lilly set her coat down on a stool behind the counter and went to the window at the front of the store to glance across the street. She grinned when she looked down at Whiskers.

"The police were over there."

"Really? Why?"

"I don't know, but it must have been something kind of big. One officer was standing by the door to prevent anyone from coming in or going out and another officer was talking to the owner out on the sidewalk."

"Hmm. There couldn't have been too many people in the shop, since it's not even officially open yet. I wonder what went on."

They didn't have to wait long for an answer. About an hour later, Ted Conover, the owner of the new tearoom, came into the jewelry shop.

"I just came over to apologize for any drama I caused this afternoon," he said. Ted was of medium build, handsome, with blue eyes.

"Oh, please don't mention it, Ted," Lilly said.

"What happened, if you don't mind me asking?" Harry asked.

"Just a disturbance with a person in the shop," Ted said, looking out the window toward the tearoom. Lilly followed his gaze, but didn't see anything. She wondered what the disturbance had been and who the person in the shop was. It didn't seem that Ted felt like sharing any details.

"Well, things happen. I've had to call the police to my shop, too," Lilly said. "That's what the police are there for."

"I guess you're right. Well, I need to be getting back to the tearoom. I just wanted to apologize to some of my neighbors. Say, are you two coming to the soft opening?"

"We're both planning on it." Lilly gestured toward Harry. "Do you think you'll be ready?"

"I think so." Ted held up both hands, fingers crossed.

"We're looking forward to it," Harry said.

Ted waved and left the shop.

"I wonder what went on over there. He sure didn't want to talk about it," Harry said.

"I can ask Bill if you're that interested."

"Nah. I'm not that interested."

Lilly stopped to see Bev after work that evening. Nikki opened the door for her, then went back to preparing a snack for Bev, who was watching television. Lilly sat down on the sofa.

"What did you do today, Mom?"

"Let's see. Nikki and I were going to go to the park, but it looked like rain, so we stayed home." Lilly gave her a confused look. It had been a beautiful day.

"Don't you believe me?" There was a challenge in Bev's voice.

"I was just thinking it was a beautiful day."

"Well, it looked like rain here. Maybe there were no clouds over by your shop."

"What did you have for dinner?" Lilly asked. She wanted to steer the conversation away from the rain.

"Hotdogs." Lilly glanced at Nikki, who mouthed the word *fish*.

"Want to play cards for a while?"

"Okay. Poker."

Lilly grinned and took up the deck of cards from the coffee table. "Nikki, are you going to join us?"

"Sure. Here you go, Bev." Nikki handed Bev a plate with sliced banana and a scoop of peanut butter.

Bev ignored her. "I'll deal, Lilly." Lilly handed the cards to her mom and waited for her to deal. Before Bev could shuffle the deck, there was a knock at the door. Nikki gave Lilly a sheepish look.

"I forgot to mention that I asked Beau to come over until Meredith gets here. I hope you don't mind. Your mom said it's okay."

"Of course it's okay," Bev piped up.

And why wouldn't I want to spend a relaxing evening with Beau? Lilly forced herself to smile. "I don't mind at all."

"Thanks. You're a gem."

Bev shuffled the cards while Nikki answered the door and Beau took off his coat.

"Hi, Lilly."

"Hi. How've you been?" Lilly and Beau spoke occasionally

because they were sharing the kids' college costs, but they didn't see each other or chat socially very often.

"Good. Work's been busy."

Lilly nodded, wishing her mother would hurry up and deal the cards.

"Beau, are you going to play poker with us?" Bev asked.

"You know it, Bevvy." *Bevvy? Please, God, let me not gag.* Beau had the grace to look embarrassed. He glanced at Lilly. "Your mom said I could call her that."

Lilly shrugged. "Fine with me. Call her whatever she wants." She cringed, knowing she sounded like a shrew.

Bev fixed Lilly with a hard stare. "You should be nicer to Beau."

"Mom, deal the cards, please. Beau, you can sit here next to Nikki." Lilly stood up and dragged a rocking chair next to her mother while Beau sat down in the spot she vacated.

Over the next forty minutes, Lilly lost fifteen cents. Nikki and Beau each lost ten cents. Bev was the big winner of the night. Lilly finally sat back in the rocking chair and yawned. "Mom, you're good. Maybe a rematch later this week?"

"You know where to find me," Bev said.

"Lilly, before you leave I'd like to talk to you about something," Beau said.

Bev's head snapped up. "What's wrong, Beau?"

"Nothing's wrong, Bevvy. I just have a quick question for Lil, that's all." *What is it now?*

Lilly leaned down to kiss her mother goodnight and then joined Beau in the foyer.

"What's up?" she asked.

"I talked to Laurel earlier today. She was telling me how much she hates school."

"Noley and I went to see her over the weekend and she was a little weepy. I don't know if she's homesick or having a hard time with her classes or what. She seems to have friends, so I don't think that's it. She and her roommate don't see eye to eye on things, so maybe that's getting to her."

"Do you think she should come home? That's what she wants."

"I think she needs to try it out for a little longer before she gives up. It's a hard adjustment, being away from home for the first time."

"If you really think that's the right thing to do, then I'll back you up. I hate to hear her so upset, though."

"I do, too. But I'd hate to see her regret the decision to come back to Juniper Junction, too."

"Yeah."

Lilly's next stop was Hassan's house to check on him.

CHAPTER 9

*H*e was sitting on the sofa in the living room, watching the news. She sat next to him and he snuggled next to her, putting his good arm around her shoulder.

"How are you feeling?" she asked.

"Better now that you're here."

She smiled. "How about your shoulder?"

"It hurts. Are you still planning to come over here tomorrow night for trick-or-treat?"

"Yes."

"Good. Maybe you wouldn't mind handing out some of the candy? I'm just thinking that if I can rest my shoulder for another day or two and not have to worry about opening the door and handing out candy two thousand times, it might help it heal faster."

"Of course I'll do that. I'll just put a big bowl of candy on my front steps and leave a note telling kids to help themselves to a piece."

"You sure you don't mind leaving your house unattended?"

"Not at all. I'll have to decide what to do with Barney, though."

"Bring him here."

"Well, the doorbell is going to ring so many times over here that he'll go mad. It won't ring at all at my house if I leave candy on the front steps, but he'll still go nuts over all the people coming and going on my block and I won't be there to calm him down. It's a lose-lose."

"Well, you know he's welcome to come here to be with you. That might make him a little less crazy."

"I'll decide tomorrow. Let me make you something for dinner before I go home, then you should get some sleep."

Lilly made sandwiches for the two of them and they ate in the living room. She told him all about the incident at the tearoom and the visit from Ted Conover.

"I'll bet his miserable ex-wife had something to do with the police being called," Hassan said. "It's taken all my willpower not to call them on her myself."

"I shouldn't have mentioned it. I don't want you even thinking about Michelle right now. You need to relax." She changed the channel and they watched one of their favorite shows while they ate.

When it was time for Lilly to leave she made Hassan promise to call her if he needed anything in the night and kissed him goodbye. Just being together, watching TV and not talking about Michelle, had helped him to relax. It was good to see him calm, even if he was in pain, and she decided against telling him about Ivy's visit to the jewelry shop, at least for the time being.

Halloween dawned sunny, brisk, and cool. Lilly was all smiles as she drove to work, past the bus stops where kids were wearing their Halloween costumes. She hardly saw any masks, probably thanks to school policies that prevented kids from wearing them, so she was thankful for that. She had fond memories of the Halloween parades Laurel and Tighe had had at school when they were little.

When she got to work she had to laugh when she saw Harry, dressed as a bunch of purple grapes, putting out the jewelry displays for the day. He wore a purple turtleneck, purple leggings, and was adorned from head to toe with big purple balloons that he had somehow attached to his clothes.

"What do you think?" He spun in a slow circle so she could see his costume.

"I love it!" She snapped a couple pictures of him so she could post it to the shop's social media pages before opening for the day. She suddenly wished she liked Halloween more so she would have felt comfortable wearing a costume, too.

Once the photos went up on social media, there were extra visitors to the shop, but mostly they were other people from the stores on Main Street who had come to show off their own costumes. Lilly took lots of pictures that day and posted all of them, figuring all the Main Street merchants could benefit from a little marketing exposure.

The sun was setting when Lilly and Harry closed the shop that night. Lilly had to hurry home to put out her candy and head over to Hassan's house. As she drove, she noticed that some younger families were already out trick-or-treating. Most kids and families tended to wait for darkness, but the little ones usually went out early. Lilly poured three big bags of candy into a huge plastic bowl and set it out on the front steps with a note that read "Have a SPOOKTACULAR Halloween! Help yourself to one or two pieces of candy!"

By the time she had placed the bowl on the steps, she noticed the first couple families with little kids heading down her block. She stood at the front window, watching as they approached, and it wasn't long before Barney started barking wildly at the prospect of having strangers near the front of the house.

"That does it, Barney. You're coming with me tonight." Barney looked up at her, cocked an ear, and wagged his tail. Lilly laughed. "That's what you were hoping for, isn't it?" She clipped on his leash and took him out to the car.

Barney didn't like going in the car if he suspected the vet waited for him at the end of the trip, but tonight he seemed excited. He panted the entire way to Hassan's house, slobbering on Lilly's seatbelt and leaping from one side of the backseat to the other, watching the kids start to fill the sidewalks.

When they got to Hassan's neighborhood there were several long folding tables set up at the entrance to the cul-de-sac. Lilly slowed the car and rolled down the window and Barney shoved his head through the opening, trying to lick the person who walked over to the car. It was Larry, one of Hassan's neighbors. He lived on the other side of Michelle.

"Hi, Larry. Is this for the block party?"

"Yeah. Are you and Hassan coming? I made chili."

"We might come."

"Come on over once trick-or-treat is done. This set-up is just an excuse for people on the block to get together. We do it every Halloween."

"All right. Maybe Hassan and I will be down later."

Larry gave her a little salute and she drove slowly down to the end of the cul-de-sac and parked in Hassan's driveway. There were already hordes of kids milling around.

Hassan was waiting for her in the foyer. "I've already used up three bags of candy."

Lilly laughed. "You're in the high-rent district. What did you expect? Go sit down and rest your arm. I'm in charge here now." Hassan grinned and did as instructed.

The doorbell rang and Lilly opened it. A little girl dressed as a fairy stood outside with her parents standing about twenty feet behind her.

"What a beautiful fairy!" Lilly exclaimed. "Would you like some candy?"

The fairy nodded shyly. Lilly put two small candy bars into the girl's plastic pumpkin and waved to her parents. A huge group of kids were coming up the walk as the fairy turned around and left, so Lilly waited for them to come up to the door, then distributed candy to everyone. The groups kept coming and coming until Hassan's candy supply was almost gone. It was getting late when she ripped open the last bag. She closed the door as another small gaggle of trick-or-treaters left.

"I ran into Larry at the end of the block," she said to Hassan. "There's chili down there if we want to hit the block party after trick-or-treating is over."

"Sounds good. Should we take something?"

"Probably. I'll whip something up if you can handle the kids again for a little while. Trick-or-treat hours are almost over, so it shouldn't be too hard on your shoulder."

Hassan took up his spot by the door and Lilly headed toward the kitchen. She had let Barney into the backyard and was opening the refrigerator door when she heard Hassan open the door to more trick-or-treaters.

Just a few seconds later, she heard loud voices coming from the front hall. "Get the hell out!" It was Hassan yelling. She left the fridge open and ran toward the front door, where she was sure Michelle had appeared to harass him.

But she was unprepared for the sight that met her eyes.

CHAPTER 10

*T*wo young men had pushed their way into the foyer, laughing. Hassan had backed into the middle of the space. His eyes were flashing, his nostrils flaring. The young men wore black and white keffiyehs around their heads and necks so only their eyes were showing. They were dressed in military-style fatigues and carried what looked scarily like real machine guns.

Lilly stopped short when she saw them. What scared her most were the keffiyehs, worn like masks, shielding the faces of the two men. She opened her mouth, but nothing came out at first.

Hassan saw her and held out his good arm. "Go back to the kitchen, Lilly. I'll take care of this." When she didn't move, he said again, louder, "Go back into the kitchen, Lilly."

She finally found her voice. "I'm not going anywhere." She directed her fiery gaze at the two people standing near Hassan. "You heard him. Get out of here before I call the police. Who do you think you are?"

The shorter of the two sneered and spoke to Hassan in a

low, deadly voice. "Get out of here and go back where you came from." He and his friend took their machine guns and pretended to spray bullets around the foyer, making *ch-ch-ch* noises with their tongues. Then they dashed out the door, which had been left ajar when they pushed past Hassan into the house.

Hassan slammed the door behind them and stood with his back against it. His eyes were wide and he exhaled slowly, his breath quivering.

"Are you all right?" Lilly asked. She reached across him to lock the door and shut off the porch light so trick-or-treaters would think the house was out of candy.

Hassan nodded. "I can't believe that just happened."

"I can't either. I'm calling Bill." Lilly whipped her cell phone out of her back pocket and dialed her brother.

"Bill? I'm at Hassan's house. Two guys just came to the door and threatened us. They were dressed up like terrorists." She could hear Barney barking in the backyard.

"Do you know who they were?" Bill asked. His voice was tense.

"No. I couldn't even tell how old they were."

"I'll be right over."

Lilly hung up the phone and turned to Hassan. "He'll be here soon. Let me bring Barney inside." She hurried through the kitchen and opened the door to let Barney in, being sure to lock the door again. From the wall in the kitchen she turned on the backyard lights and peered into the dark reaches behind the swimming pool. Seeing nothing, she breathed a sigh of relief and turned the lights off.

A moment later she returned to Hassan, who was by then sitting in the living room. Barney had accompanied her and was whining, probably from the strange scents in the foyer.

"Do you have any idea who those guys were?" Lilly sat down next to Hassan and placed her hand on his knee.

He shook his head, his thoughts clearly far away. Lilly was silent for a few minutes. Barney sat on the floor, whimpering, until Hassan patted the sofa next to him and Barney jumped up.

"Who would do something like that?" he finally said. Lilly's heart constricted at the pain she saw in his eyes.

"I don't know. Someone stupid. Maybe Bill will be able to tell us something."

"Like what? Unless he actually sees them, he won't know anything."

Lilly didn't say anything. She was just trying to be optimistic, but Hassan was right. She stood up and wandered to the front door and peered through the sidelight window into the darkened front yard. There was no movement, no one in sight, not even trick-or-treaters.

Lilly returned to the living room, where Hassan was sitting with his head in his hands.

"I don't know that I should stay in Juniper Junction, Lilly."

She sat down next to him. "Are you kidding? You'd think of moving out of Juniper Junction because of a couple jerks who don't have a shred of decency?"

"You weren't the one they were talking to, Lilly." Hassan's eyes were angry, his voice harsh.

Lilly was taken aback. She lowered her eyes and spoke quietly. "I'm sorry, Hassan. You're right."

He was quiet for a minute. "No, I'm sorry. I didn't mean to snap at you. It's just that, this is the second time I've been singled out because of what I look like. Remember the people in the bar last Valentine's Day?"

"I'll never forget. But don't let these guys scare you away.

They don't know what they're doing or talking about. People can go to jail for stuff like that, Hassan."

"I know. But they'll get away with it. We have no idea who they were and they're obviously gone by now. They would be stupid to stick around."

"They might. They're obviously pretty dumb."

"No one is *that* dumb."

The doorbell rang, startling Hassan. He stood up, but Lilly gestured for him to sit back down. "I'll get it. It's probably Bill."

Indeed, Bill was waiting on the porch, his back to the front door. He turned around when Lilly opened the door.

"I'll take a look in the backyard, but there's no one out here," he said. He turned on the backyard light and went outside. He came back in a couple minutes later and shook his head. "Nobody out there," he said. He sat down across from Hassan in the living room.

"Is there anything you can do?" Lilly asked.

"Tell me exactly what happened." Bill addressed himself to Hassan. "From the time you opened the front door."

Lilly leaned forward. She hadn't heard the story, either.

"There was a knock at the door and I opened it. Those two guys stood there under the lamp and they started laughing. The bigger one shoved my chest and pushed me back into the foyer. I yelled at him to get out, and he and the other kid, the shorter one, just walked right in. He's the one who did the talking. He told me to get out and go back where I came from. I assume he didn't realize I'm from Minnesota, and England before that." Hassan looked down at the sling on his arm. "I couldn't do much with this bad arm. Lilly came in and I'm embarrassed to say that she's the one who got them out of here, but not before they pretended to spray us and the house with bullets. I think I was just too shocked to do anything but stand there."

"And what were they wearing?"

"They had on keffiyehs, those black and white checked scarves that you see on television, worn by terrorists. Their heads and faces, except for their eyes, were covered, so there was no way to identify them."

"Did you notice anything about their eyes? Any marks, like scars?"

"No. And they were dressed in full military fatigues, carrying fake machine guns."

Bill shook his head. "I'll never understand how stupid some people can be."

"What should we do?" Lilly asked.

"Just be careful. Who knows if these guys are dangerous or just jokers. Keep your doors locked, Hassan, and don't answer the door if you don't know who's there. I'm going to see if any of the neighbors have a video doorbell or any closed circuit security cameras. We might be able to find some footage of these guys."

CHAPTER 11

a fter Bill left, Lilly poured two glasses of wine, handed one to Hassan, and sat down next to him on the sofa. "How are you doing?"

He chuckled wryly. "Great."

"Why don't we head down to the block party? Maybe it'll help take your mind off things."

"I don't think so, Lil. I'm not in a party mood."

"I'm not suggesting we go get smashed. I'm only suggesting that we get out of the house and get some fresh air. I think it would be good for both of us."

"We still don't have anything to take."

"Have you got cheese and crackers?"

"Yes."

"Problem solved. I'll slice some cheese and arrange some crackers on a plate and voila! We've got something to share."

"You're not going to let this go, are you?" Hassan tilted his head and gave her a little smile.

"Nope."

"All right. I guess we can go for a little while. Do you think we should take Barney with us?"

"Probably. He hasn't had a walk today."

They arranged cheese and crackers on a small platter, put a leash on Barney, and left, making sure the doors were locked. They left one light on downstairs so people would think someone was home.

The street was empty of trick-or-treaters. The hour had come when trick-or-treating was supposed to end, so most kids were probably at home, combing through their loot and begging for a few pieces before bedtime. Lilly carried the small tray of cheese and crackers and Hassan held Barney's leash the best he could. When they arrived at the end of the block, they were surprised to see a big crowd of people milling around.

"Hey, Hassan. Lilly. Glad you could make it," Larry said. He reached for the tray of cheese and crackers and found a place for it on one of the long tables. There was a ton of food besides the chili he had mentioned earlier. There were potato chips, hotdogs in chafing dishes, big plastic bowls full of potato and macaroni salad, buckets of candy, trays of brownies, coolers of beer and wine, and a basket of apples. Battery-operated lanterns were placed all along the table so people could see what they were eating.

"Wow! You've got quite a spread here," Lilly said.

"Yeah. We do this every Halloween. Everyone loves it." He stopped speaking when a shrill voice came from behind them.

"This is disgusting. How do we know this food isn't contaminated?" It was Michelle.

Larry groaned and leaned closer to Lilly and Hassan. "Well, almost everyone loves it." He turned to Michelle. "No one has ever gotten sick from the food we put out. If you don't want any, don't eat it."

"Humph. I highly doubt that." Michelle's face was twisted into a scowl that was visible even in the darkness.

Larry turned away from her. "I don't know why she bothers showing up. She comes and makes the same remarks every year."

Barney growled, the sound coming from deep in his throat. "It's all right, Barney." Lilly nudged Hassan. "He must sense everyone's blood pressure starting to rise."

"Michelle just likes to make trouble," said someone behind Lilly. She turned around to see who was talking.

"Oh, hi, Sally," she said. Sally Belvedere lived a few doors down from Hassan with her husband, Eugene, and their son, Oliver, who stood next to her, eating a hotdog.

"Hi, Lilly. Hassan! What happened?" she asked.

"Just a fender bender," Hassan said. "I'm all right."

"Thank goodness," Sally said. Eugene joined them a moment later.

"I saw your car in your driveway," Eugene said. "It looked like you'd been in an accident."

"Duh," Oliver said. Eugene shot him a glowering look.

Hassan nodded. "It was a couple days ago. I need to get the car looked at before I drive it very far."

"I know a good mechanic," Larry said. "I'll text you his name and number." He turned as Michelle, who had been talking to some other neighbors, raised her voice to ask a question.

"Were these apples washed?"

From somewhere in the small crowd of neighbors a voice called out, "No."

"Ugh. I'll take this home and wash it before I eat it. I'd advise all of you to do the same." Michelle turned and walked quickly away, holding the apple at a distance from her body, as if it could emit harmful death rays.

"She drives me nuts," Larry muttered. "Did you know she called animal control *and* the police about Cupcake?" Cupcake was Larry's lovable dog. She barked all the time, but she was so sweet that nobody else on the block seemed to mind.

"Did the police come to your house?" someone asked him.

"They sure did. Animal control came, too. But I hadn't done anything wrong, so they left. I don't leave him out for hours on end and I feed him and walk him, so there wasn't anything they could do."

"You think that's bad?" asked Sally. "She called the cops on Oliver because he needs a new muffler on his truck." Oliver nodded with a scowl.

"She's accused me of building my new fence six inches onto her property," Hassan said.

Lilly frowned. She hadn't brought Hassan to the block party to talk about his miserable neighbor. He was there to decrease his stress, not make it worse. Barney continued growling.

"Can we talk about something more pleasant?" she asked. "Why are we letting someone who's not even here take over the conversation? Plus, I think it's upsetting Barney."

"Lilly's right. Poor Barney," Larry said. "Hassan, what happened to your arm?"

"That's not more pleasant," Lilly said dryly.

Hassan chuckled. "I was in a fender-bender."

"Are you all right?"

"Yeah, I'm fine. The other driver was hurt more than I was."

"Also, not more pleasant," Lilly chided him. Talking about Ivy was no better than talking about Michelle.

"So let's talk about where Eugene and Sally are going on their annual Christmas cruise," Larry suggested.

"That's better," Lilly said.

"We were supposed to go to Costa Rica," Sally said. "But Eugene is getting tired of cruises and wants to stay home. So we'll be here for Christmas. Oliver is disappointed, but he's young. He'll have plenty of opportunities to go on cruises." Oliver, who went to school part-time at the community college and worked part-time at a feed store, smiled ruefully as his mom put her arm around his shoulder and squeezed him to her.

The conversation thankfully turned to the pros and cons of cruising and it was about an hour later when Hassan started yawning.

"I think it's time for us to be going," Lilly said. "It was nice to see all of you." Hassan agreed and shook hands the best he could with the men in the group. He kissed Sally on the cheek. Lilly went in search of his tray, which was now empty of cheese and crackers, and took the arm he offered. They walked back to his house slowly, enjoying the quiet of the evening. Barney had finally calmed down.

"I'm glad you made me go to the block party." Hassan hugged her arm close to him.

"It's nice that your neighbors do this every year. It's so much more friendly than just waving to someone as you head off in opposite directions in your cars."

"Which reminds me, I'll call tomorrow morning to see if Larry's mechanic can take a look at my car."

Lilly nodded and nudged closer to him. Suddenly he stopped short. "What's that?" He was pointing to something in his yard. It was high off the ground and glowed white from the light of the porch lamp.

CHAPTER 12

*L*illy squinted to get a better look. "I don't know." They hastened their steps to get a better look.

Hassan was the first to realize what it was. He groaned. "You're kidding. Don't tell me that's toilet paper in my trees."

Lilly let out a cry of dismay. "Oh, no!"

"What a mess." Hassan looked around to see if the other neighbors had been hit, too. Lilly followed his gaze, but couldn't see because of the darkness beyond Hassan's front yard.

The toilet paper quickly became a minor concern, though, when they got to the front walk and looked up at the house.

Lilly gasped.

"Oh, my God." Hassan's mouth fell open.

The words "GET OUT" were scrawled in black spray paint across the front door. The sidelight windows were broken and the mail slot in the front door was stuffed with handfuls of crumpled paper. Barney jumped up the front steps, barking.

Hassan fished for his key, wincing from the pain in his shoulder, and gave it to Lilly to open the door. When she pushed the door open, she was nearly bowled over by Barney in his haste to get inside and find the person or persons who had done this.

"I'm getting Bill back here." She already had her cell phone out and was dialing Bill's number.

"Hi. We need you back here. Hassan's house has been vandalized."

"Where are you now?"

"In his front hall. We were out talking to some neighbors at the end of the block and we came back to this. There are broken windows, paint on the front door that says 'get out,' and toilet paper in the trees out front. We can't see if other people on the block were targeted, too."

"Stay where you are. I'll be right there. Wait for me outside."

"Shouldn't we make sure everything is okay inside?"

"No."

Lilly hung up, yelled for Barney, and turned to Hassan. "Bill said not to stay inside. Do you want to sit in my car?" They closed the door behind them and stood in front of the offending graffiti.

"No." Hassan shook his head. "Lilly, I can't stay here."

"You mean, here on the front porch, or here in your house, or here in Juniper Junction?"

"Here in Juniper Junction."

Lilly clenched her teeth. She didn't even want to think about that. "Let's not make any rash decisions just yet. Let's wait to see what Bill has to say."

Hassan sat down on his front steps and for the second time that night, put his head in his hands. He looked like he'd aged ten years in five minutes.

"I don't know if it's safe for me to be here," he said.

"You know you're welcome to stay at my house."

"So that this type of thing is visited on you in your neighborhood? No way."

Lilly sighed. "Please let's not think about this right now. The police have got to be able to help."

"I wonder if the two guys from earlier came back or if this was done by someone else," Hassan said.

"It could be either, though I'd like to think that the same people were responsible. That way we'd only be dealing with one set of thugs."

Hassan didn't say anything. They waited a couple minutes in silence until Bill pulled up to the front of the house in his cruiser.

"Hassan, I'm really sorry that this has happened," he said as he came up the front walk.

"Thanks, Bill."

"Let me have a look around inside the house before you two go in."

Lilly and Hassan tried to see Bill through the windows, but they could only see him in a few rooms on the first floor, then he disappeared into the back of the house. Presently he came back outside.

"It's all clear in there. Nothing suspicious upstairs or down. You can go on in."

He followed Hassan and Lilly into the living room and sat down where he had sat just a couple hours previously.

"So tell me everything. What time you left the house, where you went, who else was there. Everything."

Hassan related the events since Bill had left, telling him about the conversations they had had with the neighbors, which neighbors he recalled seeing at the block party, and which neighbors had left.

"So this Michelle Conover is your next-door neighbor? She sounds like trouble," Bill said.

"Yes. She and I have had an ongoing feud over my new fence and the landscaping, but I doubt even she would stoop this low," Hassan said.

"Don't be too sure," Bill cautioned. "She's not above vandalism. Just ask her ex-husband."

"What do you mean?" Lilly raised her eyebrows at her brother.

"I mean that she can be vicious. She was the reason her ex-husband called us to respond to a disturbance at his new tearoom yesterday. She went in and threatened to trash the place."

"Did she? I mean, trash the place?"

"Not completely. But she did do some damage before anyone could stop her."

Hassan shook his head. "How did I end up next door to her?"

"Let me ask around and see what I can find out from the neighbors. I'll get started on this first thing in the morning." Bill stood up to leave. "We'll figure it out, Hassan. Don't worry about it."

"Easier said than done," Hassan said. Lilly gave him a sympathetic look. They both stood and accompanied Bill to the door.

"I'll probably talk to you tomorrow, Lilly," Bill said. She kissed his cheek and he left.

"I think you should go get ready for bed," she told Hassan. "I'm going to try to figure out a way to cover the window until tomorrow morning and then we can call to have it replaced. I want to get a couple pictures of the damage and I'll forward those to Bill."

"Do you want some help?"

"I think it'll be easy. I'll just find some heavy-duty tape and tape over the broken glass. You can't really help me tape it up with your bad shoulder, so I'll just do it myself."

Hassan kissed her and went upstairs. Lilly took photos of the damage to the windows from the inside and the outside and also of the spray-painted message on the front door. Then she went to the garage to find the roll of duct tape she knew was out there. She returned to the foyer and put long pieces of tape over the sidelight windows and then did the same with the other, larger, window that had been broken. She also covered the offensive graffiti with tape. Barney followed her everywhere she went, as if he didn't want her to be alone. Finally, she went upstairs to make sure Hassan didn't need anything and then left for the night.

CHAPTER 13

The next morning it was pouring when Lilly drove to the jewelry shop. Harry was full of stories about the Halloween party he and Alice, his fiancée, had attended. Lilly did her best to act interested, but Harry must have known something was wrong.

"Is everything okay, boss? You look like you're a million miles away."

Lilly blinked and shook the fuzziness from her head. "I'm sorry, Harry. Hassan had a bad night last night and I'm concerned about him."

"Is he all right?"

"Physically, he's about the same. His shoulder and arm hurt, but his head seems to be feeling better. It's his mental state I'm worried about. You know about his next-door neighbor giving him a hard time. Then someone vandalized his house last night while we were out talking to some of the neighbors at the end of the block, and as if that weren't enough, earlier in the night two trick-or-treaters showed up and made anti-Muslim threats against him."

"You're kidding. I'm so sorry to hear that. Hassan must be so upset."

"He is. We don't know if the trick-or-treaters and the vandalism are connected, but it's very possible. And now Hassan is starting to think that he should just get out of Juniper Junction completely."

"He can't do that. What would happen between you and him?"

"I'm not worried about our relationship. We're strong. What upsets me is that he feels he's not welcome here."

"But everyone loves him in Juniper Junction. He knows that."

"He does know that, you're right. But you know when someone says something bad about you, that's all you can focus on? That's how he's feeling right now."

One of the first people through the door that morning was Ivy, who came in dribbling water all over the floor. Lilly wanted more than anything to let Harry handle her, but she put on her game face and greeted Ivy herself.

"Can I help you?"

"Did you tell Hassan what I said?"

"No."

"Why not?"

"Because he's got a lot on his mind right now. He doesn't need you threatening him on top of everything else."

"I've decided to sue him."

Lilly managed to keep a poker face, though she was shaking with fury on the inside. She had figured this was coming—she just hoped it wouldn't happen so soon. "You do what you have to do, Ivy."

"Oh, I will. You tell him my lawyer's coming for him."

"Ivy, I'm going to have to ask you to leave the store now. I will not tolerate threats of any kind in here." Harry had heard the two women talking and came to stand by Lilly's side. Harry wasn't big or the least bit muscular, but she was glad to have his support. Ivy stared at the two of them for a long moment. No one spoke and Lilly stared right back, refusing to break her gaze.

Finally Ivy *harrumphed* and left the store. Lilly slumped with her back against the counter. Her shoulders and neck ached from being so taut.

"Are you going to tell Hassan?"

"I have to. I would hate for him to get a summons and find out that I knew about it all along. I just don't know when to tell him. Now is not a good time."

"I wonder how long it'll take for Ivy's lawyer to file suit."

"I don't know. Hopefully at least a week, to give Hassan time to take a deep breath."

But Ivy and her lawyer were quick. Lilly was closing up the shop that night when her phone rang. It was Hassan.

"You'll never believe what I just got." His tone was grim and Lilly's heart sank.

"What?"

"A summons and complaint. It was delivered right to my door. Ivy's suing me."

"I'm so sorry, Hassan. Ivy was in here this morning and she told me she was going to sue you. I was going to tell you, but I was hoping it wouldn't happen so soon."

"Her lawyer must be having a slow day." Hassan snorted. "Well, this is just the cherry on top of a crappy week."

"Can I pick you up and take you to dinner?" Lilly asked. "We can talk about what to do over dinner."

"The last time I left the house at your urging, someone trashed the place."

Lilly couldn't help chuckling. "Touché. How about I pick up something for dinner and bring it over?"

"I was only kidding. But I would like to stay home tonight. My arm has been bothering me a lot today."

"Okay. You sit tight and I'll get something for dinner. I'll see you in a little bit."

She found the number for her favorite diner, which was just outside Juniper Junction, and placed an order. While she waited to go pick up the food, she called Laurel.

"Hi, Mom."

"Hi, honey. What's going on?"

"Nothing."

"Are you busy with schoolwork?"

"No."

"Did you do anything for Halloween?"

"I went to a party."

"Did you have fun?"

"Not really."

"You okay, Laurel?"

"I want to come home. I don't like it here."

"I'm sorry, Laur. I want you to be happy, but I really think you should stay at school and try to tough it out a little longer. Moving away from home is a big adjustment."

"I just don't think I'm ready." Laurel sniffled. Lilly hadn't called to make her daughter cry.

"Will you do me a favor? Will you stay until Thanksgiving? Then if you really can't stand the thought of going back, you can stay home."

"Okay." Laurel's voice was quavering.

"Call me whenever you need to. Or call Dad," Lilly said softly.

"I will." Lilly could hear Laurel swallow hard.

"I'll call again in a couple days," Lilly said.

She hung up the phone and closed her eyes. Her heart

tightened and she leaned her head against the back of her chair, letting out a long sigh. Nothing was easy.

It was still raining when Lilly arrived at Hassan's house with dinner. He had spread out sheaves of papers along the length of the dining room table.

"What's all this?" Lilly asked.

"Research."

"Research for what?"

"Lawsuits."

"As in, lawsuits filed by Ivy?"

Hassan nodded. "I can't just sit here and do nothing. I need to arm myself with knowledge."

Lilly almost smiled. He sounded so dramatic. "Call my lawyer. She'll be able to help."

"This is going to cost me a fortune."

"Hopefully not. Let the insurance companies duke it out. I really believe that Ivy is just doing this to be a pain in the neck."

"I hope the judge sees it that way. I'll call your lawyer in the morning."

"Can we just relax tonight and watch a movie or something? Let's worry about this tomorrow and take a break from stress for the next few hours."

"All right. I think we can find a good movie. Want to eat in the living room?"

She picked up the bag containing dinner and carried it to the living room, then came back for the drinks Hassan had poured. He followed carrying the utensils. They snuggled up next to each other on the sofa and were soon done eating and engrossed in an old movie.

Hassan was in a better frame of mind by the time Lilly left. His shoulders were more relaxed, his face had lost a bit of its tightness, and he was actually smiling. He had made an appointment for early the next morning to get his car looked at by a mechanic, so she promised to swing by before work so she could follow him to the body shop.

He was waiting for her in his driveway when she arrived in the morning. His driving was a bit jerky because of the injuries to his arm, but Lilly stayed close behind him to make sure he arrived at the body shop safely.

The mechanic promised to look at the car that day and let him know if there was any damage to the car that was not visible to the naked eye. When they got in Lilly's car, she turned to him and asked, "Am I taking you home?"

"I think I'd like to go for a walk. Can you just take me with you to work and I'll walk around downtown for a while? I'll call a ride service to get home."

"No, you won't. I'll drive you. Want me to walk with you? I've got some time before I have to set out the displays."

"I've got so much on my mind that I don't think I would be very good company this morning." He sounded so glum. Lilly's heart went out to him.

"That's okay. You know where to find me when you need a ride back home." She parked in the alley behind the jewelry shop and gave him a big hug before they went their separate ways.

Lilly and Harry had just finished setting out the displays when there was a knock on the front window of the store. Hassan stood there holding a cardboard container with three coffees. Lilly smiled and hurried to open the door. Hassan came in and Lilly was about to lock the door behind him when she heard someone calling her name.

She turned around to see where the voice was coming from and saw Bill walking toward her.

"Hi," she said, holding the door so he could walk into the shop. "What brings you out so early?"

"I was over at the bistro picking up something for breakfast when a call came through. I saw Hassan walk past the bistro, so I figured I would find him here."

"What does the call have to do with Hassan?"

Hassan looked up from where he stood putting creamer in his coffee. "Do you need me for something, Bill?"

"Michelle Conover's body was found this morning."

CHAPTER 14

*H*assan dropped his coffee, burning his leg.

"Ow!"

Harry hurried to the office to get some paper towels to wipe up the mess. Lilly stood staring at Bill. Only Hassan was capable of speech.

"What happened?"

"We don't know yet. She was lying on the ground in her backyard and someone saw her. I don't know who it was. Apparently it looks like she's been dead for over twenty-four hours. Probably no one saw her yesterday because of all the rain we had."

"Was she sick? Or hurt? Maybe she had a heart attack."

"I don't know yet. All I know is what I've heard so far. It was just called in a little while ago and I heard from the first officer on the scene. Some guy and his bulldog found her." *Larry and Cupcake.* "I'm sure there are police all up and down your block by now."

"What should I do?" asked Hassan. "I mean, should I go

home? Should I just stay here until things calm down? Would I even be allowed to go back to my house?"

"I'm sure whoever's at the scene is going to want to talk to neighbors, so it's probably a good idea to go home for now. Is your car in the alley?"

"No. My car is at the mechanic's. Lilly drove me downtown this morning so I could go for a walk, clear my head. Things have not gone well for me this week, as you might imagine."

"Well, unfortunately, things are probably about to get worse," Bill said. "Do you need me to drive you home?"

Hassan looked at Lilly, who finally found her voice. "That's okay, Bill. I can drive him."

"All right. I've got to get back to the station. Things have been crazy the last few days and I'm only leaving work to sleep and sometimes eat. Call me if you need anything."

"Thanks, Bill," Hassan said. Lilly echoed his words, then she and Hassan stood staring at each other for several moments.

"I can't believe it." Hassan accepted a paper towel from Harry and tried dabbing some of the coffee from his pants.

"We should leave now," Lilly said. "The sooner you get back home, the better."

"Why do you say that?"

"Because you don't want the police to think you killed her and fled."

"You think someone *killed* her?" Hassan's eyes widened as the thought sank in.

"Well, maybe it's just because my brother is a cop, but that's where my mind went first," she said. "Michelle is, what, maybe thirty-five? And she seems perfectly healthy. Perfectly healthy young-ish adults don't usually just drop dead."

"Oh, my God. You're right. I'll bet someone killed her. And after the problems I've had with her, everyone'll think I did it. We need to get back to my house asap so I can be there to explain where I've been this morning." He wadded up the paper towel and threw it in the garbage. "You don't mind taking me home now?"

"Not at all. Let's go. I won't be long, Harry."

Lilly and Hassan left through the office in a hurry. They didn't say much on the ride to Hassan's house, each lost in thought. Lilly's brain was working double time. *What if they think Hassan did it? Who could have hated her enough to kill her? Maybe that apple really was poisoned. I can't say I'm sorry.*

"You know, I can't say I'm sorry," Hassan said.

"I was just thinking the exact same thing." Lilly chuckled nervously. "The good thing is that there are plenty of people who despised her. It's not like you're the only one."

"I suppose that's a good thing. It's awful to think that way, but it's the truth. I wonder if there's anyone who will miss her."

When Lilly turned down Hassan's street, a police officer stopped her.

"Where are you headed?" he asked, eyeing her and Hassan.

She indicated Hassan with her hand. "I'm taking him home."

"Where do you live?" The officer was looking at Hassan. Hassan gave him his address and the officer glanced over his shoulder. "Where are you coming from?"

"I've been downtown. Is there something wrong, officer?"

Lilly didn't know whether to be dismayed or relieved by Hassan's question. It made him look innocent, sure, but he didn't want to be caught pretending not to know what was going on, either. She kept her eyes on the officer and didn't indicate that Hassan's question fazed her.

"There's been an incident next door to you, sir. When you get in your house, please stay there and someone will be around soon to ask you some questions."

Hassan nodded and Lilly pressed the gas very slowly, easing her way down to the end of the cul-de-sac. They didn't speak again until she had parked in his driveway.

"What are you going to tell them?" she asked.

"The truth. That's all there is."

"But you made it sound like you didn't know what happened."

"I know. I probably shouldn't have done that. But I don't have to tell them I spoke to Bill."

"Just don't get in trouble. I don't want to be visiting you in jail." Lilly smiled nervously as Hassan leaned in to kiss her.

"I'll call you after things calm down and the police leave." He squeezed her hand and slid out of the car. She watched him go into his house, then backed out and drove slowly down the block. The same officer who had stopped her on the way to Hassan's house stopped her again.

"May I have your name, please?" he asked, taking out his notebook.

"Lilly Carlsen."

"Address?"

Lilly gave him her work and home addresses and her work, home, and cell numbers.

"We're getting this information from everyone who enters or exits this neighborhood," the officer explained. "We may be in touch."

Lilly nodded and drove back to work. Once inside, she called Bill.

"Do you think Hassan is going to be in trouble?" she asked.

There was a brief silence on the other end.

"Don't tell me," she said. "I already know the answer."

"Not necessarily. I'm not sure he'll be in trouble, but it doesn't look good. You must have figured that out. Between his feud with her and the vandalism on Halloween...." His voice trailed off.

"What about the vandalism?"

"We still don't know who caused the damage to his house and yard. Maybe it was Michelle Conover, maybe not. But suppose he assumed it was Michelle and he killed her because of that, in combination with all the trouble she was giving him about his fence and the landscape work?"

"You're don't actually think Hassan killed Michelle, do you?" Lilly's voice rose an entire octave.

"No, of course not. I'm just following the train of thought that any other officer would have."

Lilly blew out her breath. "It's a wonder I'm not a heavy drinker."

"Speaking of that, have you talked to Mom?"

"Mom's been drinking?!"

"No. What I mean is, you might just become a heavy drinker after you talk to her."

"Why?"

"She's been giving Nikki a hard time."

"About what?"

"Literally everything," Bill said in a wry tone.

"We can't have that. I don't even want to think about what would happen if Nikki quit."

"There's always Meredith."

"I know, but she has another part-time job. She won't be able to take care of Mom around the clock. I'll go over to Mom's house after work and talk to her. Maybe I can convince her to be nice to Nikki."

"All right. Do you want me to meet you there?"

"You don't have to. I can handle it. I think."

"Okay. I need to go over to Noley's house. I haven't seen her in a few days."

"Tell her I said 'hi.' I haven't seen her, either."

"I will."

Lilly was unfocused that morning, worried about Hassan. As much as she didn't want to admit it, Ivy's lawsuit was legitimate. Hassan had caused the car accident, plain and simple. He hadn't been paying attention while he was driving. But even though it was legitimate, it still didn't seem right. Ivy would be compensated by auto insurance for her injuries and the damage to her car—what more did she want?

Lilly knew that, when it came right down to it, Ivy was suing Hassan for no other reason than sheer vindictiveness.

And Lilly worried about Michelle's death, too. Had she actually been murdered? She could think of a few people who might have wanted her dead. More than a few, in fact. No one seemed to have liked Michelle.

And if someone *had* murdered Michelle, that meant there was a murderer walking around Juniper Junction. That was an unsettling thought, to say the least.

And she was worried about her mom ... and Laurel. And the list went on.

CHAPTER 15

*L*uckily there were several customers in the store that afternoon and the busy-ness helped keep her mind off her troubles. She was surprised when Ted Conover showed up a couple hours before closing.

"Hello, Ted. I'm so sorry to hear about Michelle. How are you holding up?"

"Thanks, Lilly. It was quite a shock, but I'm doing okay."

"What can I do for you?"

"Actually, I'm here to buy something."

"Really? What are you looking for?"

"I don't know. It's for someone special, if you know what I mean, so I just thought I'd take a look around."

Hmm. Ted has a girlfriend? Interesting. And he's getting her a gift the day his ex-wife's body is found? Also interesting.

"Well, I can show you some items, or you're welcome to have a look around by yourself."

"I think I'll browse for a bit and if I have any questions, I'll let you know."

"Sounds good." Lilly found some paperwork to do. She

tried as hard as she could to ignore Ted, but she couldn't help stealing a glance at him every now and then as he perused her display cases. *I wonder what his girlfriend looks like. I wonder if he knew her before his divorce from Michelle.*

"Lilly? Can you show me this bracelet?" His words interrupted her musings.

She walked behind the case where he was standing and unlocked it. She pointed to a couple different bracelets before she lit on the one he wanted to see.

"This is beautiful," she said. She set it on a velvet display board so he could see it better. It was a lovely bracelet—simple, bold, half-inch-wide yellow gold with a herringbone design.

"I like it, but I'd like to look around a little more."

"No problem, Ted. Let me know if you have any questions."

Ted nodded and walked around the shop slowly, stopping in front of the watches. Lilly's mind raced while he browsed. This was opening up so many questions. Finally he beckoned her over and asked to see the one watch Lilly didn't like. It bordered on looking unisex—it had a white face with no numbers and a thin leather band.

"I love this," Ted said. "I'll take it."

"Great. I'll wrap it up for you."

Ted pulled a credit card out of his wallet and handed it to her. She ran it through the machine and was surprised when it was declined. She tried it again, and when it didn't work she rubbed the card on her slacks and tried a third time.

"I'm sorry, Ted, but this card isn't working. Do you want me to call it in, or do you want to try another card?"

"Huh. That's odd. Let me get out another card." He fished in his wallet and produced another credit card, which he handed to Lilly. She ran that through the machine and it, too, was declined.

"This one's not working either, Ted. Maybe there's a problem with your bank?"

"I'd better go back to the tearoom and find out what's going on. Can you hold the watch for me?"

"Sure. Let me know when you figure out what's going on."

"I will." Ted left in a hurry, clutching both cards in his hand.

As soon as he left, Lilly put the watch in her office vault, then she returned to the front to talk to Harry.

"Harry, can you keep an eye on things out front while I'm in the office for a few minutes? There's something I need to do."

"Sure, boss."

Back in her office, Lilly reached for a pad of paper and a pencil. She needed to write down the questions she had about Ted while they were still fresh in her mind.

Who is Ted dating?

Was he dating her while he and Michelle were married?

Was the girlfriend the reason Michelle trashed Ted's tearoom before she died?

Why is he buying her jewelry right after his ex-wife's death?

Is he at all upset about Michelle's death?

Why were Ted's credit cards declined?

Is he having financial difficulties?

If so, why is he buying jewelry?

Why did Ted and Michelle divorce?

That last one—and really, if she was honest with herself, all of them—would be hard to figure out without some digging. She wasn't sure where to start digging, but at least she had written down her list of questions, and that was something.

It was almost closing time when Ted returned.

"Hi again, Ted. Have you come back for the watch?"

Ted grinned. "Yup. Got cash this time." Lilly wondered if

his credit card issue hadn't been resolved. She couldn't very well ask, either, since that went way over the nosy line.

"All righty. Let's get that wrapped up for you." She asked him to wait at the display counter while she went back into the office to retrieve the watch. She moved slowly, wondering how much information she could squeeze out of him while she rang up the sale.

When she returned to the front of the shop with the watch, she took her time entering the sale into the computer.

"This is such a lovely watch," she said. "Is it for a birthday?"

"Nope. It's just a gift for being special."

"How sweet. Lucky lady."

He winked.

She couldn't think of a tactful way to wring any more information out of him.

When Ted had paid and left the store with the watch, Lilly blew her cheeks out.

"What's wrong?" Harry asked.

"I didn't get a single useful piece of information out of him. I couldn't think of anything tactful to say."

"He's probably the type who refers to his mother as a 'special someone.'"

"It wouldn't surprise me."

The bell over the door jingled and Lilly looked up. Ivy was opening the door.

"Was that Ted I just saw leaving?"

"Yes."

"What was he doing in here?"

"Buying a piece of jewelry, not that it's any of your business."

Ivy seemed to lose interest in Ted. "Listen, Lilly. I hear Hassan got my summons and complaint. I'm here to tell you that I'm willing to settle with him."

"Ivy, the dollar signs in your eyes are showing."

"You're hilarious, Lilly. I mean it. If he wants to settle, have him call me."

"You brought the lawyers into this, Ivy. I'm sure Hassan prefers to do his communicating through his lawyer. You should have thought about that before making a huge deal out of this. Now, if you'll excuse me, I need to close up my shop."

Ivy grumbled something unintelligible and left.

"That woman gives me hives, Harry."

"I see what you mean."

That evening after work Lilly went straight to Bev's house. Nikki opened the door. She looked tired and wan, but she managed to smile as she stood back to let Lilly inside.

"How are things going, Nikki? Bill told me Mom hasn't been cooperative."

Nikki sighed. "Not really. We've had a couple rough days, that's for sure."

"Why don't you head home for the night," Lilly suggested. "I'll stay here with Mom until Meredith gets here. I think she and I need to have a little talk, anyway."

"I could use some time to myself," Nikki said. "You don't mind staying? I'd really appreciate that."

They had walked into the living room, where Bev was sitting in her favorite chair. Her arms were crossed over her chest and she wore a scowl.

"Of course I don't mind staying. Get some rest and I'll see you later," Lilly said. "Hi, Mom."

Bev didn't answer.

Nikki gathered her handbag and her jacket from the kitchen and said goodbye, then left. Lilly locked the door behind her and returned to the living room, where she sat on the sofa across from her mother.

"What's new, Mom?"

"Nothing," Bev mumbled.

"You seem to be in a pretty bad mood. What's wrong?"

"I don't like that woman."

"What woman?"

"That woman who comes here every day."

"Nikki?"

Bev shrugged.

"Do you know who she is?" Lilly asked.

"Yes."

"Who is she?"

"Why are you quizzing me?" Not only had Bev dodged the question, but she was becoming more querulous by the second. Bottom line—she didn't seem to know who Nikki was. Lilly hoped it was only a temporary lapse.

CHAPTER 16

o you feel like playing cards, Mom?"
"No."
"Want to watch television?"

Bev hesitated. Lilly knew she was thinking about it.

"What would we watch?" Bev asked. She gave Lilly a side-long look.

"Whatever you want. It's your choice."

Bev sighed. "All right. Turn it on and I'll choose something to watch."

Lilly turned the TV on and handed Bev the remote. The news was playing, so Bev turned the channel. She flipped through about three hundred channels before going back to the beginning and starting over. Lilly thought she would go mad waiting for Bev to choose something to watch. She took a deep breath and tried to remember that this was her mother, the woman who had given her life. She needed to be patient.

"Find anything good, Mom?" she asked brightly.

"I want to watch that show with the funny videos."

Lilly held out her hand. "Give me the remote and I'll try to find it for you."

"I can do it myself." Bev was scowling again.

Something dawned on Lilly. *Maybe that's the problem,* she thought.

"Is that why you're angry tonight, Mom? Is that why you're upset with Nikki? Because you want to do things for yourself?"

Bev didn't say anything, but Lilly noticed her head nodding ever so slightly.

"That's no problem. You find the show you want to watch. Now that we know what's upsetting you, we can fix it."

"Okay." Bev smiled and started flipping through the channels again. After many long minutes of trying to find the channel she was looking for, during which time she actually landed on the correct channel at least twice, Bev settled back into her chair to watch the funny home videos. Lilly had tried to keep the frustration from showing in her face while the channels looped by. If there was one thing that drove her bonkers, it was the constant switching of channels, whether it was on the television or the car radio, which Laurel used to do all the time. Relieved that she had figured out what the trouble was, Lilly leaned back against the sofa and tried to relax.

They watched television, laughing out loud at the videos, until Meredith arrived. Her smile mirrored the one on Bev's face when she walked into the living room.

"Well! Bev, you look happy tonight," Meredith said.

"I think we've had a breakthrough," Lilly told her. Then she stood up and took Meredith aside in the kitchen, out of Bev's hearing. "Mom seems to be upset because people are doing things for her. I think if we let her do things for herself, we'll see that her attitude improves."

"That makes sense. She's an adult. Adults do things for themselves," Meredith said.

If I can figure that out, Nikki should have been able to figure it out, Lilly thought. She made a mental note to call Nikki early the next morning.

Bev was still laughing at the videos when Lilly left for the evening. Lilly let herself out, making sure the door was locked behind her, as Meredith sat down to join Bev in the living room.

When Lilly got home, the first thing she did was walk Barney. The poor dog had been practically neglected over the past couple days while Lilly had been so busy with Hassan, her mom, and Laurel. She took Barney for a nice, long walk and used the time to clear her head, too.

When they got home, she fed Barney and ate a little dinner herself before collapsing on the sofa with a mystery. She hadn't even found the place where she had left off when the phone rang. It was Noley.

"Hi. Haven't talked to you in a while," Noley said.

"I know. Things have been crazy. What's new?"

"Not much." Lilly could practically see Noley shrugging her shoulders.

"Are you all right? You sound a little down," Lilly said.

"I don't know. I haven't seen much of Bill lately. I'm bored, I guess."

"I know Bill has been busy at work, and we've been dealing with Mom, as usual. Now that you mention it, though, he did say he was going to try to see you tonight. You haven't heard from him?"

"No. I texted him, but he didn't answer yet."

"I'll bet something came up at work. Want me to call him?"

"No. I can call him. I just don't want to bother him."

"If you call and he answers, then he's not too busy. If you

call and he doesn't answer, he's busy. Either way, you're not bothering him. Give him a call."

"Lilly, has he said anything to you about not wanting to see me anymore?"

So this is why she sounds out of sorts.

"No. Why? Is that what you think? That he doesn't want to see you anymore?"

"I don't know." Noley sounded miserable.

"Well, it's not true. He does want to see you. He loves you. You know what? I'm going to call him right now and tell him to get over to your house and take you out somewhere."

"No! Don't do that!"

"Why not?"

"Because if he wanted to do that, he would. Please, Lilly. Promise me you won't tell him that."

"All right. I promise. But listen, don't worry anymore. He's a police officer. Sometimes they get stuck on duty and aren't able to leave when their shift is over."

"I know."

"Would it make you feel better if you baked something?" Lilly asked. "You know how much I love your lemon poppy seed muffins."

Noley laughed, which was the result Lilly had been hoping for.

"No one can accuse you of being subtle," Noley said. "I'll bring you muffins for breakfast tomorrow."

"Thanks. Make a couple extra for Hassan, would you? He could use a pick-me-up right about now."

"Why?"

Lilly had forgotten that Noley didn't know about Hassan's recent troubles. She told Noley the whole story about Michelle.

"I heard about that on the radio. She was Hassan's neighbor?"

"Yes. And she was miserable. Everyone on the block hated her. So the police are questioning everyone."

"Let me know if I can do anything. Tell him I'm thinking about him. I've got to start those muffins if I'm going to bring them to you tomorrow."

Lilly hung up, then immediately dialed Bill.

"I hear you're ignoring Noley," she said when he picked up the phone.

He sighed. "Not you, too."

"What do you mean?"

"I mean, everyone is on my case. I can't take it." His frustration was palpable.

"You sounded fine earlier. Is something wrong at work?"

"Work has been one thing after another for days now. It's a good thing I want the overtime, because I've been working nonstop. The crazies in Juniper Junction are coming out of the woodwork. What did Noley tell you?"

Lilly thought it best not to dwell on her conversation with Noley. "Actually, not much. She mentioned that she hadn't heard from you, that's all. She didn't really say that you had been ignoring her. Those were my own words."

"All right. I'll call her, because it looks like I'm not going to have a chance to stop over there tonight. Thanks for letting me know. Maybe by next week things will calm down here at work and we can go do something together."

"Don't tell her I called you."

"I won't. Talk to you later." He hung up before she could answer.

CHAPTER 17

*B*efore leaving for work the next morning, Lilly phoned Nikki.

"Hi, Nikki. I just wanted to call and thank you again for dealing with Mom's ups and downs."

"You know I love your mom. Was she doing any better after I left?"

"Actually, I was able to get her to calm down a bit. It turned out that she only wanted some autonomy. Once I gave her the remote to the TV and told her to find whatever she wanted to watch, she was better."

Nikki sighed. "I should have known better than to try to do too many things for her. She treasures her independence. It's no wonder she was upset with me. I'm sorry, Lilly."

"Don't be sorry. You're only human."

There was silence on the other end.

"Nikki? Are you there?" Lilly could hear Nikki take a loud, ragged breath.

"The thing is, I've got a lot on my mind right now. Things are not great between me and Beau. I'm sure you don't want to hear my troubles, but I think that's why I've been frustrated when I'm with your mom. I hope you can forgive me for letting personal stuff get in the way of taking care of Bev."

Oh, God, please don't let her start spilling personal stuff about Beau.

"Like I said, you're only human. I'm sorry you and Beau are having problems. I've obviously been there."

"Maybe a couple days off would help," Nikki said.

"That's fine. Let me call the agency where we found Meredith and see if they can send someone over to replace you. Temporarily, of course. Do you mind going over today? Then you can take a couple days to recharge."

"Thanks, Lilly. I'll go over to your mom's today, and just let me know what you hear from the agency. I really appreciate your understanding."

"Believe me, I understand all too well."

When Lilly got to work she placed a call to the agency asking for a temporary replacement for Nikki. The agency was able to accommodate her with a replacement who could begin the next day, so Lilly let Nikki know.

The next phone call was to the tearoom.

"Tranquilitea. This is Ted. How can I help you?"

"Hi, Ted. This is Lilly. I should have asked you when you were in my shop, but I was just wondering if you're still going through with the soft opening today. After, you know, the tragedy with Michelle."

Ted sighed. "I think I have no choice. The invitations are out and I didn't ask for RSVPs. I can't call everyone."

"I'm sure people will understand if you postpone, Ted."

"I think it'll help me to keep my mind off things."

"Okay, then. We'll see you later."

"Bye."

The last phone call was to her mother. Meredith answered the phone.

"Hi, Meredith. How did it go last night?"

"She was fine, Lilly. She watched television for a while, then I fixed her a snack and she went right to bed. She slept all night long, which doesn't happen very often these days."

"That's good to hear. Can you put her on the phone?" Lilly waited for several moments while Meredith took the phone to Bev.

"Good morning, Mom. How are you?"

"Good. When will Nikki get here?" Good. At least she knew who Nikki was today and she didn't seem to be mad anymore.

"She should be there soon. Listen, I have a question. Remember I told you about that tearoom that's opening today?"

"You didn't tell me about any tearoom."

Lilly fought the urge to contradict Bev. "Oh, I must have forgotten. Anyway, there's a new tearoom in town and they're having sort of a celebration today. I thought you might like to go with me."

"I don't think so, Lilly. I'd rather stay home."

"Are you sure? I think it would be fun."

"I really don't like tea." Lilly shook her head. Bev loved all manner of hot drinks, including tea.

"All right. I'll ask Hassan to go with me. Nikki should be there soon, Mom. She's going to be taking a little vacation, so after today there will be someone else with you during the day. It'll only be for a couple days."

"All right. Bye-bye."

Lilly hung up and texted Hassan.

Want to go on a date with me today?

She waited for his response.
It only took him a minute.

What kind of date?
Soft opening of Tranquilitea.
Isn't that the place Michelle's ex owns?
Yes. The opening is at 2.
Ok. I need to get away from the house for a while. What time
should I be at your shop?
Come by 1:45. See you then. Love you.
Love you.

Lilly set her phone down and smiled. She was looking
forward to spending the afternoon drinking tea, trying some
new delicacies, and being with Hassan.

Hassan arrived at the jewelry shop promptly at one forty-
five wearing a handsome leather bomber jacket over a V-neck
sweater and an Oxford. His arm was still in a sling to keep his
shoulder stable, but it didn't detract from his good looks.

"Ready?" he asked.

"I am. Harry, are you ready? Is Alice coming?"

"Alice is busy this afternoon, unfortunately. I'm almost
ready. Just let me just finish putting the displays away. Are you
going to put up a sign on the front door?"

"Yes. I printed it out already. It says we'll be back at three
o'clock. I hope we can get plenty to eat and drink before then."
Lilly grinned.

Lilly locked the door behind them and they made their way
across Main Street to Tranquilitea, where they could see
people already assembling inside. Harry held the door open for
Lilly and Hassan.

The tearoom was dark and cozy. Dark beadboard and
forest-green paint covered the walls; watercolor pictures of

tearooms from around the world hung in gilt frames against the dark background. Hutches filled with all varieties of china stood here and there against the walls in the large space. In the back of the shop there was a long counter topped with elegant black granite. An array of cake stands sat on the countertop under cloches. Each cake stand was piled with dainty treats— tiny cheesecakes, one-bite brownies, finger sandwiches with a variety of savory fillings, little pastry shells filled with lemon curd and topped with fresh raspberries, and many more. Lilly took a deep breath of the exotic and earthy-scented air. Just being in such a beautiful place filled her with a sense of peace. *And tranquilitea*, she thought with a smile.

"What's the smile for?" Hassan asked. He was smiling himself.

"I was just thinking how lovely it is in here. And how tranquil, just like the name of the shop. This is just what I needed today."

"Me, too." Hassan took her hand and they wandered over to a large table in the corner where several people were already sitting. Harry followed them.

Lilly knew almost everyone in the room, since it was filled with her fellow merchants. Most of them knew Hassan and Harry. She sat down next to Ronan Quinn, the proprietor of the shoe store up the block. His shop was next door to Ivy's pottery shop.

"What's new, Ronan?" she asked.

"Not much. I've been looking forward to the opening of this tearoom. Main Street coulduse a little infusion of new blood. So to speak."

"Or an infusion of tea," Lilly said, wincing at the reference to blood so soon after Michelle's death. She gestured around the room. "Isn't this beautiful?"

Ronan nodded, then leaned in a little closer. "I hear it

wasn't so beautiful last week. Ted's ex-wife came in and did some damage to the place. She's the one who was killed the other day, you know."

"Yes, I knew that. I didn't know she had actually caused any damage, though."

"I have it on good authority that she came in here and smashed a dozen teapots all over the floor, overturned some tables and chairs, and opened the spigot on the samovar and let hot tea run all over the floor."

"You're kidding. Who told you all this?"

"Ted. Don't tell him I told you."

CHAPTER 18

So maybe Bill had been right about Michelle. Maybe she *had* been the one who vandalized Hassan's house on Halloween night. But it could have been those kids dressed up like terrorists, too. They hadn't been caught, so no one had had a chance to ask them.

Lilly was not going to allow this train of thought to stop at her station. She took a deep breath. "Let's talk about something else, shall we? The last person we need to discuss today is Michelle."

"Amen to that," Hassan said. He had been listening to the conversation between Lilly and Ronan and his countenance was darkening.

"Hassan, I hear you were in an accident with Ivy," Ronan said.

Can anyone ever talk about anything pleasant? Lilly thought.

"Yeah."

"She never shuts up about it. Too bad you had to hit someone with such a big mouth."

"Yeah."

Ronan finally seemed to sense that no one felt like talking about Ivy, either. Lilly began to worry that this outing was doomed. She looked around, happy for Ted that his soft opening had attracted such a large group of people. And not just any people, but people who were in a position to recommend his new spot to tourists and locals alike. Ted could use a boost right about now, she figured.

There was only one seat left at their big round table—in fact, there was only one seat left in the whole room—and the person who would end up taking the seat hobbled through the front door with a new cane.

Ivy Leachman. Lilly barely suppressed a rude noise. Hassan closed his eyes, as if praying that another chair would magically become vacant.

It didn't take long for Ivy's beady gaze to zero in on their table. Hassan shifted in his seat, then moved it a hair closer to Lilly. Harry was sitting between him and the empty seat. Harry noticed Hassan's discomfort.

"Don't worry, Hassan," Harry whispered. "I'll keep her talking and you won't have to say a word to her."

"Thanks, Harry."

Wincing in an Oscar-worthy performance, Ivy threaded her way around the tables and chairs, accepting the "aw"s and "poor thing"s from the assembled crowd. Her expression morphed into a sly grin when she reached the back corner table.

"Well, well. I see Lilly has her entourage here."

"It's lovely to see you, too, Ivy." Lilly frowned at her.

"Isn't anyone going to ask how I'm doing?" Ivy asked.

"How are you doing, Ivy?" Ronan asked.

"I'm in pain." She looked straight at Hassan. Lilly was glad to see him staring right back at her. She fought the urge to give him a high-five.

"Not enough pain to keep you from getting free food, I see," Harry muttered.

"What was that, young man?" Ivy fixed him with a withering stare.

"Nothing. Have a seat, Miz Leachman." Harry indicated the seat next to him, but didn't move to help her.

She hung her cane on the back of the chair and sat down quite heavily for someone so thin and wiry. She leaned her head back and closed her eyes for a moment, then addressed everyone at the table. "I'm exhausted from walking all the way over here. It's not easy to move around with injuries like mine."

No one responded. Ronan kicked Lilly gently under the table and smirked at her. Lilly rolled her eyes.

"So, Miz Leachman, how's business?" Harry asked.

Ivy looked at him as if he were a complete stranger. "You're a nosy one, aren't you?"

Lilly had to smile. Harry's plan to keep Ivy talking was starting off slowly.

Hassan was sitting rigidly forward in his seat, looking as if he would rather be anywhere else. He avoided looking at Ivy, though Lilly noticed that Ivy was doing her best to will him to look at her. She cleared her throat several times, moved her chair and let out a loud "Ooh, that smarts," and did everything but chuck her fork at him. Lilly was proud of him for ignoring her.

Finally Ivy could stand it no longer and addressed Hassan. "I trust you've had a chance to review certain documents by now, Hassan?"

Hassan glowered at her and Lilly was afraid he was about to say something uncharitable when there came the sound of a knife clinking against a water glass. All heads turned to see Ted Conover standing behind the back counter.

"I'd like to welcome all of you to the unofficial opening of Tranquilitea." He smiled as his gaze swept the room. "I can't thank you enough for coming out to support me and the tearoom today. I'm sure you've heard of the tragedy of my ex-wife's death, and I appreciate you being here to take my mind off the horror of it."

A smattering of condolences went around the room.

"You'll notice that I placed a full menu at everyone's spot, so feel free to peruse that at your leisure. Today I've prepared a number of small bites for you, all of which are on the menu. And, of course, there's tea. Lots of tea. What I'm going to ask each one of you to do is come here to the back counter with your teacups and I'll pour you whatever flavor you'd like. How about we start over here with the back table?" He indicated Lilly's table with his hand.

Hassan and Harry stood up. Hassan helped pull Lilly's chair out and Harry looked on, avoiding Ivy's scowl. Ronan was the first one in line, picking up one of each bite-sized treat and studying the menu of teas available. Hassan held out his hand, indicating that Lilly should go ahead of him. She led the way and stood behind Ronan as he agonized over his choice. She picked up a few treats and stepped around Ronan.

"Hi, Ted. Could I have a cup of Darjeeling, please?"

"You got it. Thanks for coming today."

"It's my pleasure. Say, you know Hassan, right?" She turned to Hassan, who held out his hand to Ted.

Ted didn't take the proffered hand. "I know Hassan."

"Can we move the line along a little, please? I'm in pain back here," came Ivy's grating voice from the back of the line.

Lilly held out her teacup while Ted poured the tea. Hassan indicated that he would take the same, so Ted poured his, too. Then they returned to the table.

"That was weird," Lilly muttered to him.

"I know. He doesn't seem to like me too much. I barely know him. I've hardly seen him in the six months since he moved out of Michelle's house."

There was a brief commotion behind them at the counter and they turned around to see what was going on. Ted had come around to the front of the counter and was embracing Ivy. Lilly and Hassan exchanged confused glances.

"I didn't even see you come in, Aunt Ivy. How are you feeling?" Ted cast a quick glance in Hassan's direction.

Lilly and Hassan looked at each other again. "There's your answer," Lilly said. "Ivy's his aunt. I don't believe this."

CHAPTER 19

"*A*nd he probably hates me being here because I caused the car accident in which his aunt was injured."

Ronan looked up from his plate of food. "What? What's going on?"

"Nothing," Hassan said.

"Did you know Ivy and Ted are related?" Lilly asked Ronan.

"Nope. Does it matter?"

"No. It's just interesting," Lilly said.

They continued eating in silence. Ivy sat down a couple minutes later and Ted came up behind her with her plate and teacup. "Here you are, Auntie. Enjoy. Anything you want, you just say the word. This tearoom wouldn't be here without your help." He leaned over and planted a kiss on her cheek. While he was still bent over, he whispered something in Ivy's ear. Then he left without a glance for anyone else at the table.

Ivy looked at Lilly and Hassan with glittering eyes. "Are you surprised?"

"By what?" Lilly asked. She tapped Hassan under the table

with her foot, hoping he would realize she wanted to do the talking.

"By me being Ted's auntie." Somehow Ivy didn't seem the *auntie* type.

"I had no idea. What difference does it make?"

"I wonder if you would have come today if you had known."

"Why wouldn't we come here today to support a Main Street merchant, regardless of who his aunt is?"

Ivy shrugged and picked up her fork. "I just thought you might be embarrassed."

This was apparently too much for Hassan.

"Embarrassed? Why should we be embarrassed?" He spoke quietly. Lilly hoped things would stay that way. She didn't want to make a scene. The truth was, she might not have come if she had known Ted was Ivy's nephew. Not only did she hate the idea of sharing a meal with Ivy, but it seemed somehow distasteful to be accepting Ted's hospitality after Hassan caused that car accident.

"Because of all this," Ivy hissed, pointing to her neck brace and her cane.

"All right. I think we can have this conversation somewhere else," Lilly said.

But Ivy wasn't ready to stop talking. She looked at Hassan out of the corner of her eye as she took a sip of tea, then she put her teacup down with calculated precise movements.

"Did you know Ted's father, my brother, died on September eleventh?" She avoided looking straight at Hassan, but the implication was clear.

"I'm done here. Lilly, I'll call you later." Hassan stood up, threw his napkin on the table, and stalked off. Lilly gazed after him, figuring he needed time to himself.

"Ivy, I don't know what you're trying to do, but that was hateful," she said. She glared at the older woman.

Ivy shrugged. "I was just sharing some information you and Hassan may not have known. Don't you agree that it's important to get to know your peers?"

"Of course I do. But that was over the line."

Ted had been making the rounds among the other tables, checking on guests, making sure they had enough to eat and drink. He made his way to Lilly's table just in time to hear her last remark.

"Is something wrong here?"

"No, Ted. Everything is fine. Unfortunately, I have to be going," Lilly said. She gestured toward Harry. "Harry can stay as long as he likes, but I need to get back to the shop."

She was careful not to throw her napkin down as Hassan had, but very deliberately folded it and set it next to her plate, which still had several pieces of food on it.

"Can I put the lemon bar and the molasses cookie in a to-go box for you?" Ted asked.

"No, thank you. Everything was delicious, but I need to head out. Thanks for inviting us." She shot one last glare in Ivy's direction and weaved her way through the room to the exit, stopping briefly to greet the other merchants there.

When she emerged from the tearoom onto Main Street, Hassan was nowhere to be seen. She strode back to the jewelry store, hoping she was walking fast enough to get out her angry energy. She set out the displays she and Harry had put away, then unlocked the door and turned the sign to "Open." It wasn't long before the bell over the door jingled and Hassan walked in.

She gave him a sympathetic look. "How are you doing?"

He made a harsh scoffing sound. "I've had it. I've had it with

Ivy, I've had it with Michelle, I've had it with Ted and his tearoom, I've had it with stupid people."

"I can't believe Ivy said that."

"I can. She's the most miserable woman I know, now that Michelle is dead. Who says that to someone?"

"I'm embarrassed for the whole town of Juniper Junction. I had no idea these feelings were out there."

"They're everywhere, Lilly. This is not unique to Juniper Junction."

"I'm really sorry." Lilly couldn't think of anything to say. She couldn't very well say she knew how he felt, because she didn't. Not exactly.

"I know you are. I'm just so tired of it."

"What can I do to help?"

Hassan shrugged. "I don't know that there's anything you can do. I wonder if your brother has had any luck finding out who those guys were who came to the door on Halloween night."

At least he's not talking about moving away. "I don't know. I'll call him and find out. Are you ready to head back to your house?"

"I suppose. I need to get some work done."

"I'll drive you back as soon as Harry gets here."

"Thanks."

Harry returned from the tearoom a short while later. Lilly and Hassan gave him expectant looks.

"I'm sorry for what happened, Hassan." Harry took his coat off and slung it over a stool behind one of the display cases.

"Thanks, Harry."

"Did anyone say anything after we left?" Lilly's eyes blazed. Now that she had talked to Hassan, she was even more angry at Ivy. And at Ted for refusing to shake hands with Hassan.

"Ivy chattered on and on to Ronan about the injuries she

got in the car accident." Harry's glance shifted to Hassan briefly. "Sorry. Are you sure you want to hear this?"

Harry nodded tensely.

"She said that she might have permanent nerve damage in her arm and she's having 'vicious' headaches every day."

"There's something vicious, all right, but it's not a headache." Lilly realized she was clenching her jaw and tried to relax.

CHAPTER 20

"I know what she's doing," Harry said. "She's trying to make it known to everyone that she's hurt so when she sues Hassan, there'll be witnesses. Ronan as much as told her to shut up, that he's sick of listening to her complaints."

"And she's already sued me," Hassan said. Lilly realized she hadn't mentioned that to Harry yet.

"Oh, geez, Hassan. I'm sorry. I didn't know that."

Lilly remembered something. "Harry, did you happen to hear what Ted whispered to Ivy when he brought her plate to the table?"

"Yeah. He said, 'please rethink your decision.'"

"I wish I knew what that was all about," Lilly said.

Hassan shook his head. "I just can't believe any of this."

"Hassan, I'm taking you home. You need to relax." Lilly pulled her car keys out of her pocket.

"Thanks. I won't be able to relax, though." Hassan followed Lilly through the office and out the back door of the jewelry shop.

"As soon as I drop you off I'm going to call Bill and see if any of the neighbors got a glimpse of those guys from security cameras or doorbell footage."

"Whatever."

"I know you're discouraged right now, but if the police can catch the people who barged into your house on Halloween, they can be arrested and charged. The same with whoever vandalized your house while we were out, assuming it wasn't those same guys. Everyone will know it's not acceptable to treat people like that."

"Everyone should know that already."

"I agree."

Lilly turned into Hassan's driveway and turned off the car. She faced him and he gave her a tired smile.

"I appreciate all you're doing and saying. Really I do. I'm sorry I haven't been very good company lately." He took her hand and kissed it.

"You've had a lot on your mind. This is what couples do, and I want to help you however I can."

"You're already helping." He leaned forward and kissed her, wincing as he did so.

"Am I that bad?" Lilly asked, laughing.

He laughed along with her, then chucked her under the chin. "You're the best."

He got out of the car and walked around to her side.

"Don't forget that," she teased.

"I won't. Why don't we plan to go out to dinner tomorrow night? The Water Wheel? While I still have some money, I want to spend it so I don't have to give it all to Ivy."

"You won't have to give all your money to Ivy, I promise. But yes, The Water Wheel sounds good. Just tell me when to be there."

"I'll call you later." He leaned down and kissed her again. Then she went back to work.

The first thing she did when she got home that evening was call Bill.

"Hey," he greeted her.

"Hi. Doing any better?"

"Things are slowing down a little bit, if that's what you mean."

"Good. I'm calling to see if you or someone else was able to talk to any of Hassan's neighbors about doorbell video footage or security footage."

"I haven't gone over to his neighborhood at all since that night. Something came up the next morning and I haven't been able to get over there personally. Let me check the file and I'll see if anyone else has had any luck. If Hassan hasn't heard anything, there's probably nothing to hear."

"That's what I figured. I told Hassan I would ask, though. Call me if you hear anything."

"I will. Wait, before you go, is Noley mad at me?"

"Not that I know of. She certainly hasn't mentioned it. Why?"

"I can't get ahold of her. I thought you might know what's up."

"I'll find out and let you know."

"Thanks."

After they hung up Lilly fixed something quick for dinner and took Barney for a walk. She knew she should call her mother and she figured she should probably call Noley, too, but she was not ready for more drama just yet. What she needed was a little bit of time to relax and unwind. Spending time with Barney always worked like magic, so she took him around the block a second time, much to his delight.

And she was right—she felt much better when she returned home. She poured herself a glass of wine, got into her comfy pajamas, and sat down on the sofa with Barney next to her.

At first she thought she might turn on the television to watch the news, but she decided to make those phone calls first.

When she called her mother, Meredith answered the phone. "She's just drifting off to sleep right now," she said in a quiet voice.

"Oh, darn it. I'm sorry I missed her."

"Honestly? It was probably good that you did. She's not too happy with you tonight."

"Me? What did I do?"

"You told Nikki she could have a few days off and your mother isn't too happy about it."

"That doesn't surprise me. I'll talk to her about it tomorrow. Thanks, Meredith."

She hung up and called Noley next. When Noley answered, it was immediately clear that something wasn't right. She sounded stuffed up and her voice quavered a little.

"What's wrong?" Lilly asked.

"Nothing."

"You're lying. Tell me what's wrong, Nol."

"It's Bill." A surge of panic seized Lilly's heart and it constricted, sending her pulse racing.

"What about Bill? Is he all right? Is he hurt?"

Noley sniffled loudly. "No. It's not that. He's fine. I just, I just...." She started to cry.

"Don't cry, Nol. It's all right. Did Bill say something to upset you?"

Noley was quiet for a few moments while she composed herself. Lilly could hear her swallow hard. "He didn't say anything. That's just the problem. He called for five minutes last night and then he had to go. Someone at the station needed him. Do you think he's seeing someone else? Or maybe he just doesn't feel the same way toward me anymore?"

"No way on both counts. He's been so busy, Noley. He's

taking on a bunch of overtime and it's overwhelming for him. He just told me a little while ago that he couldn't get ahold of you and he thought something was wrong."

"I didn't answer the call because I'd been crying and I didn't want him to know that.

"Lilly, I just don't know if I'm cut out to be in a relationship with a police officer. I worry about him all the time and now that he's taking all this overtime, I'm lonely. I'm too needy, Lilly. I just can't handle it."

Lilly was stunned into silence. She had had no idea Noley was feeling this way.

"You have me, Noley. You have Hassan. You have other friends, too. We're all here for you when Bill's not."

"No offense, Lilly, but none of you are Bill."

Lilly smiled to herself. "Well, duh. We're just here to bridge the gap, that's all."

"Thank you. But I want Bill."

"I know. He feels terrible that he hasn't been able to see you. But this is something he has to do. Every job has times when you're busier than other times. This is just his time."

"But he's a police officer. I worry about him constantly. I don't know if I can deal with the worrying anymore."

"That's when you reach out to other people for company. You know, he's my brother. Don't you think I worry about him?"

"Do you?"

"Of course I do. I've worried about him every day since he went to the police academy. My mother was a basket case when he went. You should have seen her."

"So how do you deal with it?"

"First, I just have to trust that he's going to be careful. Second, I had to learn that there's nothing I can do to protect him. I can only control my own behavior. So I decided that I'm going to live my life and support him and trust that he's where he needs and wants to be."

"That's not an easy thing to learn."

"I know, believe me. But I can't let my worry paralyze me or I'll never do anything. And then he would wind up feeling guilty and everything would be a big mess."

"Okay."

"Do you feel any better?"

"Not really. But you've given me some things to think about."

"He loves you."

"I know. I love him, too. It's just so hard."

"I know. But staying busy helps. Want to meet me for lunch tomorrow?"

"Yeah, we can do that."

"All right. Chin up. See you tomorrow."

"Thanks, Lilly."

"That's what I'm here for."

They hung up and Lilly immediately texted Bill.

For the love of God, text Noley and tell her you miss her.

Then she shut off the phone. That way he couldn't bug her with a lot of questions.

"Time for bed, Barney."

* * *

When Lilly turned on her phone the next morning it pinged incessantly with missed texts. Two were from Hassan, letting her know what time he had made reservations for dinner and another wondering where she was. Two more were from Laurel, begging to come home. Lilly made a mental note to call Beau and discuss the situation. Nikki also left two messages, wondering how Bev was doing in her absence. Noley had called to thank her for their talk the night before. The last one was from Bill, telling her that he texted Noley and hadn't heard back from her.

She called Hassan on her way to the shop. Thank goodness for hands-free dialing. Being able to talk on the phone while she was driving was a huge time saver.

"Sorry I didn't answer the phone last night. I turned it off so I had plausible deniability when Bill accused me of ignoring him."

"What's going on with Bill?"

"I texted him and demanded that he text Noley. She's having a hard time dealing with him working all the time. And him being a police officer."

"Working hard is one thing. Having a problem with his entire profession is totally different."

"I know. She worries about him a lot and I think it's getting to her. No one wants to worry all the time." She told him what she had shared with Noley and he agreed it was the best thing she could have said.

"So we're having dinner at seven tonight? I can't wait," she said.

"Can you pick me up?"

"Of course. I'll see you at six-thirty. Has the mechanic called you back yet?"

"No. I'll call him today and see if he's made any progress."

Lilly had arrived at the shop by the time she hung up with Hassan. She dashed off a quick text to her brother, then one to Noley, asking how she was feeling today. She got a text back immediately.

Feeling better. Heard from Bill last night but was already in bed.

Replied this morning. Assume you had something to do with it.
Thanks. U R the best.

Lilly texted back with a heart emoji and put her phone away. The only thing she still had to do was get in touch with Beau so they could discuss Laurel's situation.

CHAPTER 21

*S*he and Harry were both helping customers later that morning when Bill came into the shop. He stood to one side, but his hands were clasped at his waist in full cop mode while Lilly spoke to a man about designing a custom piece for his wife's birthday. Shoppers looked askance at Bill, worried looks on their faces. Lilly tried to keep her flustered thoughts to herself. She wished Bill wouldn't do this—didn't he know a police officer in the shop would freak people out?

Lilly's customer promised to return in a couple days with a decision about which piece he wanted to buy for his wife, then left the store in a hurry, looking over his shoulder at Bill as he walked out the door.

Lilly turned to Bill and rolled her eyes.

"Don't do that."

"Do what?"

"Stand there like you're waiting to haul me in. It scares people off."

Bill relaxed his stance. "Oh. Sorry. I wasn't thinking."

"What's up?"

"I came over to tell you that none of Hassan's neighbors caught anything on Halloween night either on a security camera or a doorbell camera. The officer in charge of the case is probably calling Hassan to break the news to him as we speak."

"That stinks. So what happens next?"

"The truth is, not much. I hate to say it, but very often things like this go unsolved. The resources have to be used for bigger problems."

"This is a hate crime, Bill. Doesn't that deserve resources?"

"We don't know that it was a hate crime, Lilly. Without more evidence, we can't be sure."

Lilly put her hands on her hips and raised one eyebrow. "That's ridiculous. Of course it's a hate crime."

"You might very well be right, but we have bigger fish to fry right now."

"Like what?"

"Like the murder of Michelle Conover, for one." Bill gave her a stern look. "Listen. I agree with you. This is probably a hate crime. But we have a dead body and that case has top priority right now."

"If I have to get the evidence myself, I'm going to make sure those guys are arrested for what they did." Lilly glared at her brother.

"I may just haul you in after all."

"I mean it, Bill."

"Don't get involved, Lilly. Leave this to the professionals. You've gotten in trouble before by going off half-cocked and trying to do the job of the police."

"Well, if the police aren't going to do it, who is?"

"Let us get Michelle's murder solved, then we'll concentrate on Hassan's issue."

"Humph."

"You sound like Mom."

"Way to make things better, Bill."

He smiled and kissed her cheek. "Gotta run. I'll check in later."

"Wait. What about Noley?"

"What about her?"

"Did you talk to her yet?"

"No. I texted her last night at your command. She texted me back this morning, but I haven't actually spoken to her yet today."

"She's meeting me for lunch. Why don't you join us? You two need to talk."

"I can't, Lil. I've got to get back to work. And why do you say that?"

Lilly didn't want to reveal everything Noley had told her, but she needed to find a way to alert Bill that this was more important than he realized.

"Because she's your girlfriend and people who are dating need to communicate with each other or their relationship suffers, if you get my drift."

Bill shook his head. "You're talking in riddles. I've got to go. I'll call Noley as soon as I get a chance. I needed to talk to you first about the guys at Hassan's house."

Lilly shook her head as she watched Bill leave the shop.

She was still fuming when Noley arrived to go to lunch a little while later.

"What's wrong?" Noley asked.

"That stupid brother of mine."

"What did he do?"

"He's trying to tell me that the police don't have enough 'resources' to work on Hassan's case rightnow." She used her fingers to make air quotes.

"They're probably busy on the Michelle Conover murder."

"You sound just like him."

Noley chuckled. "It's a good thing you're my best friend or I might take that the wrong way."

That got a laugh out of Lilly. "Where do you want to go for lunch?"

"How about the tearoom? Is that open?"

"No way. Let's go to the bistro." While they walked to Armand's small French restaurant, Lilly told Noley what had happened at the tearoom's soft opening.

"I can't believe it. Ivy actually said those things to Hassan?"

Lilly nodded grimly, clenching her jaw.

"And Ted Conover is Ivy's nephew?"

More nodding and jaw clenching.

"Poor Hassan must think Juniper Junction is nothing but a hotbed of bigots," Noley said.

"He doesn't think that, but I couldn't blame him if he did."

"I'm boycotting that tearoom for as long as Ted owns it." Noley opened the door to the bistro. They were pleasantly assailed by the scents of fresh croissants and coffee. Lilly took a deep breath and let it out slowly.

"This place calms me right down," she said.

Noley laughed. "Me, too. Who would have thought that a year ago?" On July Fourth of the previous year, Armand's wife had been poisoned at a community celebration where Noley had been in charge of the catering. Noley had been under suspicion for the murder until the real killer was found, and Lilly was amazed that Noley had been willing to patronize the bistro after that.

Noley ordered first. "Hi, Armand. I'll take the *pan bagnat*, but no anchovies, please. I'd like red peppers on it, but go easy on the onions. And please slice the tomatoes extra thin and sprinkle them with a little *fleur de sel* before putting them on the bread."

Lilly rolled her eyes. Ordering with Noley was always an adventure.

Armand smiled. "*Mais oui,* Noley. What can I get you, Lilly?"

"Just a coffee, please."

Noley looked at Lilly in surprise. "You're only getting coffee? Why did we come out for lunch, then?"

"Because I forgot that Hassan and I are having dinner at The Water Wheel tonight and I don't want to spoil my appetite."

Famous last words.

After work that night Lilly hurried home, changed from business casual to dressy, and drove over to Hassan's house. He was waiting for her with a glass of wine.

"Thanks. I needed that." She took the wine and sat next to him on the loveseat in the living room. A fire burned low in the fireplace and she held one hand out to its warmth.

"Long day?"

"Yes. I talked to Bill and he told me that someone was going to call you with the news that they didn't find any security camera footage that they could use to find out who those guys were on Halloween night. He also told me Michelle's murder takes precedence right now."

Hassan nodded. "Yeah, someone from the station called to tell me. Frankly, it's what I expected."

"It's not fair."

"Maybe not, but that's the way it is. We'll have to wait until the murder is solved, then hope there's some way to find out who the mask-wearing creeps were."

"I don't like the thought of you living right next door to where a murder took place."

"I don't, either. But I think I'm pretty safe. I think the

person who killed Michelle is probably someone she pissed off. There have to be a million of them out there."

"Let's think of something else. Like dinner. You ready to go?" Lilly finished her wine and stood up.

"I'm starving. Let me get my coat."

Lilly helped him get his coat on. She was reaching for the door handle when there was a sharp rap on the door.

She frowned and said in a low voice, "Now what?" She opened the door and was surprised to see two police officers standing there.

"Hassan Ashraf?" the stouter one asked.

Lilly turned aside so Hassan could step forward, exchanging a worried glance with him.

"Going out?" the officer asked.

"Yes, sir. We have reservations at The Water Wheel for seven o'clock."

"I'm afraid that's going to have to wait. May we come in?"

Lilly felt her stomach drop as Hassan gestured for the officers to enter. She was going to give Bill a piece of her mind for not warning her about this.

"We'd like to ask you a few questions. Is there a place we can sit down?" the stout officer asked.

Lilly helped Hassan shrug his coat off and hung it up in the hall closet. She followed the men into the living room, where the tall, skinny officer sat down on the loveseat, the stout one sat in an armchair, and Hassan sat down on the sofa. She sat on the sofa, too, a few feet away.

"How can I help you?" Hassan asked.

Lilly was amazed at how calm Hassan looked. He sat up straight, but was not perched on the edge of the sofa like some nervous, guilty perp. On the other hand, her palms were sweaty and she was pretty sure the officers could see her heart beating right through her blouse. Hadn't the police already questioned Hassan?

"Tell me about Ivy Leachman," the stout one said. Apparently he was going to do all the talking.

Hassan blinked. Clearly he had been expecting questions about Michelle, as had Lilly.

"Um, what do you want to know?"

"I want to know who killed her."

CHAPTER 22

*L*illy gasped.

Hassan's mouth hung open as he shifted his gaze from one officer to the other and back again. "Someone killed Ivy? Who? What happened?"

"That's what we're trying to figure out, sir. She was found unresponsive in her place of business this morning, having been bludgeoned with a large piece of ceramic."

"I didn't even know she was dead. I just saw her yesterday," Hassan said.

Wrong thing to say.

"That's what I hear. Tell me about it."

Hassan slumped back against the sofa cushion. "She and I were involved in a car accident the other night." He lifted his arm as proof of his injury. "It was my fault, really. I wasn't paying attention to where I was going."

"And?"

"And she made a big show of her injuries yesterday when we happened to be at the same place for lunch."

"Where was that?"

"The new tearoom, Tranquilitea."

"What else happened?"

"She made a comment about the tearoom owner's father having been killed on September eleventh. It was a thinly veiled jab at my faith."

"I see. Is it true that she filed suit against you over the car accident?"

"Yes, sir."

The officer went on to ask Hassan about his activities all day. Of course, Hassan had been home alone all day and there was no one who could corroborate that.

Finally the stout officer stopped asking questions and it was the other one's turn.

"I have some follow-up questions for you about Michelle Conover, Mister Ashraf," the officer said.

"Certainly."

"We've learned a little more about your disagreements with her. Why didn't you tell us about those when we first questioned you?" The officer took out a small notebook and pen. He held the pen poised over the paper, poised to write down whatever Hassan said.

"Because I didn't think it was relevant."

The officer's eyes widened. "You didn't think an argument with the victim over property rights was significant in a murder investigation?"

"Not really. I didn't kill her, so I didn't see the need to discuss it."

"You need to let the detectives make that decision, sir."

Hassan nodded.

"Tell me about this property dispute."

"She thinks—thought—that I had my new fence built six inches onto her property."

The officer waited a long moment before speaking again.

"And did you?"

"No. I had a surveyor come out before the fence was installed to make sure it would be entirely on my property. He even came out to double-check the measurements."

"Do you have the number of the surveyor?"

"Sure." Hassan pulled his cell phone from his pocket and scrolled through his emails. "Here it is. This has his name, his email, office address, and phone number." He held out the phone to the officer, who took it and scribbled things down as he glanced back and forth between his paper and the phone.

"Tell me about the other problems you've had with Michelle Conover."

Hassan shifted uncomfortably, the first indication that the officers' questions were getting to him.

"She didn't like the noise that the landscapers made with the machines they used. You know, like the leaf blower and the lawn mower."

The officer waited again before saying anything. "And what did she say to you?"

Hassan proceeded to tell the officer a watered-down version of his confrontations with Michelle. He didn't divulge how angry Michelle had been, nor did he divulge how angry he had been in return.

"And did you know Michelle Conover?" the officer asked, turning his attention to Lilly.

"Yes, but not well."

"Have you ever spoken to her?"

"Yes."

"About what?"

"I told her to leave Hassan alone."

"She was really bothering him, huh?"

Uh-oh. I should have known he'd twist my words. I am going to have such a talk with Bill.

"It's not that. It's just that he had been in a car accident and I wanted to keep people away from him so he could rest."

"Let's circle back to that car accident, Mister Ashraf. From what I hear, you were so upset over something Mrs. Conover had said or done that you weren't paying attention to the road."

Hassan shifted again. He moved closer to the end of the couch and rested his sore arm on one of the throw pillows.

"It happened right after Michelle approached me about my fence encroaching on her property. I had a lot on my mind, and it wasn't just Michelle. The accident happened because I just wasn't paying attention."

"It sounds like she made you pretty mad."

"It's not like that. Like I said, I had a lot of things on my mind that had nothing to do with Michelle. I just wasn't paying attention."

Another long pause. Did this officer think Hassan was going to magically confess to Michelle's murder? "Are you aware that the driver of the car you hit, Ivy Leachman, is the aunt of Mrs. Conover's ex-husband?"

"I found out afterwards, yes."

"And how did you find out?"

"When we were at the tearoom. Ted Conover mentioned it."

Pause. "You have a lot of things going on, don't you?"

"Yes. But I didn't kill Michelle or Ivy."

"No one said you did." The officer raised his eyebrows. Lilly was fighting the urge to wrap her hands around his neck and squeeze as hard as she could.

In the silent stare-down that followed, Lilly was pleased that Hassan's gaze didn't leave the officer's face. Finally he put his notebook away and both officers stood up.

"Thank you for your time. I'm sure someone will be in touch. Don't go far, because we're going to have more questions for you."

Hassan and Lilly followed them to the door, then locked it when they left. Hassan leaned against the door and closed his eyes.

"I can't believe Ivy's dead."

"Me neither."

Silence.

"They think I killed both women."

"I doubt it. They were just trying to sweat you into saying something, anything, that might help them find out who killed them. I'm sure of it."

Hassan gave her a doubtful look.

"Listen, that's my story and I'm sticking to it." Lilly tried to smile. "Let me call Bill and see what he can tell us. He didn't say a word about anyone coming over here tonight to question you."

But when she dialed Bill's number, it went straight to voicemail.

"I think his phone is off. He's probably at home, sound asleep. He hasn't gotten much time off lately."

"Do you still want to see if there's a table at The Water Wheel?"

"Not really. Let's just stay in and have sandwiches. Do you have cheese and bread?"

"I'm sure I do."

"Then grilled cheese, coming right up. You sit down and relax."

"There'll be no relaxing for me until they find out who killed Michelle and Ivy and I'm off the hook."

"I'm sure I'll talk to Bill tomorrow."

"That'll be great, as long as I'm not arrested before then."

CHAPTER 23

hile the grilled cheese sandwiches cooked, Lilly set the table. She lit candles and poured wine, just as if they had been at The Water Wheel. When she went to the living room to tell Hassan dinner was ready, she found him on his phone, scrolling through websites for local defense lawyers.

"Did you talk to my lawyer?"

"Yes, but only to discuss the lawsuit Ivy filed. I'm going to have to call her again and ask for a recommendation for a good defense lawyer."

"We already know one. It's Gretchen, the woman Noley hired last summer. But you're not going to need a defense lawyer. They'll find out who did it."

Hassan looked up at her. "It can't hurt to be prepared, right?"

"I suppose not. Dinner's ready."

Hassan smiled for the first time all evening when he saw that Lilly had lit the candles and poured wine in the crystal goblets. "Thank you for doing this," he said, nuzzling her neck.

"You're welcome," she giggled. "Now sit down and let's eat before I starve to death."

After she left Hassan's house that night, she stopped at her mom's house before heading home. Meredith was there and opened the door for her.

"Hi, Meredith. How's Mom?"

"She had a pretty good day, from what I heard from Nikki's sub, Susan. She said your mom even agreed to go for a walk this afternoon."

"Really? Wow. I'm impressed. Is Mom awake?"

"Yes. She's in the kitchen eating a snack."

Lilly headed for the kitchen and Meredith followed her. They found Bev sitting at the table, staring straight ahead.

"Hi, Mom."

Bev blinked slowly. "Hello, Lilly."

Lilly pulled out a chair and sat across from her mom. "You okay, Mom? You look a little out of it."

"My arm hurts."

"Where on your arm?"

Bev pushed up the sleeve of her cardigan, but it got caught on her elbow and she couldn't get it up any farther. She squeezed her eyes shut, wincing.

"Can I help you, Bev?" Meredith asked. She leaned over Bev and gently helped her push the sleeve up. Lilly gasped when she saw the deep purple bruise all around the elbow.

"Mom! No wonder your arm hurts. What happened?"

"I don't remember."

Meredith looked at her with concern. "Bev, it looks like you took a nasty fall. Do you remember falling today? Or maybe yesterday?"

Bev frowned in concentration. "I fell today."

"When?" Meredith bent down to look at the elbow more closely.

"Outside."

Lilly and Meredith exchanged glances. Maybe the walk outside hadn't been so good, after all.

"Susan didn't say anything about Bev falling. I can ask her tomorrow."

"If I have anything to say about it, Susan will not be here tomorrow." Lilly's face was grim. "I'm going to call the agency right now and leave a message with their answering service. I'll have them send over somebody different tomorrow."

"I miss Nikki." Bev's voice sounded small and sad.

"I know, Mom. But it's only for a few days. She needed some time off."

"I can't take time off," Bev said.

Lilly and Meredith exchanged glances again. "Take time off from what, honey?" Meredith asked.

"From being sick."

Lilly's heart almost broke listening to her mom. She often wondered whether her mother realized that her mental health was declining, but moments like this made it all too clear: she knew. Lilly thought it might be better if Bev didn't realize what was happening.

She went around the table and put her arm around her mother's shoulders, hugging her close. "Nikki will be back before you know it, Mom. We'll get someone else here tomorrow instead of Susan, and hopefully Nikki will be back the next day."

"Why did Nikki leave?"

"She just had some things she needed to do."

"What things?"

"Oh, just some personal things." Lilly tried to speak breezily, but this brought back memories of when her kids were toddlers. Everything was "why?" and "what?" and "how come?"—constant questions needing explanations and answers.

"What personal things?"

"I don't know, Mom. I didn't ask. It's none of my business."

"Well, you don't have to get mad about it."

"I'm not mad, Mom."

"I can tell you're mad. Meredith, I'm ready for bed."

Lilly straightened up and grinned with teeth gritted. "Mom, I'm not mad. But I'll leave you alone for the night so Meredith can help you get ready for bed. I'll talk to you tomorrow, okay?"

"Yes."

"Love you, Mom." Lilly bent down to kiss Bev's cheek, but Bev turned away. Lilly shook her head. She didn't need this tonight. She looked at Meredith, who winked at her and nodded to let her know that she would take care of everything, and Lilly left for home. The first thing she did when she walked into the house was to call the care agency, demand an investigation into Susan's time with Bev, and request another aide until Nikki could return. She hoped it would only be one more day. She hated that Bev's life had to be disrupted because of a problem between Nikki and Beau.

It wasn't until midmorning the next day that Lilly finally got Bill on the phone.

"Did you know someone was going to go to Hassan's to question him?" She tried to keep the accusation out of her tone.

"I just found out this morning. I didn't even know about Ivy until just a couple hours ago. I'm not working either case, Lil, so I'm not in the loop. And I've been so busy that I didn't have a chance to talk to any of the guys working it."

"It's like he's the prime suspect."

"Like I said, Lilly, I don't know anything about it."

"You mean it's really possible that he's the prime suspect?" Lilly could barely keep her voice even.

"I didn't say that at all." Bill sounded tired. "All I said was that I am not privy to the details of the investigation."

"But you can find out, can't you?"

"Yeah. It's just going to take some time. I know Hassan didn't do it. We'll get the person who did."

"All right. Let me know when you hear anything, will you? And how's Noley?"

"Fine, I guess. Listen, I have to run. I'll talk to you later." He hung up. Lilly was incensed that the police were bothering Hassan with their nosy questions and their suspicious attitudes. Couldn't they see he was not a killer?

One thing was sure: if the police were going to keep harassing Hassan, she was going to take matters into her own hands. She was going to find out who killed Michelle. And Ivy. The two murders had to be related.

CHAPTER 24

*L*illy called Nikki when she got home from work that night. Hassan had said he had an overseas phone call that was expected to go long, so she didn't bother going to his house.

"Hi, Nikki, I was just calling to see how everything's going." What she wanted to say was, *When the heck are you going back to work?*

"It's going much better with Beau, thanks."

"Mom's been asking about you." Lilly hoped Nikki could be guilted into going back to work quickly.

"Does she miss me?" There was a smile in Nikki's voice,

"She sure does. And the replacement the agency sent took her out for a walk and didn't mention that Mom fell. She's got a huge, ugly bruise on her elbow."

"That's awful! Is she all right?"

"She's okay, but she missed you a lot."

"Well, you tell her I'll be back soon."

Lilly was hoping Nikki would feel so bad that she would head back to Bev's house first thing in the morning, but that wasn't happening. Lilly supposed a couple days was the most she could ask for. She had given Nikki the time off, after all. She couldn't blame her for wanting to take the time.

After they hung up, Lilly went in search of a pad of paper and a pen. When she had what she needed, she curled up on the sofa with Barney next to her.

"I'm going to write out a list of the people who hated Michelle and Ivy, Barn. At least the people I knew about. There are surely others I've never met. I'm going to need a lot of paper and ink. It would probably be easier to make a list of the people who liked them."

In the "Michelle" column the first name she wrote down was Ted Conover. She thought he had a pretty good reason to want Michelle dead. After all, she had apparently done a number inside his tearoom the week before the opening. If someone had done that to Lilly's jewelry shop, she was pretty sure she would wish death upon them. She wouldn't actually go through with it, but she could sympathize with the feelings of anger. And Ted hadn't seemed too devastated by Michelle's death.

Second, she wrote down "co-workers." She didn't know any of them, and in fact she didn't even know where Michelle worked, but she knew she couldn't stand to spend her working hours with someone so disagreeable and horrid. She made a note to find out where Michelle worked and pay a visit to the place.

Third, she wrote down the names of all the neighbors she could think of. There were Eugene and Sally, Larry, and probably everyone else who lived on the block. Michelle seemed to have left no neighbor unsnubbed in her crusade to sow hatred up and down the cul-de-sac.

Finally, she wrote down Ivy's name. Was it possible that Ivy had such an affection for her nephew that she had killed his ex-wife? Lilly doubted it. Ivy might have been one of the most miserable people she had ever known, but she didn't strike Lilly as a killer.

But then again, neither had any of the other killers she had met.

The "Ivy" column was shorter and only included the words "neighbors," "co-workers," and "other business owners." She contemplated putting Ted's name on the list, but didn't. They appeared close.

She found it easier to concentrate on the Michelle list because it seemed a bit more specific. She needed to find out who Michelle's co-workers had been.

The next day Lilly placed another call to Bill.

"What is it now?" he answered.

"You're a grouch. Can't you be any more pleasant?"

Bill cleared his throat and Lilly figured he was counting to ten, as she often did. "How can I help you today, my dear sister?"

"That's better. You can tell me where Michelle Conover worked."

"No can do."

"Why not?"

"Two reasons. First of all, it would look a little weird if I went to the officer in charge of the case and asked for that information. And second, it sounds to me like you might be gearing up to put your nose where it doesn't belong."

"Well. Don't hold back, Bill."

"Lilly, I'm sorry. It's just that I know what's coming. I'm going to tell you to butt out of police business and you're going to insist that you're not getting involved.

"If I find out in time, I will tell you if it looks like Hassan is going to be questioned again as a possible suspect in either Michelle's or Ivy's death, but I'm not going to help you investigate this outside the police department. Or have you forgotten the many times I've told you I could get fired for that?"

"It sounds like you got up on the wrong side of the bed."

"Not helping, Lilly…." Bill was using his Big Brother voice, the one that warned her she was on thin ice.

"Okay, all right. Forget I asked."

"I will."

"All right."

"All right."

They hung up at the same time.

I'll just have to use my own sources, thought Lilly.

At lunchtime Lilly walked across the street to the tearoom. She hadn't thought of what she was going to say, but she figured the words would come as she needed them. She was surprised that the door was locked. She peered through the window and could see Ted standing behind the back counter, his back to the window. She knocked on the glass. He spun around and walked to the front door.

"Hello, Lilly. How can I help you?" He didn't invite her inside. His eyes were red-rimmed and puffy.

"Hi, Ted. I wanted to say I'm sorry about Ivy's passing."

"Thank you."

Lilly didn't say anything for a moment.

"Is there something else you need, Lilly?"

"Oh. Uh, no. I mean, yes. I was just wondering if I could get a few copies of your menu. You know, to pass out to people who might ask for restaurant recommendations. Ski season is coming up, you know. It's going to start getting busier."

"Oh, sure. That would be great. Thanks, Lilly. Just a minute." He closed the door and hurried to the back. He returned a couple minutes later holding a sheaf of menus.

"I appreciate you doing this, especially after the way things ended the other day…." His voice trailed off, as if he didn't know what to say next.

"Yeah, well, the Main Street merchants need to stick together. Say, speaking of sticking together, how are you holding up? You know, Michelle … and Ivy…." *That was smooth.* Lilly made a mental note to rehearse the next time something like this came up.

Ted heaved a long sigh and his gaze clouded. "As well as can be expected, I suppose. Of course, it will be hard getting used to Auntie being gone. She helped my father raise me after my mother passed, you know. And as for Michelle, we may have been divorced, but a part of me will never stop loving her. Are you married?"

"No. Divorced."

"Then you know what I mean."

Uh, no. I have no idea what you mean. Lilly kept her mouth shut.

"I know a lot of people thought Michelle could come on a little strong, but that was her superpower. That was how she got where she did. In business, I mean. Michelle always got what she set out to get."

Bingo. The perfect segue. "I can imagine. Where did she work? Her co-workers must miss her terribly." Lilly tamped down the urge to make a retching sound.

"Well, she used to work on Wall Street. That's where we met." The pride in his voice was unmistakable.

"I heard that somewhere. So where—"

"When we moved to Juniper Junction, I got out of the business and became co-owner of a vegan grocery store in Lupine. She took a job at an investment firm right next door." *Excellent. I know exactly where that is.* Ted was still talking. "Mostly she worked out of the house, but she went into the office about once a week. I'm sure the staff appreciated it when she was around. More work got done and they had some direction."

I can just imagine the direction they craved when she was around —right out the front door.

"How nice that you could work near each other. Well, Ted, I need to get back to work. Thanks for the extra menus."

"No problem. Thanks for coming by, Lilly." He turned and walked back into the tearoom, locking the door behind him.

Harry was waiting to ask a slew of questions when Lilly got back to the jewelry store. The first thing she did was to dump the tearoom menus in the garbage. She had no intention of steering anyone there even if they were dying from lack of tea and snacks.

"Why'd you go to the tearoom? I thought you'd never go back there after what happened. Did Ted say anything about what happened at the soft opening? Or Michelle? Or Ivy? What did you guys talk about?" he asked.

"Easy there, inspector. First, I went with the pretense of asking for more menus. What I really wanted was to find out where Michelle worked. Otherwise, you're right. I never want to go back there. Second, Ted implied that he thought I'd never come back because of what happened at the soft opening. Third, I did learn that a part of him will always love Michelle. His words, not mine. And finally, he thanked me for my condolences for Ivy's death."

"So did you find out where she worked?"

"Yes. She worked in Lupine and didn't go into the office very often. I think I'll head over there tomorrow and ask a few questions."

"Why aren't the police doing it?"

"They are, but Bill hasn't been in a position to get the whole scoop for me. He's not working the case."

"In other words, you're going off to investigate a murder on your own."

"I wouldn't put it that way. And don't tell anyone."

"Maybe I should go with you. You know, for muscle." Lilly grinned. Harry was practically see-through.

"Thanks, Harry, but I'll need you to stay here and take care of customers while I'm gone. The investment firm where she worked probably doesn't have evening hours, so I have to go while the jewelry shop is open."

"Got it. No problem, boss." He saluted and she shook her head, smiling.

CHAPTER 25

That evening Lilly called Noley. "Want to go with me to the place where Michelle Conover worked?"

"The woman who was murdered? No, thanks. Remember what happened the last time I went with you to talk to someone who might have been involved in a crime? I hung out with strippers and you got knocked out. I'm not exactly eager to do that again."

"No strippers this time, I promise. In fact, the exact opposite. Everyone you'll meet will be in power suits."

"Somehow that sounds even worse."

"You won't go?"

"Well, I probably should go with you just to make sure you survive the experience. When are you going?"

"Tomorrow sometime. Whenever you're free."

"I'm doing a cooking show from my kitchen tomorrow. I don't know when I'll be done."

"That sounds cool. What's it for?"

"An internet cooking show. They ask cooking columnists

from around the country to make something entertaining and show viewers their home kitchens. It should be fun."

"What are you making?"

"*Pain au chocolat.*"

"Sounds delicious and complicated."

"It is delicious. It's not complicated, but it does have a lot of steps. It takes some time to make it."

"So you want to go with me the day after tomorrow instead?"

"Let me call you when the taping is done and we'll see what time it is. We're supposed to get started pretty early in the morning, so maybe it won't go too late."

"Sounds good. How are things with Bill, by the way?"

"We've been talking a little more. I just don't want him to feel like I'm nagging him for attention or like he has to appease me somehow."

"He doesn't feel that way, so don't worry about it. Hey, if you have any *pain au chocolat* left after you make that video tomorrow, remember who your best friend is, okay?"

"I always do."

* * *

It was three o'clock the next afternoon before Noley called. "The video crew just left my house. Are you ready to go over to Lupine?"

"Sure. I can pick you up. I'll be over in just a little while."

"What should I wear?"

Lilly looked down at her outfit. "I have a plan. I'm going to change into total casual, but you should change into hard-charging business attire."

Noley groaned. "I don't think I like your plan."

"You don't even know my plan."

"All right. I'll change and see you in a bit."

Lilly put Harry in charge of the shop and left a short time later, after taking off all her makeup, putting her hair up in a high ponytail, and changing into yoga pants and a tee shirt that she had in her office.

When she pulled into the driveway, Noley came out of her house swinging a small paper bag. Lilly grinned. *Pain au chocolat.* Being friends with such a good cook had some great perks. As usual, Noley looked great. Her blond hair was up in a French twist and she wore dark green capri dress slacks and a matching jacket over an ivory blouse. She wore gorgeous dark green suede pumps.

"You look perfect. Here's my plan: you're going to be the prospective client and I'm your sloppy friend who's just along for the ride."

Noley cocked one eyebrow at Lilly. "You look like you just got out of bed."

"I know. You look rich and I look dumpy. I want them to pay more attention to you than me."

Noley sighed. "Remind me why I agreed to this?"

Lilly grinned.

Lupine was bigger than Juniper Junction and not as pretty. Whereas Juniper Junction had a quaint main street, Lupine had a blocks-wide downtown with cramped parking spots and too much traffic. Lilly frowned as she hunted for a parking spot. She finally found one two blocks away from the investment firm. While they walked to their destination they talked about what information Lilly wanted to glean from the visit.

"So what am I supposed to be doing?" Noley asked.

"You're looking for an investment firm that will fit your needs. You have a large amount to invest because you're a famous person. That part you don't have to fake."

"I don't have a large amount to invest."

"But you are a famous person. Stay with me here, Nol."

Noley grimaced. "How much money?"

"A couple million."

"A couple *million*? I can't fake that kind of money."

"What do you know about how millionaires act? They're just like you and me."

"Somehow I doubt that."

"Just be yourself, but with more money, okay? Let me take care of the rest."

The firm was located in a squat brick building that looked like it had housed a gym at one time. Big square windows in front, now tastefully covered with glare-blocking shades. Double glass doors, now frosted to look secret and important.

Lilly opened the door and stood aside for Noley to enter first. A soft-spoken middle-aged woman greeted them from behind a large semicircular desk.

"Good afternoon. How may I help you?"

Lilly looked at Noley, who looked nervous. Lilly was beginning to worry that perhaps she should have coached Noley a little more when Noley spoke.

"My name is Noley Appleton. This is my friend, Louise." She gestured toward Lilly, who bestowed a gracious smile on the receptionist.

"I am interviewing investment firms in the area. I would like to consolidate some of my bank accounts into an investment account and I need some guidance."

"Certainly. We can help you with that. Let me see who's available to meet with you." The receptionist put on the glasses that hung on a lanyard around her neck and scanned the computer screen in front of her. "It looks like Gerald McIntosh is available. Let me ring him and see if he can meet with you."

"I know I should have made an appointment, but Louise

and I were walking by this building and just decided on a whim to stop in."

"Well, we certainly appreciate that," the woman said with a smile. She picked up her handset and touched a few numbers on her phone. "Mister McIntosh, I wonder if you have a few moments to meet with a potential client out here."

She hung up the phone and said with a smile, "He'll be right out. Can I get you anything? Coffee? Tea? Mineral water?"

"No, thank you. We're fine." Noley was doing a good job of sidelining "Louise." Lilly smiled.

They sat down in upholstered taupe chairs and Noley commenced reading a financial news magazine that sat on an occasional table next to her. Lilly pulled out her phone and pretended to read texts. There was one real text there, too—one from Laurel, who asked if she could come home for Thanksgiving a few days early because "who needs those last few classes before the break, anyway?"

She typed a quick "Busy. We'll talk about it later" before a man stepped into the lobby and held out his hand. Not surprisingly, he seemed to instinctively know which of the two women was his prospective client. Noley set the magazine aside and stood up to greet him, then introduced Louise. Mister McIntosh led them back into a sparsely furnished office space which confirmed Lilly's suspicion that this, indeed, had been a gym in a former life.

CHAPTER 26

The high ceilings were raftered with iron bars; big pendant lights with glass shades hung from the rafters. The "offices" were actually long tables scattered throughout the huge space in an industrial-looking format. It was surprisingly quiet. There were several employees talking on phones, and though it seemed like everyone would be able to hear everyone else's business, that wasn't the case.

Mister McIntosh led the way to a table near the back of the huge room. He gestured to two chairs on one side of the table and he took a seat opposite Lilly and Noley as they sat down.

"So tell me a little bit about yourself," he said to Noley.

Noley launched into her spiel about her job, her alleged assets, and her investment needs. Lilly fidgeted a little while she spoke, wondering how best to intercept the conversation and steer it toward Michelle. Finally she nudged Noley with her foot, hoping she would get the message that it was time to cut to the chase.

Noley cleared her throat. "I'm interested in knowing a little more about the employees here. Does each person have access to all the other advisors' client accounts? In other words, say I need something done and you're out that day. Can I rely on someone else to take care of my needs?"

"Yes, of course." Mister McIntosh turned to a sleek file cabinet that stood next to the table. He rifled through files for a moment, finally pulling out a shiny brochure. He handed it to Noley with a smile. "This brochure identifies all our employees. There's a biography of each one detailing their credentials and their specific strengths. I think you'll find that you'll be in capable hands no matter which one of us helps you."

Noley nodded her thanks and glanced at the brochure before handing it to Lilly. This was what Lilly had been waiting for. She barely restrained herself from snatching the brochure right out of Noley's hand.

She looked through the brochure, giving the impression that she wasn't really interested in what it said. She was looking for a blurb about Michelle. When she found it, she read it quickly and looked up with a look she hoped smacked of genuine confusion.

"Excuse me." She interrupted Mister McIntosh as he droned on about returns on investments and prime-plus-one interest rates.

"Yes?"

Lilly pointed to the photo of Michelle, which was attractive in an assertive sort of way. It reminded Lilly of a velociraptor. "Isn't this the woman who has been in the news?"

Mister McIntosh nodded. "Yes. We haven't had new pamphlets printed yet. She worked here after she left her job on Wall Street."

"It's terrible, what happened to her," Lilly said.

"Yes, it was."

"I'm sorry for your loss." Lilly lowered her gaze in an

attempt to look sorrowful. Noley merely watched the exchange.

"Thank you. I've only been here for a couple years, so I didn't really know her very well on a personal level, even though she worked here for several years before her death. She only came in once a week. The rest of the time she worked from her home."

"Itmust be devastating to lose a co-worker in such a horrifying manner."

"I suppose so, but I wasn't close to her, like I said." Mister McIntosh turned his attention back to Noley and was about to say something when Lilly spoke again.

"Do you know what happened to her?"

Mister McIntosh looked like he was trying, unsuccessfully, to curb his annoyance at Lilly's questions. "No, I don't. I only know what I've read in the paper."

"I hear they haven't caught the person who did it. She looks like such a nice person. Who would do such a thing?"

"Looks can be deceiving," Mister McIntosh said.

Lilly leaned forward. "Really? She wasn't as nice as she looks?"

Mister McIntosh squirmed in his seat. "I don't think I should be speaking ill of the dead."

"I'm just curious. I'm studying to be a psychologist, so I find it fascinating to learn about the things that motivate people to act." *I am getting really good at this*, thought Lilly. "So you're saying that maybe her true nature was hidden under a pleasant façade?"

"That's exactly what I'm saying."

"So if she wasn't a nice person, why did the investment firm keep her on?" Noley asked.

He seemed grateful to turn his full attention back to Noley. "She was an excellent financial advisor and, after all, she only came in once a week. We could deal with her more easily when we knew she would only be here a fraction of the time." He paused. "I really shouldn't be talking about her like this."

"Don't feel bad about it." Noley waved her hand breezily. "It's important for potential clients to know these things."

"Well, let me tell you more about how our commissions work and then I'll give you some information to take with you to study."

Lilly had hoped to glean more information from this man, but he clearly wasn't interested in saying more about Michelle. Luckily, there was still one way for her to get the lowdown on Michelle. The receptionist.

When Noley was done talking to Mister McIntosh and he had loaded her arms with folders full of statistics and financial data about the firm, she stood up to shake his hand.

"Let me walk you out," he said. Lilly grimaced. She was going to have to think fast in order to get some time with the receptionist out of Mister McIntosh's hearing.

"Um, do you have a restroom? I need one—quick," she said. Mister McIntosh cocked one eyebrow at her and pointed in the direction of the ladies' room. "Thanks," she said. Then she turned to Noley. "I may be a few minutes. It must be that burrito I had for lunch." Noley suppressed her laugh with a dainty cough, and Mister McIntosh looked like he couldn't get away from Lilly fast enough. She dashed off in the direction of the ladies' room, then waited there for several minutes before deciding that Mister McIntosh had surely gone back to his work station. She peered around the restroom door and saw Noley chatting with the receptionist. That was a good sign.

A moment later Lilly strolled into the lobby. Noley turned to her and smiled, gesturing toward the receptionist. "Louise, this is Dot. She's been working here for twelve years. Dot, you've already met Louise."

"It's nice to meet you, Dot." Lilly held out her hand.

"We were just talking about Michelle." Noley gave her a look and raised her eyebrows almost imperceptibly.

"I can't believe you knew her," Lilly said, her eyes wide with interest.

"Oh, yes. I knew her." Dot smirked.

"I've heard she could be a bit demanding," Noley said. Lilly could have hugged her for taking the conversation down this road.

"That would be an understatement," Dot said.

"Really?" Lilly looked at her with an open expression, silently inviting her to dish all the dirt she had.

"Well, I don't want to speak ill of the dead, but no one got along with her around here," Dot said in a conspiratorial tone. "Thank God she only came in once a week. Once a month would have been better."

"She was that bad, huh?" Lilly asked.

Dot scoffed. "You have no idea. She would come in here like she owned the place, ordering people around, demanding that I bring her coffee. Like that's my job. I don't think so. And she would scream at anyone who she thought was being too loud on the phone or just talking to someone. And she even stole a big client from one of our advisors." She mouthed the words *Mister McIntosh.*

CHAPTER 27

So Michelle had stolen a client from Gerald McIntosh?

"You're kidding," Noley said.

"Nope. She was awful."

"Gerald McIntosh is our newest analyst. I think he would have confronted her if he had been here longer. I feel terrible for him. He needed that commission. He's got a wife and four kids." Dot was speaking almost in a whisper.

"That's awful." Lilly and Noley exchanged glances as the phone rang and Dot excused herself to answer it.

Once she hung up, Noley reached out her hand. Dot stood up and shook it. "I'm sorry we've taken up so much of your time, Dot. It was lovely talking to you. Maybe I'll see you again soon." Dot smiled and thanked them for coming in.

On the sidewalk, Lilly turned to Noley with a grin. "It sounds like Gerald McIntosh had a house full of reasons to kill Michelle Conover."

"I agree."

""I'm glad Dot was so chatty. Say, you make a convincing millionaire. You were great in there."

"So were you. But a burrito? Really?"

* * *

When they got back to Juniper Junction Lilly dropped Noley off and went back to the jewelry shop. Harry was holding court with three women who had come in to browse for souvenirs of a girls' weekend in town. She didn't want to interrupt the fun, so she stayed in the office until the women left. She turned on her computer and while she waited for it to boot up she checked her texts. Another one from Laurel with another reason she should be allowed to come home early for Thanksgiving—she felt she should be home to learn how to make a proper Thanksgiving dinner. Lilly replied that the bulk of the Thanksgiving feast wouldn't be prepared until Thanksgiving Day, so there was no need for her to come home early for that.

When her home page popped up, Lilly put her phone away and concentrated on the screen. She typed in "Gerald McIntosh" and waited to see what she could discover.

There he was on the roster of the investment firm they had visited, as well as the Lupine school board. It didn't take long to find out that he was the perfect husband and father—photos of him and his lovely wife at a springtime charity gala, with one of his daughters at a Daddy-Daughter dance, helping another daughter at a food drive, coaching his twin sons' baseball team, and with his parents at a charity auction for their church. He had even been Lupine's Man of the Year two years prior. Lilly rolled her eyes. *This guy is too good to be true.*

She clicked on one link after another, opting to avoid the sites offering to find Gerald McIntosh's criminal background and home value. She didn't care about his home value and she could ask Bill about his criminal background.

Harry poked his head into the office when the women had left. "I am a magician," he said proudly. "Those three women each bought a necklace and matching earrings. Souvenirs of their girls-only weekend, they said."

Lilly grinned. "That's terrific, Harry. I could see you had them eating out of your hand, so I didn't want to bother you."

"How did your field trip go?"

Lilly told him what they had learned from Dot and what she had found online about Gerald McIntosh.

"Nobody is *that* good," Harry said. "He's got to be hiding something."

"That's what I thought."

Lilly stopped by her mother's house before heading home. Meredith met her at the door. "Your mom is furious. Maybe it would be best if you wait until tomorrow to see her."

"What's wrong now?"

"She's upset because you didn't ask her about sending someone new over. Apparently she liked Susan. She's madder than a wet hen."

"Susan, who let her fall down and didn't tell anyone? Like I was going to let her back into Mom's house." Lilly sighed. "I don't get no respect, Meredith."

Meredith threw her head back and laughed. "I respect you, Lilly. So does Nikki. And your mom does, too. Usually."

From inside the house came the sound of Bev yelling. "Who's at the door, Merry?"

Meredith turned her head to yell into the living room. "It's Lilly."

"Tell her I'm mad at her."

"I already did."

"Is she coming in?"

"Do you want her to?"

"Yes." Lilly could just picture Bev sitting there in the living room, arms crossed over her chest and a scowl on her face.

Meredith stepped aside to let Lilly in the house, giving her a wink as she did so. Lilly tentatively stuck her head around the door jamb and looked into the living room. Sure enough, Bev was sitting in her favorite chair and she looked mad. Her arms weren't crossed over her chest, but her hands were balled into fists. Lilly ventured into the room.

"Hi, Mom. Before you say anything, let me tell you that we couldn't have Susan back here because she let you fall down and didn't tell anybody. You could have been hurt badly and we wouldn't have had any idea." Lilly got all her words out in a rush before Bev could interrupt.

"Bah. If I was hurt, I would have told you. From now on you have to tell me whenever you change anything." Lilly could hear a hint of the old Bev, who had thrived on busy-ness and the efficient management of her household.

"All right, Mom. I'm sorry. I should have told you that Susan wouldn't be coming back."

"I liked Susan. She let me do whatever I wanted."

"That was the problem, Mom. Her job wasn't to let you do anything you want. Her job was to keep you safe, and she failed at that." Lilly sat down across from Bev as she was speaking.

"I wasn't badly bruised, Lilly. You're making too much of it."

"Mom, if you were bruised at all—and even if you weren't bruised—Susan should have told us that you fell. That's important. What if you had a head injury that didn't show up until later? Meredith wouldn't have known what to look for."

"Bah. You're making mountains out of molehills."

"Well, back to the point. I'll tell you from now on if there's going to be a change."

"Thank you. That's all I ask and you can certainly do that much for me."

Lilly counted to ten before answering Bev. "You're right, Mom. Now if you don't need anything, I'm going to head home. I need to get some dinner."

"I don't need anything. Thank you for stopping by."

Lilly kissed her mom's cheek and Meredith walked her to the door. "If you can get past her anger, you can see she's having a pretty good day," Meredith said in a whisper.

"I noticed that. She seems pretty lucid. I'm going to call Nikki when I get home and see if she'll be ready to come back tomorrow."

When Lilly got home she poured herself a bowl of cereal and took out her phone. Before she could dial Nikki's number, though, the phone rang. It was Beau.

"Rats." Lilly debated whether to answer the phone or let it go to voicemail. After the fourth ring, she decided to pick up. "Hello?"

"Hi, Lilly. It's Beau."

"I know. What's up?"

"Uh, I just called to say hello."

"No, you didn't. You never call just to chat, Beau. What's up?"

"I called to see how Bev is doing. I miss the old girl."

Lilly wanted to tell him not to call her mother "the old girl," but decided it wasn't worth the effort. "She has good days and bad days. Dementia is like that. Some days she's just like her old self, and other days I barely recognize her."

"Huh. Maybe I should go see her," Beau suggested.

"Beau, you didn't really call to ask about my mother. Why did you call?"

Beau hesitated for a moment, then asked, "Do you think we should let Laurel come home early for Thanksgiving?"

"So she's been texting you, too? I don't think it's a good idea. We've paid for these classes, and I expect her to pass them. Her chances of passing go down if she skips classes. Even if she doesn't return to school next semester, she may go back someday. She needs to have passing grades if she wants to get into another college at some point."

"I guess you're right. She really hates it there, though."

"I know. I think we need to be prepared for her to refuse to go back after this semester. But while she's still enrolled, she needs to do her best. Coming home early is not doing her best."

"It'll be kind of nice to have her around if she doesn't go back to school, don't you think?"

"Let's not cross that bridge until we get there, Beau."

"All right."

Lilly called Nikki after she hung up with Beau and was thrilled to learn that Nikki would be returning to Bev's the next morning.

CHAPTER 28

*L*illy stopped in to see Bev the next evening right after work. She was delighted to see Nikki when she answered the door.

"It's good to see you, Nikki. How's Mom?"

"She's good. I think she's happy to be back to the routine."

Lilly smiled. "I know I am. She must be thrilled."

"She talked my ear off today. I've noticed she's a little more unsteady on her feet, but she's in a good place mentally for the moment."

"How unsteady?"

"She started to tip over when she got out of her chair in the living room to go to the kitchen, but I'm always standing next to her when she moves, so I was able to help her."

"Thank you. This is so soon after she fell with Susan. Do you think it's time for us to start worrying more about her physical safety?"

"Not yet. Not as long as someone is here with her. Once she got on her feet, she was able to walk into the kitchen without my assistance."

Lilly nodded, making a mental note to tell Bill.

She chatted with Bev and Nikki for a little while, then went home and called Hassan. "How was your day?"

Hassan sighed. "The police have been at Michelle's house all day. I can't get any work done knowing they're over there, looking for something to incriminate me."

"Have they taken anything out of the house?"

"A computer and lots of paper bags that look heavy. Probably papers and notebooks."

"That's good. That means they're looking in other directions for the person who killed her. That can only be good for you. You never communicated with her over email, did you? Or put anything in writing at all after one of your run-ins with her?"

The line was silent for a moment, then Hassan groaned. Finally he said, "Actually, there was one time. She emailed me to tell me that the landscapers were making too much noise and that her resulting headache was so bad that she couldn't leave the house or even lift the phone to tell me."

"And what did you say?"

"I said something like, 'I don't know how you got my email address, but don't contact me again unless you're looking for trouble.'"

"Oh, geez. You really said that?"

"Yes. Or something like that. I was furious and I lost my cool. I could kick myself."

"Let's hope the police are looking for emails from someone else and they don't even see that one."

"Do you think I should tell them about it?"

"I don't think so. If you call now to admit to a nasty email, you'll only draw attention to yourself."

"All right. But something tells me I haven't seen the last of that email."

"You might be right. But you can just explain to them that you were angry because she was constantly on your case and you were trying to get her to stop. You would tell them that it wasn't a physical threat, but a legal one."

"You mean like, I might sue her if she kept it up?"

"Yeah. Maybe you were thinking of suing her for harassment."

"This gets worse and worse."

"I know. But hopefully they'll catch who did it and everything will be back to normal soon. And you'll get a new neighbor who's a lovely person."

"What are you doing tonight?" he asked.

"Nothing. What are you doing?"

"Nothing. Want to come over? I can throw some steaks on the grill."

"Sounds good. I'll be there in a few."

Barney must have realized he was going in the car, because he started prancing around the kitchen, panting and shaking his head. Lilly laughed as she clipped his leash onto his collar.

"You want to go see Hassan, Barn?"

Barney's ears perked up and he barked once.

"I thought so. Maybe you can even have a bite of steak."

Hassan was as happy to see Barney as Barney was to see him. He rubbed Barney's ears and the dog rolled immediately onto his back, offering Hassan his stomach for some rubbing. When the two of them were done playing, Hassan let Barney out into the backyard, where Barney promptly ran to the back fence in search of squirrels and other woodland friends.

Hassan draped his arm around Lilly's shoulder as they watched Barney in the yard. "He is so much fun."

Lilly grinned. "He loves you. We can walk him after dinner. I haven't walked him today."

"Sounds good. Let's eat. I'm starving."

Two steaks were coming to room temperature on the counter. Hassan grilled them while Lilly fixed a quick dip for fresh vegetables and they ate on the patio with Barney sitting quietly next to them. "You wouldn't know this patient, polite guy is the same one who was on his back begging for tummy rubs earlier, would you?" Lilly asked with a chuckle.

Hassan picked up a small piece of steak and held it out to Barney, who gobbled it up quickly and waited for more.

"One more, Barn, then let's go for a walk." Lilly watched his reaction to her words with a smile. His head shot up and he started jumping around the patio with frenzied excitement.

Hassan laughed. "I'll do the dishes when we get back. Let's go, Barney." He and Lilly picked up their dishes and deposited them in the sink before heading out the front door with a very eager dog on the end of the leash.

CHAPTER 29

*I*t was a warm evening, at least by Colorado standards in early November. Several people were out, taking advantage of the relatively mild temperature. Barney stopped every few feet to sniff the ground, which smelled different from his neighborhood. They were in front of Michelle's house, stopping for the third time already, when a terrific noise came from the end of the block.

"What's that?" Lilly asked in alarm.

"It's Oliver. I don't know how anyone can stand driving without a decent muffler."

"Michelle complained about that, didn't she?"

"Endlessly."

"Who could enjoy a sound like that?"

Hassan shrugged. "Oliver, I guess. Hopefully he's planning to get the truck fixed. Sally told me that Eugene is refusing to pay for Oliver's truck expenses, since he's got a part-time job. Maybe the kid just hasn't saved up enough for a new muffler."

"I'd be glad to make a donation."

"So would every neighbor on the block."

The truck with its unearthly racket drove by slowly. Barney started barking and stood still, staring as Oliver rolled to a stop next to them.

"Hi, Mister Ashraf. Sorry about the noise. Hi, Mrs. Carlsen."

"Hi, Oliver."

"Did you get a new dog?" Oliver asked Hassan.

"No, this is Lilly's dog, Barney. He comes over sometimes to sniff the grass on our block." Oliver smiled and pulled away. As soon as his truck started moving, Barney set up another hue and cry.

"Hush, Barn," Lilly said.

"It's okay if he barks. Michelle was the only one on the block who had a problem when a dog barked."

"I know. But there's no need to annoy people unnecessarily." Barney stopped barking as if he could understand what Lilly was saying. The trio kept walking and a few minutes and several stops later they saw Larry walking toward them. Beside him was his dog, Cupcake.

Barney started making snuffling noises as Cupcake approached, then the two dogs led each other around in circles as they introduced themselves for the hundredth time.

"We heard you were the one who found Michelle's body, Larry," Lilly said.

"Sure was. Cupcake actually found her. She smelled something and just made a beeline for the woman's backyard. And there she was, face-down in a big puddle. Looked awful."

"That must have been terrifying for you," Lilly said.

"Oh, I've seen dead bodies before. I was in the service, you know. Truth is, this neighborhood's going to be a lot nicer now that she's gone. I hope you don't think I'm speaking out of turn."

"We understand what you're saying." Lilly glanced at Hassan.

Hassan had clearly had enough of the conversation. He bent down and scratched Cupcake's head when she had had enough of Barney's attentions. "How are you, Cupcake?" he asked. Lilly bent down and stroked Cupcake's back. Cupcake was a sturdy bulldog with bulging muscles and dark eyes. She licked Hassan's hand and gave Barney a sidelong glance. It was like she was teasing him.

"Did you see that?" Larry asked. "She's a smart one, Cupcake is. She knows it torments Barney when you guys pet her." He shook his head. "Typical woman, I suppose."

Lilly gave him a dark look which he probably didn't see because it was already dark outside and even under the light of a nearby lamppost, he was watching Cupcake, not Lilly. She straightened up and said, "I've read that sometimes we humans tend to anthropomorphize animals when we want to believe that they're exhibiting human characteristics." Hassan squeezed her hand, a clear signal to be quiet, and Larry gave her a blank stare.

"That's a big word," he said. "And I don't know what it means, but I know Cupcake is teasing that boy of yours." He chuckled and kept walking.Lilly could hear him talking to Cupcake as they meandered away. "How could that mean old Michelle ever have called the police on you, girl?"

"Sorry," Lilly mumbled to Hassan. "He couldn't stop at insinuating that Cupcake charmed Barney witless, but then he had to go and say she's a *typical woman*. Ugh."

Hassan laughed. "Don't worry about Larry. He doesn't realize what he's saying sometimes. He's harmless."

"Yeah, well."

Hassan leaned over and kissed Lilly's cheek. "Want to turn

around and head home? I think the temperature is starting to drop."

Indeed, it was getting colder. They coaxed Barney away from the clump of leaves that was holding his fascination and went back to the house. Lilly was mixing a pan of her home-made hot chocolate mix when there was a knock at the door.

Hassan went to open it, with Barney barking at his heels. Lilly could hear voices in the foyer and went to see who was there.

She was shocked to see two police officers standing there. Hassan and the officers turned to look at her and she realized she must have let out a surprised noise.

"And you are?" the first officer asked her.

"I'm Lilly Carlsen."

"Wife? Girlfriend?" he asked Hassan.

"She's my girlfriend. How can I help you, officers?"

"We're here to arrest you for the murder of Michelle Conover."

CHAPTER 30

"What?" Lilly cried. "He didn't kill Michelle! You can't arrest him!"

The officers ignored her while one read Hassan his rights and the other eyed Barney warily. Lilly reached for Barney's leash and clipped it on him so she could control his movements while the police were in the house.

"Lilly, it's all right," Hassan said. His voice, normally low and warm, sounded frightened. No wonder. He was being charged with a crime he hadn't committed. "I'll go with these officers and cooperate. Will you please call that woman who represented Noley last year? Gretchen. Have her meet me." He turned to the policemen. "Where are we going?"

"The police station downtown."

"Have her meet me there," Hassan instructed.

"Should I call your parents, too?"

"No. Don't call them." Hassan's voice was urgent. "I don't want to drag them into this." Basra and Amir Ashraf lived in Minneapolis, but had purchased a home in Juniper Junction the previous year. Though the home had been badly damaged by fire shortly after the purchase, Basra and Amir had remodeled it and enjoyed spending vacations in Juniper Junction. Lilly could understand Hassan's reluctance to call them.

Lilly watched, her breath constricting in her throat, as the officers led Hassan to the police car that sat in the driveway. Thank God they had waited until after dark, when there wouldn't be a block-long spectacle of observers. That would only have added to Hassan's embarrassment and frustration.

She immediately called Gretchen, whose number was still in her list of contacts, and asked her to meet Hassan downtown, then she called Bill. As soon as he answered she lit into him.

"Why didn't you let me know ahead of time that Hassan was going to be charged with Michelle's murder?" She was yelling, but she couldn't stop herself.

"What are you talking about? Hassan's been arrested?"

"Yes! Why didn't you warn me?"

"I'm really sorry, Lilly. I had no idea. You know I would have told you if I had known. How's he doing?"

"About as well as can be expected, under these preposterous circumstances."

"Let me look into it and see what I can find out. I'll get back to you." Bill hung up abruptly.

Lilly paced the length of Hassan's house, waiting for Bill to call. She tried calling Noley, but the call went right to voicemail. Her anxiety was clearly affecting Barney, who followed her every step, whining and whimpering. Finally she went into the kitchen and finished the dishes. Hassan would be coming home soon, she hoped, and she didn't want him coming home to a sink full of dishes. Surely the police would realize they had the wrong person in custody.

When she finished, Bill still hadn't called her back. She

couldn't wait any longer to talk to someone about this, so she called Noley again. This time her friend answered.

"Hi. Sorry I missed your call earlier."

"That's okay. Hassan has been arrested."

"What? Why?"

"They've accused him of killing Michelle. That woman is still causing trouble, even after she's dead."

"Why do they think Hassan did it?"

"Who knows? I'll go see him as soon as I can. Maybe they've told him why they think he did it. I assume the lawyer will call me as soon as I can go see him."

"Have you talked to Bill?"

"He had no idea it was going to happen. I don't know what's wrong with him, Noley. He's normally on top of things and this time he's let me down every time I've talked to him."

"I wish I had an answer for you, but I don't. I haven't talked to him much, though he's been better about calling me in the last couple days."

"Well, I called him and let him have a piece of my mind. I'm waiting for him to call me back."

"Let me know what he says. I'm worried about Hassan."

"Me, too. I'll call you as soon as I know anything."

Once Lilly hung up the phone, she locked up the house and took Barney home. He was subdued in the car, as if he knew something was going on.

Bill called as Lilly was walking into her kitchen. She whipped out her phone.

"Yes?"

"Hi. They've got the timeline where he can't prove where he was at the time of Michelle's murder, they have the ugly history and recent confrontations between the two of them, they have a threatening email, and they have an affidavit that you're not going to like."

"What do you mean? What affidavit? Whose affidavit?"

"Ivy Leachman swore out an affidavit that she saw Hassan sneaking around Michelle's backyard the day before the murder."

"You've got to be kidding me. It's a lie. Both she and Hassan were in pain that day from the car accident. I'm sure she didn't go anywhere near Michelle's house and Hassan certainly wasn't sneaking around anywhere. If Ivy weren't already dead, I swear I'd kill her."

"I did not hear that."

"Whatever. That's not enough to charge Hassan with murder, is it?"

"I don't know. But don't forget—these people don't know Hassan like you do and like I do. They're following the evidence."

"Following the evidence, my foot. They've arrested the easiest person and they're not looking for the real killer."

"They think he offed Ivy, too." Bill's voice was quiet.

"What?!" Lilly shrieked. "That's impossible!"

"It's not impossible—that's the problem. The evidence against him is all circumstantial in Ivy's case, but I've seen people convicted on less. But he hasn't been arrested for it— he's only a suspect."

"Oh, my God. I'm going to lose my mind, Bill."

"Take it easy. We know it's all a big mistake, and at least they're still looking for evidence that someone else killed Ivy. Listen, I have to go. Can I call you later?"

"Only if you have new information about Hassan. Otherwise, call Noley. I'd rather you talk to her in the few spare minutes you have. Or call Mom. She loves talking to you."

"Have you seen her?"

"Mom? Yes. She's been mad at me because Nikki took a few

days off. Like it's my fault. And she's been unsteady on her feet."

"Is she all right?"

"I think so. Nikki was there to help her. We'll just have to make sure someone is keeping an eye on her all the time."

"It makes me nervous."

"Me, too. But it's all part of the disease, and we just have to make sure Mom doesn't get hurt."

"Okay. I'll talk to you later. Thanks for staying on top of everything with Mom."

"No problem. Get some rest and thanks for checking on Hassan's case for me."

The next morning, Lilly arrived at the shop wound up like a clock.

"You okay, boss?" Harry asked.

"No. Hassan was charged with Michelle Conover's murder last night."

Harry stared at her, mouth agape, a pearl necklace swinging gently from his hand, which had frozen as he was putting the necklace onto its display. "Hassan? What are they thinking? I can't believe it."

"Well, believe it. And to make matters worse, Bill has been useless. He didn't even know they were going to arrest Hassan. When I called to talk to him about it, that was the first he had heard."

"What can I do to help?"

"I'm afraid there's nothing to do right now. I'm waiting to hear from his lawyer and then I can go see him."

That evening she texted the lawyer, since she hadn't heard a word from her. She was longing to see Hassan, even if it was in a jail. Memories of Noley's time in the county lockup the previous summer were uppermost in her mind, and she knew how scared and lonely Hassan must feel inside his cell.

She hadn't expected a text back from the lawyer, so she was surprised when the woman called her almost immediately after she sent the text.

"Hi, Lilly. It's Gretchen."

"Hi, Gretchen. Any news? How's he doing?"

"He's doing all right. He's not happy with the situation, obviously. But he's holding up. I'm hoping to get him out of there before long so he can at least be at home."

"That would be great. Can I go see him?"

"Sure. You can see him any time after ten tomorrow morning until seven tomorrow evening, I think. Check the visiting hours to be sure, but I think that's when you can visit. Just remember that you can only be there fifteen minutes a day."

"Got it. Thanks, Gretchen. What happens next?"

"They've let people go in cases where there's been far more convincing evidence, so I'm just going to keep trying. I don't know why they're so dead set on keeping him. No pun intended."

Lilly hesitated to ask the next question, but she forged ahead anyway.

"Gretchen, do you think it's possible they're keeping him because he's Muslim?"

There was silence on the other end for a moment, then Gretchen answered. "I'd like to think that wouldn't happen here, but the truth is, I don't know. I guess anything is possible. They have to tell me what they've got on him in terms of evidence, so I don't think they know anything more than what they've told me."

"Do you know if they've looked into anyone who worked with Michelle?"

"I think they determined that the murderer wasn't someone she worked with."

"Hmm. I don't know about that."

"What do you mean?"

"I mean, I happen to know that she worked with someone who was really mad at her."

"Lilly, how do you know that?"

"I have my methods."

"Listen. I know I'm not your lawyer, but I don't want to see you get hurt. Don't do anything stupid."

"Is 'stupid' a legal term?"

"Yes."

Lilly hung up and went to bed, but not before replying to a text from Tighe. He was worried about Laurel because she hated being at school.

I'll call her tomorrow. Thanks for letting me know. Love you.

CHAPTER 31

*L*illy's first task the next day was to call Laurel.

"What's up, Laur? Tighe texted me last night and said I should call you."

A sob erupted on the other end of the line. "Please let me come home, Mom. I'll get a job, I'll go to community college, I'll do anything. I hate it here."

"Let me talk to your dad and see what he thinks, okay? That's the only thing I can promise right now."

"Okay." Laurel snuffled and let out a hiccup. "I'm sorry I've disappointed you."

"You haven't disappointed me, Laurel. You went away from home and you've stuck it out like I wanted you to. That's a huge accomplishment and I'm proud of you for it. I just don't want to see you do something you'll regret."

"I know. Can you call me later?"

"Sure thing. Have a good day, honey."

"You, too." Laurel hung up.

Lilly sighed and dialed Beau's number. It was time to admit that she'd been wrong.

"You're up early," he said when he picked up the phone.

"I get up this early every day."

"Huh. I remember when you used to love sleeping in."

"Beau, I didn't call to discuss my schedule. I called because Laurel's melting down at school."

"Yeah. I figured. Do you think it's time to let her come back to Juniper Junction?"

"I'm afraid so. I was really hoping she would finish out the semester and decide it wasn't so bad after all, but I don't think that's going to happen. She's totally miserable."

"I can go pick her up any time."

"Before we tell her we're letting her come home, I think we should have a plan in place."

"I just told you I'll go pick her up."

"Not that kind of a plan. A plan for her future, at least in the short term."

"Oh."

"I think she needs to get a job and she needs to have a plan for continuing her education."

"Okay, I can agree with that."

As if I would take "no" for an answer.

"Do you want me to call her and tell her?" Lilly asked.

"I can call her."

Oh, no you don't. You're not going to be the one to give her the news she's been waiting to hear since August.

"Why don't we both go up to campus and tell her in person?" Lilly suggested.

"You want to go this weekend?"

Lilly didn't really want to go anywhere that weekend. She wanted to stay local so she could be there if Hassan needed anything or if there was a change in his status. But this was important, too. "I guess so. Let's go this weekend, tell her, and plan to pick her up the following weekend. That way she has time to pack and say goodbye to her friends. Can you leave Saturday, early in the morning?"

"How early?"

"I don't know. How about seven o'clock?"

"You're kidding."

"Beau, I have to work on Saturday so I need to get back to town."

"Oh, all right. Have it your way. I'll pick you up at seven on Saturday morning. God, that's early."

"Quit your complaining. I'll see you then."

Lilly couldn't wait for her lunch hour that day. As soon as the clock struck one, she told Harry she was off to see Hassan.

"Tell him I said to hang in there," Harry said.

"I will. I'll be back soon."

Once at the jail, Lilly experienced a strange sense of *déjà vu* when she entered the large lobby area where people sat while they waited to see their incarcerated loved ones. Had it only been fifteen months since Noley was on the inside? What did the universe have against Lilly that everyone she loved ended up in jail?

She sat up straight in the ugly plastic chair with her handbag on her lap.

When the guard finally called her name, she found that she was suddenly nervous to see Hassan. What shape would he be in? Would he be happy to see her or angry because he was stuck in jail while she was free to roam?

The guard took her through two sets of doors, then into a pale yellow room that stank of sweat and sadness. She sat down in a chair in the middle of the room, her toes touching the line of tape that separated the room in half. There was another chair directly opposite her where Hassan would sit when he came in.

Lilly only had to wait for a minute or two. This jail was

punctual, she had to give them that. As soon as she saw Hassan being led into the room, she stood up, beaming.

"Sit down," the guard barked. She sat immediately.

Hassan gave her a meek smile as he sat down across from her. The guard left the room, but Lilly could see him standing just on the other side of the metal door.

"How are you doing?" She leaned toward Hassan, trying to read his eyes.

He blinked. "Okay, I guess, considering the circumstances."

"I talked to Gretchen late last night. She said she's hoping to get you out of here."

"That's what she tells me. But I don't know, Lilly. They seem to be sure I'm the one who killed Michelle."

"Did you go to Michelle's house the day before Halloween?"

Hassan looked away. "Yes." She could barely hear him.

"Why in the world did you do that?"

"Because I wanted to measure her backyard. I was trying to prove that my fence wasn't on her property. She had left to go somewhere, so I went over."

"Ivy saw you and she swore out an affidavit that you were there, sneaking around."

Hassan closed his eyes. "Oh, no."

"Well, we can explain that away. I hope. On to other topics. I have some news that you might find interesting. I can't believe I forgot to tell you this the night you were arrested. I found out that Michelle stole a lucrative client from one of her co-workers."

Hassan ran a hand over his eyes. He looked world-weary. "Lilly, you're not investigating this murder on your own, are you? There's a killer out there. I don't want you doing anything that's going to jeopardize your safety."

"Don't you worry about me. I'll be smart about it, I promise."

"Have you told Bill what you're doing?"

She tilted her head and raised her eyebrows at him. "What do you think?"

He shook his head. "Lilly, you make me nervous. I don't need to be worrying about you on top of everything else."

"I told you. Don't worry about me. Oh, and Beau and I have decided to tell Laurel she can come home. We're going up to campus this weekend to tell her."

"Why do you have to go to campus to tell her? Can't you call her?"

Lilly smirked. "Beau wanted to tell her, and I know it's stupid, but I have no intention of letting him be the bearer of good news. So I suggested we go together."

"If I were the jealous type, I would not be happy to hear you and Beau are going on a road trip together."

"Luckily, you're not the jealous type, and even if you were there would be nothing to fret about." She reached over and put her hand on Hassan's knee. "I can't wait to get you out of here."

They talked for several more minutes. Lilly kept checking her watch to see how much more time they had.

At the end of fifteen minutes the guard opened the door and glared at them. "Time's up," he said to Lilly. He jerked his head toward the door. "You gotta go."

She stood up and kissed Hassan on the cheek before the guard could stop her. "I love you," she said.

"I love you, too. Will you come back tomorrow?"

"Of course."

"I said, time's up." The guard glowered at her.

"I'm leaving." The last thing she wanted to do was antagonize him. He opened the door for her and she swept through it without a backward glance. She was pretty sure she would start crying if she saw the guard lead Hassan away.

But the hydraulic contraption that closed behind her was slow, and she could hear the guard talking to Hassan.

"Let's go, Taliban," he said.

Lilly whirled around in time to see the guard prod Hassan in the back, but the door closed and she lost sight of the two men. She could feel her skin getting hot and she forced herself to take a deep breath. They had the wrong man in custody—and now they had to treat him like this? It was wrong.

She stormed out of the jail and called Bill the moment she was in the parking lot.

"Bill, you are not going to believe this."

"What?"

"I was just visiting Hassan and the guard called him 'Taliban.'"

"You're kidding."

"I wish I was kidding. Who can I talk to about this?"

"I don't know, Lil. I suppose you could go to the warden."

"Do you think I should?"

"Are you sure of what you heard?"

"A hundred percent sure."

"I would think before popping off about it. You don't want to make things harder for Hassan."

"How would I be making things harder for Hassan?"

"Families that make noise about an inmate's treatment often find that the inmate is singled out after that, and not in a good way."

"That's terrible."

"I know, but that's the way it is. You don't want more misery for Hassan to be on your conscience."

"But ... but ... I can't believe they would take it out on him if I'm the one who says something."

"They can't take it out on you, so they take it out on the next closest person. I wish it weren't that way, Lilly, but sometimes it is."

Lilly sighed. "All right. I won't say anything." *At least until he's out, then I'm telling everyone.*

"I think that's smart."

Lilly grumbled goodbye, then returned to the shop.

CHAPTER 32

*L*illy stopped at Bev's house on her way home from work that night. Nikki answered the door with a smile.

"How's Mom today?"

"She had a pretty good day," Nikki said.

"I'm glad to hear it. Has Bill been by?"

"No. He called earlier, but told your mom he had to work late tonight."

Lilly shook her head. "That boy has been working way too hard."

"That's exactly what your mom said."

"Mom thinks that even when Bill is on vacation." Lilly rolled her eyes. Nikki chuckled and led the way into the living room.

"Hello, Lilly. How are you, dear?" Bev asked, looking up from a photo album in her lap.

"I'm good, Mom. How was your day?"

"It was lovely. Nikki and I made soup together and it was delicious."

Lilly glanced at Nikki, who was smiling. "It was Bev's recipe. She said she used to make it all the time when you and Bill were kids."

"Not baked potato soup," Lilly exclaimed.

"Yes, we made my famous baked potato soup." Bev beamed, clearly pleased that Lilly had remembered.

"Is there any left?"

"Sure. Want some?" Nikki asked. Bev started to stand up, but Nikki waved her down. "I'll get it, Bev." Bev didn't seem to mind that Nikki was doing something for her.

A few minutes later Lilly was sitting on the sofa enjoying a hot bowl of soup and crusty French bread.

"This bread is good, too," Lilly said. "It tastes like Armand's."

"It is Armand's," Nikki said. "Your mom and I went over there today to pick it up."

Lilly looked at her mom in surprise. "You went out today? That's great!"

"We did." Bev nodded. "And that Armand is so French and so handsome. You should try a little flirting with him, Lilly."

Lilly smirked. "Mom, I have someone in my life, remember? Hassan?"

Bev gave Lilly a blank look. "Hassan? I don't know anyone named Hassan. I would remember that." Lilly decided now was not the time to announce that Hassan was being held in the local jail.

Her mother broke into her thoughts. "It can't hurt to find out if Armand is available."

"Mom, his wife was killed last summer. Her name was Cerise and he is still mourning her passing. And even if he weren't, I'm very happy with Hassan."

Bev waved her fingers dismissively. "Bah. You're single. Live a little!"

Lilly's eyes widened and she looked at Nikki as if to say *Who is this woman??*

Nikki shook her head and chuckled silently. Lilly decided the wisest thing was to change the subject.

"Mom, I'm going to be bringing Laurel home soon."

"Is it Thanksgiving break already?"

"Unfortunately, no. She's coming home for good."

Bev turned her head and gave Lilly a sharp look. "What do you mean by that?"

"I mean, she's dropping out of college for now. She is very unhappy there and Beau and I have decided to let her come back to Juniper Junction."

Bev shook her head and kept shaking it while she spoke. "You're making a mistake, Lilly. I'm surprised at you. What Laurel needs is to stay in school. How else will she ever get a job?"

"I think she'll eventually go back to school, but it's not the right thing for her at this point. Maybe she just wasn't ready to leave home. Once she matures a little bit she might want to go back. And in the meantime, she can take classes at the community college."

"I still think you're making a mistake."

"We'll just have to wait and see. Hopefully not."

"Well, you are."

Lilly took a deep breath. She wasn't going to have this argument with her mother. "I've got to get home, Mom. Thanks for the soup. It was delicious."

"Goodbye, dear."

Nikki accompanied Lilly to the door. "Sorry your mom is being so contrary. It's not like you don't have enough to worry about right now without your mom telling you you're wrong. But I think you and Beau are doing the right thing. I've heard Laurel crying to him when I'm at his house and it's heartbreaking. And Lilly, I heard about Hassan. It's terrible. I know they've got the wrong guy. Tell him I'm thinking about him."

"Thanks, Nikki. I just hope and pray they come to their senses and let Hassan go home. And as far as Laurel is concerned, I really believe this is the right step. I was against it at first, but I've come around to Laurel's way of thinking. I'll stop by tomorrow to see Mom."

When Lilly got home she sat on the sofa with Barney for a while, stroking his head and talking to him.

"I miss Hassan, Barn. I mean, I love you, but it's nice to see him every night or at least talk to him. We need to get him home." Barney looked up at her, his big brown eyes questioning. She laughed. "I know. I don't know how we're going to do it, either."

The next day Lilly left the shop around mid-morning to visit Hassan. She had decided he might be her best bet for getting at least a couple answers to her questions about Ted, since they had been neighbors for a short time. She had also decided to ask him about the guard's "Taliban" comment.

He had shaved and looked better than he had the day before, though he still had bags under his eyes. The same contemptible guard had escorted him into the room.

"How are you holding up?" she asked, ignoring the guard.

He shrugged. "Okay, I guess." The guard left the room and the door clanged shut behind him. Lilly didn't say anything for a moment, then took a deep breath.

"Hassan, I—"

"Don't tell me you're leaving me," he interrupted. "Because I can't take it right now." He closed his eyes.

"Why on earth would you think that?" Lilly stared at him, her mouth hanging open. "Whatever gave you that idea?"

"That's not why you're here?"

"Of course not. I'm here to see how you're doing. What are you even—why—what are you talking about?"

"Never mind." He shook his head. "It was just something stupid. The guard—never mind."

"Did the guard say something? That guard who just brought you in here? Because he's one of the things I needed to talk to you about."

"What about him?"

"First, you tell me what he said."

"It was nothing, really. I should know better than to listen to anything he says."

"Did he say something about you being brown and me being white?"

Hassan gave her a suspicious look. "What makes you think that?"

"Because I heard the terrible name he called you yesterday. That's what I wanted to ask you about."

Hassan nodded. "Yeah, he said something about the differences between us. You heard that? I'm sorry."

"Sorry? Sorry for what?"

"Sorry you had to hear that."

"Hassan, don't be sorry. I'm sorry that he called you that. *He* should be sorry he called you that. But here's my question: do you want me to tell someone? I mean, do you think I should report him to his higher-ups?"

"God, no. Don't do that."

"Why not?"

"Because he'll make life miserable for me, that's why. Just let it go, please. I know you want to help, but I don't think it's a good idea."

"All right. I won't say anything. But after you get out of here I'm saying something to someone. They can't just get away with treating people like that."

"Anyone can say anything they want if I can just get out of here."

"I know it feels that way now, but what he said is outrageous. Now. Enough of that. I need to pick your brain about a couple things."

CHAPTER 33

"First, do you know who Ted might be dating?"

"Ted's dating someone? That's news to me."

"All right. So obviously you don't know who it is. Next question. Did you ever see a woman besides Michelle around the house before Ted and Michelle divorced? I'm thinking maybe he was seeing someone while they were still married."

Hassan was shaking his head even before Lilly got the question out.

"Do you know why they divorced?"

Hassan shook his head again. "I have no idea. Maybe each of them realized the other was awful."

"Could be, but there has to be something else. I'm just trying to figure out what it was."

"Why all the interest in their marriage all of a sudden?"

"Because I'm trying to figure out who killed her. Do you think Ted could have done it in a sort of if-I-can't-have-you-then-nobody-can-have-you way?"

"I doubt that very much. Besides, I'm sure the police have checked Ted out thoroughly. What has Bill said about it?"

"Not much. He's been working overtime and I've barely talked to him."

"Lilly, leave this to the police. I can't protect you from yourself if I'm in jail, and I worry that you're going to get hurt or put yourself in a position that you can't get out of."

"Oh, pshaw. Don't worry about me. I'm being careful. The more I can learn, the quicker we can get you out of here. Has Gretchen been in to talk to you?"

"Yes. She says she's trying every angle to get me out. But since I travel a lot, I'm considered a flight risk. And because it's a murder, they're less inclined to let me post bail."

"But what about the complete lack of real evidence?"

Hassan gave a dejected shrug. "I don't know. All I know is, I'm still in here, so there must be enough circumstantial evidence to hold me."

"Well, I'm doing everything I can to get you out. Keep your chin up. We'll be having dinner again at The Water Wheel before you know it." She reached for his hand, and he held hers limply.

"You have a deadbeat boyfriend," he said.

"Stop that. I have the best boyfriend—the only one I want." She leaned over and kissed his cheek while casting a nervous glance toward the door where the guard still stood on the other side. "And don't listen to any of that bigot's nonsense. He's just a meathead on a power trip."

Hassan snorted. "Will I see you tomorrow?"

"Yes, barring any unforeseen circumstances."

The guard came in and stood over them with his arms crossed while Lilly pushed her chair back and scowled at him. He muttered something under his breath that sounded like "traitor."

"What did you say?" Lilly demanded.

The guard smirked. "Nothing. What did you hear?"

Lilly glared at him and pressed her lips together in a thin line. Finally she turned away and walked to the door, waiting for him to open it for her. As soon as he did, she hurried away without looking back. She swallowed hard, glad to be out of there. She felt a surge of anger and helplessness as she thought of Hassan, stuck behind the bars of the jail with that monster.

By the time Lilly got to work, she had calmed down a little bit. She had to remind herself over and over that the guard was an uninformed, unenlightened dirtbag and was just trying to get under Hassan's brown skin.

Harry was waiting on a couple who had come to purchase matching watches as wedding gifts for each other. They were a mature couple, probably in their seventies, and Harry chatted them up like he was one of the older crowd. They loved him. The gentleman pumped his hand several times after Harry had boxed up the watches, and the woman kept calling him "a dear boy." Lilly smiled. Harry was meant for this job.

After work she decided to swing by Hassan's house to check on everything. The neighborhood was quiet when she drove down the block and pulled into Hassan's driveway. She was glad Hassan had had his door repainted and all the broken glass replaced quickly, because the front of the house had looked downright eerie when the vandalism was still evident. She doubted whether she could have summoned the courage to visit his house alone if the damage had still been visible. Michelle's house was completely dark, and Lilly shivered as she got out of the car and rummaged for Hassan's house key in her purse.

Hurrying up the front steps, she glanced over her shoulder to make sure she was alone. She would have laughed aloud at the silliness of it if she hadn't been terrified. Her fingers trembled as she fumbled with the key to let herself in the front door. The lock finally clicked open and she rushed inside and locked the door behind her. She leaned against the door and took a deep breath.

"I wish Barney was here," she said aloud. Hearing her own voice helped her to calm down just a little bit. She figured if she talked her way through the house it might help to keep her fears in check while she looked around to make sure everything was in its place and undisturbed.

She flipped on lights in every room as she went through the house.

"Kitchen looks good."

"Dining room, check."

"Living room, check. Wait. No, I forgot to take care of those glasses on the end table." She picked up the two wine glasses she and Hassan had used the night he was arrested and carried them into the kitchen, where she washed them in the sink and set them in the dish rack. While she was drying her hands, she wandered over to the French doors leading out to the patio and peered into the darkness. She realized suddenly that anyone standing outside could see her because the kitchen lights were on, so she flung out her hand and grappled for the light switch.

When the light flooded the patio and she saw the man standing in the yard, she let out a scream that probably curdled the blood of every living thing within a half-mile radius. The man grinned and waved, and only then did Lilly realize that it was Larry from down the block. She whipped the French door open with all the fury she could muster in her terrified state.

"Larry! You scared me half to death! What are you doing out here?"

"I'm sorry if I scared you, Lilly. I can't find Cupcake. We were out for a walk and she was off the leash. A rabbit ran in front of her and she took off. I could have sworn I saw her run back here, so I followed her."

Lilly's heartbeat had barely slowed while Larry explained what was going on. She managed a smile as she placed her hand across her chest. "I can help you look, if you'd like." She closed the door behind her and stepped onto the flagstones of the patio. "Cupcake!" she called. Larry called the dog, too. They listened for any response, then called again and again.

A couple minutes later, Larry sighed. "I wonder where she's gotten to. Thanks for your help, Lilly."

"I won't be here long, Larry. If you want, I can cruise around in my car looking for her before I head home."

A noise from the direction of Michelle's house startled them. Lilly stiffened. Larry jerked his head in that direction and a wide grin spread across his face when Cupcake trotted onto the patio. Her large bulldog features looked almost comical in the floodlit darkness. She snuffled the ground near Larry's feet, seemingly unconcerned that she had spent several minutes being a Lost Dog.

Larry clipped the leash onto Cupcake's collar and straightened up. "Sorry again for scaring you, Lilly. But I'm glad Cupcake's back." He looked down at the dog, shaking his head. "What were you doing over at Michelle's house, you crazy dog?" He laughed aloud as if Cupcake had answered him with some witty response, then bid Lilly goodnight and left around the side of Hassan's house.

Lilly went inside and closed and locked the French doors behind her. She wished again that Barney had come with her. He would have alerted her to Larry's presence on the patio before Lilly had realized Larry was there. Then again, Lilly thought, if Barney had been here, growling and barking at something Lilly couldn't see, she would have been terrified.

The longer she stayed in Hassan's house, the more jittery she became. She bounded up the stairs as if the hounds of hell were chasing her, did a quick check of each room, and bolted down the stairs. She scooped up her purse, turned off all the lights except one lamp burning in the living room, and let herself out the front door. It wasn't until she reached the end of the cul-de-sac that she breathed a sigh of relief.

She couldn't wait to get home. But first she had to stop at her mother's house. Nikki greeted her at the door. "Your mom is in bed already," she said in a low voice.

Lilly was surprised. "How come? Is she sick?"

"No, but she had a long day. Not a very good one, I'm afraid."

"What happened?" Lilly stepped into the foyer while Nikki closed the door behind her. They spoke in whispers.

"She tripped over the edge of the rug in the foyer and that upset her. She wasn't hurt, but it scared both of us. It seemed to get to her more than I would have expected. She cried and cried and Lilly, I felt so bad for her. I offered to take her for a ride in the car, I offered to bake with her, I offered to play cards, but nothing worked. She was just glum all day long. She sat in the living room and looked out the window for hours."

Lilly's shoulders drooped. "Poor Mom. Is there anything I can do to make tomorrow better?"

"I doubt it. I'm hoping she'll have forgotten it when she gets up tomorrow morning. If she's no better when I get here, or if she's worse, I'll give you a call and we can go from there. She's safe, though, so don't worry about anything right now."

Telling Lilly not to worry was like telling the sun not to rise.

CHAPTER 34

*T*he next morning Lilly had no sooner walked into Juniper Junction Jewels than Nikki called her cell phone. Lilly's stomach tightened when she saw the caller ID.

"Hi, Nikki. Is everything all right?"

"I just called to tell you that your mom fell. I've called an ambulance and they're on their way."

Lilly held the phone like a vise. "Is she okay? I'll be right there. How long 'til the EMTs get there?"

"Probably a few minutes. I called you as soon as I hung up with the 9-1-1 dispatcher. I really should get back to her now."

"Wait—is she okay? Where is she hurt?"

"It looks like she may have broken her arm. Right now she's sitting in her favorite chair. She's conscious and complaining about the pain, so that's a good thing, Lilly. I would be a heck of a lot more worried if she were unconscious. I called 9-1-1 just as a precaution, but I could probably have taken her to the doctor's office in my own car."

"I'll be there as soon as I can." Lilly hung up and swung

around to talk to Harry, who had approached her as she talked to Nikki.

"Everything okay, Lilly?"

"My mom took a fall and her nurse called the paramedics as a precaution. Harry, I hate to do this, but can you take care of things while I run over there? I don't know how long I'll be."

"You know I will. Just get out of here and let me know how she's doing."

"Thanks, Harry. I appreciate it." She threw him a thankful glance and jogged back to her car. Before she pulled out of her parking space she dialed Bill's number, then spoke to him as she drove.

"I've already heard. I'm on my way there now," he said in greeting.

"All right. I'll see you there. Did Nikki tell you how it happened?"

"No. I hope Mom wasn't in a place where Nikki could have prevented a fall."

"Let's not worry about that just yet. I'll meet you there and we'll figure out what happened and why."

It only took Lilly a few minutes to reach Bev's house. She parked in front of the neighbor's house so the ambulance could park as close as possible. She was getting out of her car as Bill arrived in his police cruiser. She ran ahead of him up the front steps; Nikki was already at the door waiting for everyone. "She's in the living room," Nikki said.

Lilly and Bill rushed past her while she waited to show the paramedics where to go. Bev was lying on the sofa, holding her arm, her lips pressed in a thin white line.

"How are you doing, Mom?" Lilly asked.

"I hurt. How do you think I'm doing?"

At least her attitude wasn't hurt, Lilly thought.

Bill put his hand on Lilly's forearm and gave her a nudge. She moved out of his way.

"Mom, we're not trying to annoy you. We've been worried ever since Nikki called. How did it happen?"

"I fell in the bathroom, if you must know."

At least she's as miserable to him as she is to me. Lilly immediately regretted the thought. This was about Bev, not about Lilly. They both stepped back as the paramedics entered the room.

"Hello, Bev. We're here to check you out," one of them said to her.

"That's very nice of you."

Lilly and Bill exchanged glances. Nikki came up next to them. "She couldn't wait until you got here," she whispered. "She kept asking for both of you. Don't let that gruffness fool you."

"So she fell in the bathroom?" Bill asked.

"Yes. It's the one room she goes into completely alone." Nikki shook her head. "I hate to take away any more of her independence, but maybe we should think about having her keep the door open. Or maybe I should help her in and help her when she's done, too."

Lilly looked skeptical. "Maybe this was just a one-off. Let's see how she feels about it before we go suggesting changes to her routine."

Bill and Nikki nodded. They watched as the paramedics asked Bev a series of questions, then stood up.

The first paramedic addressed Lilly. "Are you her daughter?"

"Yes. My name is Lilly and this is my brother, Bill." She indicated Bill with a wave in his direction.

The paramedic nodded. "Good to know. I wasn't sure if someone had also called the police."

"No," Bill said. "Nikki called me and Lilly after she called for you guys."

"How you want to handle this is up to Bev and you," the paramedic said. "You can make an appointment for her to see her own doctor to get the arm set, or we can take her by ambulance to the hospital. That's the route I recommend, since we can check her out more thoroughly there, get some X-rays, et cetera."

Lilly looked at Bill. "I think we should let them take her over to the hospital. What do you think?"

"I agree."

"Do I get a say in this?" asked Bev in a querulous voice.

"Of course," the paramedic answered.

"Then I want to go to the hospital."

Lilly was surprised. She had expected Bev to object to being taken anywhere, even to her own doctor.

"The hospital it is, then." The paramedic jotted something down on the clipboard he was carrying and turned to his partner. "Let's get her prepped." They went outside and came back just a couple moments later wheeling a stretcher. It took several minutes to get Bev situated in relative comfort on the stretcher, then they left. Bill rode with Bev in the back of the ambulance and Lilly and Nikki followed the ambulance in Lilly's car.

"I'm so sorry about this," Nikki said.

"I know, but what were you supposed to do? We had all agreed prior to this that you wouldn't go with her into the bathroom. You were just doing what we asked you to do."

"I know. But I still feel bad. She's in my care, and this happens. Given how upset she was yesterday after she tripped on the rug, I'm surprised she didn't fall apart."

"Let's just be glad she didn't. I hope she doesn't have a delayed reaction to the broken arm."

"We'll have to wait and see. This may scare her, Lilly. I just want you to be aware. She rarely wanted to go anywhere before this, and now that she's very likely broken a bone, I wouldn't be surprised if she refuses to leave the house from now on."

"We'll just have to come up with fun places to go to entice her out of the house once in a while."

"Hmm," was all Nikki said.

When they arrived at the hospital, Lilly and Nikki made their way to the emergency department in search of Bev and Bill. Nikki found a quiet corner of the ER where she could phone in a report of Bev's accident to her agency office while Bill and Lilly sat on each side of their mother in a curtained-off space. Bev was dozing, but the pain in her arm kept jolting her awake.

CHAPTER 35

"Mom, is there anything we can do to make you more comfortable?" Lilly asked.

"You can find out where the doctor is," Bev said. "Have they all disappeared?" She frowned.

"They're busy in here, Mom," Bill said. "I'm sure someone will be in to see you as soon as possible."

"I hope so. I have things to do at home. Isn't that a TV?" She pointed to a small television on the end of a giant metal arm that hung from the ceiling.

"Looks like it," Lilly said. She stood up and moved around the bed, looking for a remote control. "I don't see how to work it. Let's give it a few minutes. If someone comes in, we can ask."

That quieted Bev for several minutes, but eventually she grew impatient. "Can't one of you go ask how to work the TV? You're not much use sitting around staring at me."

Bill stood up and tried to hide his smile. "I'll check." He went in search of the elusive nurse-who-wasn't-busy, but came back a short time later shaking his head.

"I can't find anyone who isn't with a patient. Let's look for the remote again."

Bev started pushing all the buttons on the side of her bed, and that's how they found the controls for the television. A nurse poked her head around the curtain, having been summoned by one of the buttons Bev pushed.

"Can I help?" she asked with a perky smile.

"You can tell me when a doctor is going to show up around here," Bev said.

The nurse's smile didn't budge. "We'll get someone in here very soon." She disappeared into the bowels of the emergency room and Lilly, Bill, and Bev were left alone again.

"Mom, can I fix your pillow?" Lilly asked.

"No."

Lilly grimaced and sat back in her chair. She prayed the doctor would be in soon to deflect some of the tension in the room. Presently the curtain was pulled back and Lilly sat forward expectantly.

It was Nikki. "Bev, how is your arm?"

"I think I'll live. Lilly, Billy, can one of you go find a chair for Nikki?"

"I'll find one myself," Nikki said. She left and Lilly and Bill looked at each other. It seemed Nikki was the favorite child at this point.

Nikki was back just a minute later, lugging a heavy chair. Bill hopped up and took it from her, then set it on the floor close to the head of Bev's bed. Nikki would get the place of honor.

The doctor came in just a few moments later. She was brisk and efficient while still radiating warmth. Lilly liked her immediately.

"Do you mind if I call you 'Bev'?" she asked with a smile.

"That's my name."

The doctor ignored the rude remark while Lilly's face turned every shade of pink. Bill looked at the ground to hide his embarrassment.

"Tell me what happened," the doctor said.

After Bev had explained how she had fallen and Nikki had told the doctor about Bev's history of dementia, the doctor performed a quick examination, ordered X-rays for Bev's arm, and promised to return as soon as the X-rays were complete.

Without any discussion, Nikki accompanied Bev to the X-ray room when the tech came to take Bev away in a wheelchair. Lilly and Bill sat next to Bev's bed, waiting.

"How do you like that?" Lilly asked. "Why are we even here?"

"For moral support, I guess."

"She doesn't seem to want it."

"You're right. Maybe we're just here so you can give us all a ride home." He smirked.

"How's work going?" Lilly asked.

"Pretty good. It's actually starting to slow down a little bit, so that's why I'm able to stay here this morning. Last week I couldn't have sat here waiting."

"I'm glad to hear it. Any news floating around the station about Michelle Conover's murder?"

"There doesn't seem to be much discussion about it, but I'm not in that loop right now. I've been working on other things."

"Can you find out about it?"

"I can try. I'll ask a couple of the people working on it. How's Hassan doing?"

"He can't wait to get out of there."

"I'm sure. He doesn't belong in there, but my word isn't enough to set him free. He must be getting pretty sick of the way he's been treated since he bought the house in town."

"I'm sure he is. We don't talk about it that often. I think because he's embarrassed by it."

"Why is he embarrassed?"

Lilly shrugged. "I told him there's no reason for him to be embarrassed. He still doesn't like to talk about it, though."

"Did you ask him about what the guard said?"

"Yeah. He wants me to let it go. He doesn't want to rock the boat."

"As much as I hate to say it, that's probably wise."

A few minutes later an orderly wheeled Bev back into the room with Nikki in their wake. Bev stood up a little shakily and got herself onto the bed, then four pairs of hands—Lilly's, Bill's, Nikki's, and the orderly's—tried to make her comfortable as she lay back against the pillow.

"I'm fine, all of you. Let me do it myself," Bev said in a grumpy voice.

Everyone stepped back so Bev could struggle with the pillow alone, then she leaned back with a loud sigh. "When will the doctor be back in?"

The orderly answered. "I'll let her know the X-ray is done. It's being read right now."

"Thank you, young man."

The orderly smiled and left the small group alone. They all sat in silence for several minutes while Bev closed her eyes. Nikki scrolled through her phone and Lilly stood up to walk the corridors of the emergency department. Finally Bill came to find her. "The doctor is in with Mom."

They hurried back to Bev's bed as the doctor was addressing Bev and Nikki. The doctor turned to Lilly and Bill.

"I was just telling them that your mother has sustained a distal humerus fracture."

"English, please," Bev said.

The doctor smiled her calm smile. "You've broken your elbow. We'll get that set and you'll be on your way in no time."

"Wanna bet?" Bev asked.

Lilly had no idea how the doctor kept her snark in check in the face of grouchy patients. The doctor beckoned to her and Bill while Nikki stayed next to Bev.

"I understand from your mother's nurse that this is the second fall she's had in the past couple days."

Lilly and Bill nodded.

"And you mentioned earlier that your mother has been showing more and more signs of advancing dementia."

"I guess so," said Lilly.

"Yes," Bill said.

The doctor looked from Lilly to Bill and back again. "Just make sure she talks to her regular doctor about the falls. The time may come when you need to discuss alternative care arrangements."

She excused herself and went into the neighboring curtained-off area for the next patient. Lilly and Bill looked at each other.

"Maybe it's just that she's getting older. Older people fall sometimes," Lilly said.

"That's true." Bill paused, as if collecting his thoughts. "I do think we need to make an appointment for Mom to see her doctor, though. Maybe there's something he can do to help with her balance."

Lilly sighed. "Everything stinks."

Bill put his arm around her shoulders and they returned to Bev's bedside.

CHAPTER 36

*A*fter Lilly had driven everyone back to Bev's house and made sure that Bev was comfortable and didn't need anything, she escaped from there and went straight to work.

"How's your mom?" Harry asked.

"She has a broken elbow and she's as mad as a hornet, but I suppose that's better than being sad, which is how she reacted the last time she fell."

"Has she been falling a lot?"

"No. This is the second time this week, though. Her dementia seems to be getting worse."

"But it could also just be her getting older, right?"

"It could." Lilly shrugged. "But the thing is, she's been so mad lately. Not all the time, but erratically. I've gotten used to her bluntness, but it seems to be getting more pronounced. I hate to say it, but there are times I don't look forward to seeing her. It seems like my very presence irks her."

"I'm sure it's not that, Lilly." Harry gave her a sympathetic look.

"I wish I was sure."

Only a few customers came in that afternoon, so although there were practically no sales, it was blessedly quiet and Lilly needed the time to think. Harry puttered around the shop all afternoon, glancing at her with concern every so often.

"Harry, let's close up a few minutes early tonight. I need a glass of wine and a bath. I'm so tense my head hurts and my shoulders and neck ache."

"Sure, boss. I'll lock the front door." Lilly nodded and busied herself with stacking invoices she had gotten in the mail.

Harry had almost reached the front of the shop when he said, "Oh, here's Bill."

Lilly looked up in surprise to see her brother coming into the store. She felt a little knot of worry in her stomach and pressed her hand against her abdomen as if to smooth out the knot.

"What's up?" she asked Bill. "Is something wrong with Mom?"

He was still in uniform and he looked worn out. Lilly noticed for the first time that his uniform wasn't hanging on his frame as tautly as it usually did and she was concerned that he was losing weight.

"Not that I know of. I was in the neighborhood and I thought I'd stop by to let you know that I was sent to a call this afternoon on Hassan's block."

"Really? What for?"

"Do you know Eugene and Sally Belvedere?"

"Yeah."

"There was—um, a disturbance at their house."

"But you're going to tell me what it was all about, right?"

"Yeah." Bill looked around. Harry had gone back into the office. "Domestic issue," he said in a low voice.

"You mean like Eugene beat up Sally?"

"Or the other way around."

Lilly gasped. "Sally beat up Eugene?"

"Looks that way."

"Is he all right?"

"I think he will be. Their son came home in the middle of it, after another neighbor had called in an anonymous tip, and he had broken up the fight before I got there."

"What caused it?"

"I'm not exactly sure. What do you know about them?"

"Not much. The son drives a pickup truck with no muffler and it makes people crazy. That's about it. And I guess Michelle Conover filed a complaint with the police because of the noise the truck made."

"Well, neither Eugene nor Sally wanted to discuss the issue, so I left. Eugene didn't want to press charges, so there wasn't much for me to do."

"I never would have guessed Sally would be capable of something like that."

"People surprise me every day, Lil."

"So why did you come here to tell me about it? Do you think it had something to do with Michelle?"

"I don't know. I did hear someone yell something about Michelle as I was going up the front walk, but I don't know if it was Eugene or his son."

"Have you told the detective in charge of Michelle's file?"

"I'm on my way back to the station to let him know now. I had to stop at the tearoom to talk to Ted Conover about something first."

"What did you have to talk to him about?"

"A complaint we've received about him. Nothing to do with Michelle."

"Anything I should know about as a fellow Main Street merchant?"

"Nah. It's nothing. It didn't even happen in Juniper Junction."

"If you say so. I'm headed over to Mom's. Want to come with me?" Lilly rolled her eyes. "It promises to be great fun."

Bill chuckled. "I promised Noley I would go see her as soon as I get off work, so I'll go see Mom after I leave Noley's house."

"All right. Thanks for coming by."

Bill hesitated before turning toward the door.

"What is it?" Lilly asked.

"I need some help."

"I'll help you if I can. What do you need?"

"I'm going to ask Noley to marry me."

CHAPTER 37

*L*illy let out a squeal and threw her arms around Bill's neck. "I can't believe it!" she squeaked. "I'm so excited for you!"

"Easy does it, Lilly. I haven't even asked her yet. She might say no."

Lilly cocked her head and put her hands on her hips. "Don't be silly. Of course she won't turn you down!"

"Well, I've gotten myself pretty worked up over it."

"There's absolutely no reason for that. When are you going to ask her?"

"I haven't decided yet. First I have to pick out a ring. That's why I'm here. I almost came in earlier to do it, but I chickened out. Luckily I had some information to share with you, so I didn't look stupid coming in here for no reason."

"I'm so excited!" Lilly squealed again. "Come into the back and let me show you what I've got."

Bill looked at the empty display cases. "Why don't I come back when you've got stuff out? I don't want you to have to go rummaging through the vault to show me rings. I figured you'd still have the jewelry out."

"We put it away early. I'm beat."

"All the more reason for me to come back."

"Can you come back tomorrow?" Lilly couldn't hide the eagerness in her voice. How would she ever manage to keep this secret from Noley?

"I don't think so. I'm still working a lot of overtime. I have to pay for the ring somehow, and I don't want to dip into my savings. If Noley and I get married, I'm sure we'll want to buy a house, so I'm saving for that, too."

"Is *that* why you've been working yourself to death? So you can save up money for a ring?"

"Yeah. It hasn't been so bad."

"Sure. The weight you've lost looks great on you." Lilly smirked.

"I know, I know. I didn't need to lose any weight. It's not overwork that's done that, it's worrying about asking Noley to marry me. I can't eat, I can't sleep. I might as well be working. At least that way I'm making some money."

"I'll bet if you asked Noley she would say she'd rather you had spent the extra time with her."

"All right, you win. But now I'm ready to ask her and I need a ring. Can I come by the day after tomorrow?"

"Sure. Come first thing in the morning. I'll put the ring displays out and you can browse before Harry gets here."

"Sounds good. Thanks, Lilly. It's good to have a relative in the jewelry business. I assume you can pass along your employee discount?"

"Of course. I'll see you day after tomorrow. I'll let you know if I see anything at Mom's house that you need to know about."

"Don't tell Mom about this, okay?"

"Now, why would I do that? I'm not about to ruin the surprise."

"Thanks. If Noley says no, it'll be better if Mom doesn't know anything about it."

"We've been through this. Noley is *not* going to turn you down."

Bill smiled and left.

Lilly hurried over to Bev's house as soon as Bill was gone. When she walked into the living room she wasn't surprised to find Bev scowling at the television.

"What's the matter, Mom?"

"What do you think is the matter? My arm hurts."

Lilly glanced at Nikki, who had seated herself in a chair next to Bev. "How'd this afternoon go?"

"The pain pills worked, but now they're starting to wear off. She can't have more for another hour, though."

Lilly gazed at Bev for a moment, feeling sorry for the negative feelings she had nursed toward Bev in the past eighteen hours. Here was her mom, miserable and in pain, andLilly was annoyed at her for being unpleasant. *How selfish can I be?*

"Is there anything I can do to make you more comfortable, Mom?"

"No. If I need something, Nikki can do it. That's why we pay her, right?"

Lilly was taken aback at her mother's words. She glanced at Nikki, who shook her head slightly as if to say, *Don't worry about it. I'm used to it.*

Now Lilly felt bad for both of them. She wondered if Nikki would stick around if Bev's nastiness worsened. The good thing was that Bev generally seemed to be more agreeable toward Nikki than anyone else, so that was something.

She sat down on the sofa across from her mom and watched television with her and Nikki for a little while. The game show that was on was one of Bev's favorite shows and she didn't like to miss it. She also didn't like interruptions.

Lilly's phone rang just as one of the contestants was miraculously giving the correct answer to a trivia question about walruses. Bev glared at her.

"Sorry," Lilly whispered. She grabbed her phone and hurried out into the kitchen to take the call. She glanced at the caller ID—it was Tighe.

"Hi, honey. Good to hear from you. What's up?"

"Mom, I'm worried about Laurel. I don't want to keep nagging you about her, but I think she's super unhappy."

"Did she call you?"

"Yeah. She's bawling. She's upset because you won't let her quit school."

"As a matter of fact, I am going to let her quit school. Your father and I are headed up there this weekend to tell her."

"I wouldn't wait if I were you. She's more upset than I've seen her in a long time."

Now Lilly was worried. If Laurel was reaching out for help from her brother, who was busy with his own life in college, she must be desperate.

"All right. I'll call her and tell her the news. That should cheer her up."

"I think that's a good idea. Will you call her right now?"

"I'll run over to your father's house and we'll talk to her together. We want the message to come from both of us so she knows we're both on board with it."

"Okay, but you should hurry."

"Tighe, do you know something I don't know? Why the sudden rush?"

"I don't know, Mom. It's just this feeling I got from her. She's really out of her mind."

"All right. Thanks for calling, honey. Let me get going to Dad's right now."

After she hung up Lilly returned to the living room. "Nikki, can I talk to you for a minute?"

Nikki started to rise from her seat, but Bev put out her good hand. "Whatever you have to say to Nikki, you can say in front of me. No secrets in this house, young lady."

Lilly sighed. "Fine, Mom, though this has absolutely nothing to do with you."

"We'll see about that."

Lilly turned her attention to Nikki. "I have to run over to Beau's house. Can you call him and let him know I'm coming? It's urgent."

"Of course." Nikki was already reaching for her cell phone, but she paused as she listened to the exchange between Lilly and Bev.

"Why are you going to his house? He's not your husband anymore," Bev said.

Now she remembers. "I know that. I have to talk to him about Laurel."

"What about Laurel?"

"Mom, I've gotta run. I'll talk to you later. It's nothing for you to worry about."

"If you're going to say things like that right in front of me, I think I deserve to know what you're talking about."

"Mom, you demanded that I talk in front of you. I have to go to Beau's so we can call Laurel together. We both need to talk to her."

"About what?"

"About bringing her home from college, that's what. Nikki, you'll call him?" Nikki nodded. "Thanks. I'll see you tomorrow, Mom."

Bev waved her hand at Lilly in more of a gesture of dismissal than goodbye, and Lilly hurried out to her car.

She raced over to Beau's and he was waiting for her at the door when she arrived. She normally wouldn't have rushed to call Laurel, but the tone of Tighe's call had worried her and she wanted to talk to Laurel as soon as possible.

She and Beau greeted each other tersely. Nikki had obviously called with a heads-up that something was going on with Laurel, so Beau wanted details as soon as he closed the door behind Lilly.

"Tighe called. He's very worried about Laurel, who is apparently hysterical about wanting to leave college. I think we need to call her—right now—and let her know we're coming for her this weekend." Lilly had spilled all her words in such a hurry that she took a big gulp of air.

"All right. Do you have her number?"

She squinted at him. "Of course I have her number." She hadn't meant to sound cross, but shouldn't he know his own daughter's phone number?

He held out his cordless phone to her and sat down next to her at the kitchen table as she dialed Laurel's number then hit the button to put the call on speakerphone. Laurel's phone rang once.

CHAPTER 38

"Hi, Dad." Lilly began to tremble suddenly and tears sprang to her eyes. She clenched her teeth, telling herself sternly to keep it together. She hadn't realized how worried she had been about Tighe's phone call until she heard Laurel's voice.

"Dad?"

Lilly swallowed. Beau was staring at her as if she had sprouted wings.

"Hi, Laur," he said.

"It's actually Mom and Dad," Lilly finally said.

"Oh. Hi, Mom."

"How are things going?" Lilly asked.

"They suck."

"Well, that's why we're calling."

"Laurel, we're going to let you quit school and come home," Beau said. Lilly could have punched him. She might have known he would manage to be the bearer of the good news. She balled her hands into fists and remembered that the important thing wasn't who told

Laurel she was coming home, but that Laurel would be very happy.

And she was.

"You're kidding!" she shouted. "Really?"

"Really," Lilly said. She was smiling now, happy because Laurel was happy. "We were going to come up to school this weekend to tell you, but I had a worrying phone call from your brother and it convinced me to push up the good news by a couple days." *Take that, Beau.*

"And I agreed completely," Beau said. He grimaced at Lilly and she smiled in return.

"When can I come home?" Laurel asked. Lilly could practically see her daughter dancing with excitement.

"Is Sunday too early?" Lilly asked, glancing at Beau. He nodded.

"No way. I can have everything packed up tonight, even."

"No need to rush. If we come up on Sunday, that way I can work at the shop on Saturday. Now that I know you're all right and not about to do anything drastic, I'd like to go into work so I don't have to ask Harry to be in charge again. I've done a lot of that lately."

"This is so great, you guys," Laurel said. "I really hate it here. I can definitely get through the next few days if I know I'm coming home on Sunday."

"And you'll take care of telling the administration and doing everything you need to do to withdraw?" Lilly asked.

"Yes. I'll do everything first thing tomorrow morning."

"All right. Just make sure you're allowed to stay in the dorm until Sunday. We'll call the bursar and see what the deal is with tuition and room and board."

"Thanks, you guys. I love you both so much," Laurel said. Lilly could hear the relief in her voice.

"We love you, too. I'll text you and let you know what time

we'll be there on Sunday," Lilly said. Beau hadn't said anything, so Lilly looked at him, raised her eyebrows, and nodded toward the phone.

"Love you, too, Laurel," he said. Clearly the man wasn't used to expressing his love for his daughter out loud.

After they all hung up, Lilly stood to leave. "Thanks for calling Laurel with me. Are you good with getting an early start on Sunday? We may have to take two cars to fit all her stuff."

"I'm good with that. I'll drive my car and follow you up."

"All right. Let's plan to leave at seven. That way we can take all the time we need to clear out her room and get back to Juniper Junction."

Beau nodded and Lilly left. She couldn't wait to get home. This had been a very long day.

* * *

The next day Lilly visited Hassan at lunchtime. He looked tired and his skin was sallow.

"How are you holding up? Are you eating?" She was concerned that stress might be preventing him from having meals.

Hassan shrugged. "I eat if I'm hungry. The meals are terrible."

"We'll get you out and you'll be having steak on the grill in no time. I have some ideas about new avenues of inquiry, so maybe I'll be able to find something that will spring you from here."

"Lilly, you have to let the police do their jobs. I don't want you going out and looking for information that could get you hurt. There's a murderer out there somewhere."

"I'm being careful, I promise. Now, listen to what I've learned."

"All right. But I want you to tell Bill all about it when you leave here if he doesn't already know."

"He knows about one thing because he's the one who told me about it."

Hassan lifted his eyebrows.

"See? I knew you'd be interested in that. He came by the shop last night to tell me he had been called to a 'domestic disturbance' at Eugene and Sally's house." Lilly used her fingers to make air quotes.

"Really? Is Sally all right?"

"I'll say she is. She's the one who attacked Eugene."

"You're kidding."

"Nope. It's true. Oliver had to pull her off Eugene."

"So is Eugene okay?"

"Probably. He didn't want to press charges and Bill didn't say anything about him having to get checked out by a doctor, so I assume he's okay."

"I can't believe it. I never would have thought that of Sally."

"So here's my question: what if Eugene had a thing for Michelle and Sally killed her in a rage? After last night, we know that Sally is capable of violence. We've also heard Sally speak ill of Michelle, but we've never heard Eugene say anything against her."

Hassan looked thoughtful, but finally shook his head. "I just don't see it, Lilly. Even knowing that Sally has a violent streak, she seems too level-headed to pop off and kill someone."

"Maybe. But I'm keeping her on my list, just in case."

"What else have you learned?"

Lilly had been ruminating over whether to tell Hassan that Larry had been looking for Cupcake in Hassan's backyard. She didn't want Hassan to worry that she wasn't safe going to check on his house by herself.

She decided to tell him, though, and her fears were confirmed.

"I went to your house to check on things, you know, just to make sure everything is locked up tight and peaceful, and I was startled to see Larry on your patio."

"Larry was on my patio? As in, Larry the Neighbor? Why?"

"Cupcake got away from him when they were out for a walk and Larry thought he got into your yard."

"Was the gate open?"

"I don't know and I didn't think to check when I left."

"Was Cupcake back there?"

"She was actually in Michelle's yard, but she wandered over into your yard while I was talking to Larry."

"So the gate must be open."

"Oh, yeah. I guess you're right."

"I don't like the sound of that. I don't want you to check on my house anymore. You might not be safe there. Promise me you won't go over there alone again."

"I promise I won't go over there alone again."

"Thank you. You know, we really don't know Larry all that well, but we *do* know that Michelle called the cops on Cupcake, so that gives Larry a reason to despise her. Now, do you have any good news to share? I need to hear something positive."

"Do I ever! I was saving this for last because I knew you'd be happy about it."

Hassan's face brightened and he smiled for the first time since Lilly had walked in. "Really? What is it?"

"You know how I told you Bill came into the shop to tell me about Eugene and Sally last night?"

"Yes."

"Well, that's not the only reason he came in. Guess what. He came in to look for a ring because he's going to ask Noley to marry him!" She was squealing by the time she blurted out the good news. She stole a glance at the guard, who was standing on the other side of the metal door. He caught her eye and glared at her. She turned her attention back to Hassan, who was beaming.

"That's terrific! It's about time. I hope I'm out of here soon so I can congratulate them."

"He's worried that she'll turn him down."

"No chance."

"That's what I told him. I'm so excited!"

The guard opened the door and approached Lilly and Hassan. "Time's up, loverboy," he said. Lilly shot him an annoyed glance.

"Tell Bill I said congratulations," Hassan said before kissing Lilly on the cheek. "I'll kiss you properly when I get out of here," he whispered.

"No whispering," the guard bellowed. Hassan rolled his eyes and turned to leave. Lilly watched him walk away next to the guard and her fists clenched. She could not wait for Hassan to get out of there so she could report that loathsome guard.

CHAPTER 39

The next morning Bill came into the shop early, before Harry got there. It didn't seem right that Harry should know about Bill's plans before Noley did, so Lilly wanted Bill to be able to look at engagement rings without anyone else knowing about it.

Lilly brought out all the engagement rings she had in the vault. "Do you know Noley's ring size?" she asked.

Bill shook his head. "I figured I could just eyeball them. Her fingers are pretty thin. If I asked her ring size, she'd know what I'm planning."

"I would buy one that's too big and then I can resize it for her," Lilly said. "If you were to pick out one that was even one size too small, she might not be able to put it on her finger when you give it to her and you'd both be disappointed."

"Good point. See? I told you I would need help."

"When are you going to ask her?"

"I don't know. I wanted to have the ring first so the most important thing is taken care of."

"*How* are you going to ask her?"

"I haven't decided yet. I want it to be really amazing."

"Of course you do. I'm sure it'll be amazing no matter what."

They pored over rings for at least an hour before Bill decided on a radiant cut diamond in a yellow gold setting. He couldn't take his eyes off it once he picked it out.

"What do you think? Do you think she'll like it?" he asked Lilly a hundred times.

"She'll love it. It will be perfect with her skin tone. And she prefers yellow gold jewelry, so the setting is perfect, too. You'll have to go with gold bands when the time comes. Are you good with a yellow gold ring on your finger?"

Bill took a deep breath. "It sounds so real when you say it. What if she says no?"

"Stop it. She's not going to. Now you need to get out of here before Harry gets in. I'll box up the ring for you and you can pay for it, then be off with you."

Bill grinned. "Do I get a fancy box, too?"

"How does navy velvet sound?"

"Perfect." He fished around for his credit card while Lilly placed the ring carefully in the velvet box, then he paid for the ring and left. He wore the biggest smile Lilly had ever seen when he left after thanking her for all her help and the use of her employee discount.

It was mid-morning and there were several customers in the store when Noley came in. "Can I talk to you?" she asked as Lilly was turning her attention to someone at the counter.

"Sure. Give me a couple minutes. You can wait in the office, if you'd like."

When the rush was over, Lilly asked Harry to mind the front of the shop while she talked to Noley in the office.

"What's up?" she asked.

Noley looked at her with watery eyes. "I just don't think I can see Bill anymore."

What?!?! Not now!

"What's wrong?" Lilly asked, sitting down across from her friend.

"I just never see him. He's working all the time and he doesn't have any time for me. If this is what it's going to be like from now on, I just can't deal with it." Noley folded her hands in her lap and looked down, but Lilly could see the tears falling on her skirt.

She stood up and walked around the desk and put her arms around Noley's shoulders. "This crazy amount of overtime is only temporary, I promise. I know you two are meant to be together. Give him one more chance, please? I'll even talk to him if you want me to."

"I don't want you to!" Noley looked at Lilly with horror. "How embarrassing. What are we, in seventh grade? No. I don't want you to talk to him."

Well, I'm going to, like it or not.

"Okay. But will you give him one more chance?"

"I guess so. It's not like I have anything better to do."

"That's the spirit ... sort of," Lilly said with a smile. That got a short chuckle out of Noley. "Call him," Lilly urged. "And if he doesn't pick up, then leave him a message."

"Okay. Thanks, Lilly. Sorry to come in here and bother you, but I just had to talk to someone and get this off my chest."

"You're not bothering me at all. I've got to get back to work, though, so why don't you go to Armand's, grab some sandwiches, and come back here for lunch?"

"Okay." The two women walked to the front of the store and Noley left, walking slowly up Main Street. As soon as she was out of sight, Lilly whipped her cell phone out of her pocket and called Bill.

"What's up?" he answered.

"Trouble. I can't talk now because I've got customers, but you need to ask Noley tonight."

"That's impossible. I haven't planned anything yet."

"You'll be planning to ask another woman on a date if you don't, because Noley is thinking of leaving you."

"What? Why?"

"Because, you doofus, you've all but totally ignored her in your quest to make money for her engagement ring. She thinks your whole life together would be like this."

"Oh, no. This is a disaster. You've got to talk her out of it."

"I'm doing my best. She's coming back here for lunch. Think of something quick, Bill."

"I will. I'll call you later."

Harry must have figured out something was wrong when Lilly dropped a chain on the floor and got it all tangled up in itself. "Is everything okay, boss?" he asked.

"I'm just fidgety today, I guess." Lilly gave him a sheepish grin.

"Try cornstarch on that knot. It should come right out."

"I've heard that works with shoelaces, but I don't know about sterling silver chains. And I'm fresh out of cornstarch here in the shop."

"Give it to me and let me try it. Lilly, your hands are shaking. Are you sure everything is okay?"

Lilly grimaced. "Other than Hassan being in jail, Laurel quitting college, my mother falling more and more often, and trouble between Bill and Noley, yeah. Everything's fine."

"You've got a lot on your plate. Why don't you go out for a walk? Clear your head. You might feel a lot better if you get outdoors."

Lilly smiled at her assistant. "Thanks, Harry. Maybe I'll do that. Noley's bringing lunch back for the two of us, but maybe a walk around the block would do me some good before she gets back. Then you can go out for lunch and the two of us can eat in the front of the shop."

"Sounds like a plan."

Lilly set off down Main Street at a brisk clip. After several minutes, she finally slowed down to a stroll, her breathing having become less ragged and her blood pressure having fallen a good ten points. Harry was right—getting some fresh air worked wonders for the soul and the mind.

She was on her way back to the jewelry shop when she passed Ted's tearoom. Something was taped to the front door.

Tranquilitea is closed until further notice.

Lilly looked around as if the answers to the questions posed by the notice were swirling around in the crisp fall air.

What in the world does this mean? Closing a store before it even has a chance to get off the ground is definitely not a good move. Where's Ted, and why did he close the store?

CHAPTER 40

She wondered where she could turn for answers. Should she bother Bill again? She decided against it. He probably needed a break from her and her bad news and her questions for a little while.

By the time she got back to the shop her mind was reeling with questions about Ted.

"Did you know Tranquilitea has closed?" she asked Harry.

He looked at her in surprise. "No. Why would Ted do that?"

"I don't know. It's strange. It leads me to believe there's something really wrong."

"Like what?"

"Well, other than the deaths of his aunt and his ex-wife within a day or two of each other? Maybe he's having health issues or serious financial problems. There was the day he came in here to buy that watch and his credit cards were declined. Maybe he's bitten off more than he can chew and he couldn't pay his bills."

"I'll bet that's the reason," Harry said. "He probably went

broke opening the tearoom and doesn't have enough capital to keep it afloat until he's in the black."

The bell over the door jingled and Noley walked in, holding up two brown paper bags.

"I'm just dropping these off," she said. "They're cold sandwiches, so we can eat anytime. I need to run to the bank before lunch. Is that okay with you?"

"Sure. Take all the time you need," Lilly said. Noley left again. Lilly peered into the bags and knew immediately which one was hers and which was Noley's. One bag held a *jambon-beurre*, a simple ham sandwich on a baguette, and one bag held a salad and four tiny containers for items on the side. There was one little container with vinaigrette, one with a few croutons, one with freshly grated cheese, and one with a wedge of lemon. Noley was so picky. She always balked at the word "picky" and preferred "discerning," but it boiled down to her being picky. Lilly smiled at the thought of Armand rolling his eyes in his good-natured way at Noley's quirks.

Noley was back about a half hour later.

"Harry, you can go to lunch now," Lilly said. She reached for the bag with the *jambon-beurre* and pushed Noley's bag over to her.

"How did you know which bag was which?" Noley asked.

"Really?"

"I'm not picky."

"Okay, you're not picky. Now listen because I've got news."

"What news?"

Lilly was happy to have something to talk about that wasn't Bill. She wanted to distract Noley from her problems with Bill long enough for Bill to decide how he was going to pop the question. "Did you go past Tranquilitea today?"

"No. Why?"

"There's a sign on the door that says the tearoom is closed until further notice."

Noley's eyes widened. "You're kidding. I thought that place would be a sure thing. Why is Ted closing it?"

"I don't know. Harry doesn't know, either. But I'm wondering if Ted is having financial problems." She felt a slight twinge of guilt over discussing the man's money issues, but, she reasoned, anyone standing in line behind Ted, if there had been anyone, would have been able to see the same thing Lilly saw. So she told Noley about Ted's credit cards being declined and him returning to pay for the watch in cash.

"Hmm. I'm not sure that's a financial problem. I mean, watches sold at jewelry stores tend to be pretty expensive and he ended up paying cash for the watch, right? So he can't be *too* desperate for money."

"I suppose," Lilly said, taking a bite of her sandwich. "It just seems strange that a business that just opened would suddenly close like that."

"It's definitely strange. But maybe he did it for another reason."

"Well, I'm going to try to figure it out."

"And how are you going to do that? You have a backlog of issues at the moment, if I'm not mistaken."

Lilly made a face at her friend. "I don't know. But I'll figure it out."

"Why all the interest in Ted Conover?"

"I don't know. I guess it's because two women whom I know were in his life are now dead."

"That is a little too coincidental."

"Want to come over for dinner tonight?" Lilly asked, changing the subject.

Noley wagged her finger at Lilly. "Listen, I know what you're doing. You're trying to take my mind off Bill. But it's not going to work. That is all I can think about right now. So I can have dinner with you, but I'll still be thinking about Bill."

"Guilty as charged," she said, gathering her sandwich crumbs into her hand. She tossed them in a wastepaper basket nearby. "But you have to give me credit for trying."

Noley finally smiled. "I do give you credit for trying. But I have to work this out with Bill."

"Does that mean you aren't going to leave him?" Lilly couldn't keep the excitement out of her voice.

"No. But it means I'll listen to an explanation of why he's been practically absent for weeks."

Lilly had to clench her mouth shut to prevent herself from telling Noley exactly why Bill had been taking so much overtime. She busied herself taking care of the lunch debris.

"Well, I'm sure he has a good one."

"So are you still coming over for dinner?"

"Do you really want me to?"

"Sure. But all I have is cereal right now."

"Then thanks, but I'll pass." Noley grinned.

After Noley left Lilly found the page of questions she had written about Ted and his strange behavior. She had a few more queries to add.

Why did Ted close his tearoom?

Is it closed for good?

Where does Ted live?

Does he have any business partners?

A couple of those questions would be relatively easy to answer. When Harry returned from his lunch break, Lilly went into the office to retrieve her laptop. She set it up on one of the display counters in the front of the shop and opened a new tab. There was no time like the present to start learning more about Ted.

"Whatcha doing, boss?"

"Trying to find a little information on Ted Conover."

"You're really interested in that guy, aren't you?"

"Sort of."

Her first search was the state government's online compilation of business information that was available to the general public. She was amazed at the number of businesses with the word "tranquil" in the name. Mostly spas.

She ran her finger down the list and finally came to Tranquilitea.

She clicked on the business name and was shocked by what she saw.

There on the screen were the name of Ted Conover's business partners: Gerald McIntosh and Ivy Leachman.

Ivy wasn't that much of a surprise. After all, she was family. But Gerald McIntosh? It had to be the same Gerald McIntosh who had worked with Michelle. The same Gerald McIntosh who had lost a client to her.

Lilly wasn't sure what all of this meant, but she was pretty sure it meant something. She made a note on her paper to ask Bill if the police knew about it, but they had to know. It was public information.

She delved further into the database to see if she could find home addresses for both men. Sure enough, there was Gerald's address in Lupine. And to her surprise, Ted lived in Lupine, too. She had assumed he lived in Juniper Junction.

"You all right, boss?"

Lilly looked up to find Harry staring at her.

"I'm okay."

"I wondered because you're sitting there with your mouth hanging open and you look like you just saw the ghost of Zebulon Pike." Lilly had to think for a moment before she realized who Harry was talking about—the man for whom Pike's Peak was named.

Lilly quickly closed her mouth. "I just found out who Ted Conover's business partners are. One is Ivy, or was Ivy, and the other one is a guy I sort of know." It wasn't technically true, but she had at least met him.

"Oh. Interesting."

Clearly it wasn't that interesting to Harry, who turned away to greet someone coming into the shop. Lilly's fingers flew over the keyboard as she tried, in vain, to find out more information about Tranquilitea. Specifically, she was looking for the financials. She had assumed they wouldn't be public, and she was correct.

On a hunch, Lilly tried another search. She was right—Ted had moved to Lupine even before his divorce was final, since Michelle was still living in the house in Juniper Junction.

She needed to go back to Lupine, and specifically, to Michelle's old firm. Tomorrow.

CHAPTER 41

That night she went to visit Hassan after work. "I feel like we're getting close to a breakthrough," she told him as soon as the guard had left them alone.

He wrinkled his brow. "What kind of a breakthrough?"

"I mean, threads are starting to come together. I need to sort out my thoughts and figure out what's going on."

"I have a bad feeling about this."

"Don't worry about me. Worry about getting reservations at The Water Wheel to celebrate your release." She grinned.

He didn't grin back. "If something happens to you because you're off half-cocked to follow an idea that sounds dangerous to everyone but you, there's nothing I can do to help you from in here. Let the lawyer and the police work this out and you stay out of it, please."

"I can't. The police are getting nowhere and Gretchen is a lawyer, not a detective."

"You're not a detective, either, remember?"

"Yeah, well, I appear to be the only one who can help you at the moment. So do you want to get out of here or don't you?"

"Of course I want to get out. But I want you alive and well when it happens."

"I'll be alive and well, don't you worry."

She kissed Hassan goodbye when the guard came for him, and ignored the guard's sneer. *Let him think what he wants in that bigoted head of his,* thought Lilly. *I'll be reporting him to his superiors in no time flat.*

Lilly had a hard time sleeping that night. She tossed and turned, playing over and over in her mind what she was going to say in the morning when she arrived at Michelle's former firm. When she got up, she dressed in a conservative black suit, slicked her hair into a severe style away from her face, and put on loads of makeup. A pair of stilettos completed the look. She transferred everything in her everyday quilted purse to an expensive leather bag that she had bought years before. She had immediately regretted the purchase when she made it, but it was coming in handy today.

She drove to Lupine early so that she could be at the firm when it opened. She parked a block away so no one would see her sedan—she needed to project an image of wealth and sophistication and her car didn't figure into that image. She would walk.

When she arrived at the door of the financial firm precisely at eight o'clock, her feet already hurt. *How do people wear high heels every day?* She swore she would never again complain about the low-heeled pumps she usually wore to work.

Before pushing the door open, she said a silent prayer that no one would recognize her from her previous visit. She had a different role to play this time.

Dot, the receptionist who had been there the previous visit, looked up from her computer as Lilly entered the building.

"Can I help you?" she asked.

"I certainly hope so. I have just come from a highly unsatisfactory meeting at my broker's office and I am in the market for a new financial firm. I've heard Gerald McIntosh is excellent. Is he available right now?"

The receptionist scrambled from her chair. "I believe so. Let me check and I'll be right back."

"Thank you, miss." *Phew. Dot didn't seem to recognize me.*

Lilly sat down on the edge of one of the chairs in the lobby and crossed her legs, swinging one of them in a tight, controlled manner. So far, so good.

A couple minutes later Dot returned and smiled at Lilly. "He'll be right with you," she said.

As she was speaking Gerald McIntosh stepped into the lobby and smiled at Lilly.

She stood and extended her hand to Gerald. "Good morning, Mister McIntosh. My name is Bernice Plumpton. I am looking for a new financial advisor as my former one has become highly unsatisfactory. I have heard that you are a bright young man."

Gerald smiled. "Thank you, Ms. Plumpton. Would you care to come back to my office where we can chat?"

Lilly followed him through the familiar door into the shared industrial workspace that had so intrigued her on her prior visit. She looked around and nodded. "Modern and forward-thinking. I like it." Gerald turned around and smiled at her as they continued walking. She followed him to a table in the back of the room.

Gerald extended his hand and gestured for Lilly to have a seat. He went around to the other side of the table and opened a sleek laptop.

"Tell me about yourself, Ms. Plumpton," he said.

"Oh, I'm not interesting. Just a wealthy middle-aged divorcée. I would like to hear about *you*. I want to know who's handling my money."

Gerald leaned forward and folded his hands on the table in front of him. "Smart woman." Lilly inclined her head toward him to acknowledge the compliment and he continued. "I am a lifelong resident of Lupine, except for the five years I was away in college. And even then I didn't go far. I stayed in-state and graduated with a business degree and an MBA."

"Where did you rank in your class?"

"Right up near the top. You're in good hands, Ms. Plumpton. Don't worry about that."

"Community groups? Family? Hobbies?" Lilly asked. She knew she was treading in territory that might be considered inappropriate, but she would cross that bridge if she came to it.

"Yes to all three. I have a wife and four children and I'm active with their sports teams. I'm also involved in the local food bank and other charitable organizations in Lupine."

Now to move in for the kill. "Any conflicts of interest?" Lilly asked.

"I'm afraid I don't know what you mean, Ms. Plumpton."

"I mean, I like to invest a certain portion of my money locally. In other words, I like to keep a percentage of my money in Colorado. I believe I have a responsibility to give back. Do you personally hold any financial interests that might affect how you deal with my investments?"

"You are a shrewd investor, Ms. Plumpton. I can see you're quite well-versed in investing."

"I am. It's my money. But you didn't answer the question, Mister McIntosh."

"It's funny you should ask, Ms. Plumpton. In fact, just this week I divested myself of a financial interest in a local business in Juniper Junction. Other than that, I have no significant investments locally."

Bingo. Now to learn more about that. This is almost fun.

"Oh, Juniper Junction? A lovely town. I have been there many times. If you don't mind my asking, what business did you have an interest in?"

"Tranquilitea. It's a new tearoom right there on Main Street. Very nice place." *And apparently the state website hasn't been updated to reflect this development.*

"Yes, I am familiar with Tranquilitea. A charming little tea shop. I stopped in there one day for a cup of their Darjeeling. Have you tried it? Very refreshing."

Gerald nodded.

"And may I ask why you no longer have a financial interest in the business?" She was really pushing her luck.

Gerald seemed to agree. He pressed his lips together and said, "Personal reasons. If that's all, Ms. Plumpton, I do have another appointment in just a few minutes, so if you'd like to take a folder containing literature about the firm and read the material at your leisure, I will be happy to talk to you again when you're ready."

This was almost too good to be true. He was going to let her go and she didn't even have to discuss phony financial information with him. Good. She had been worried that the numbers would muddy her ability to think clearly and stay in the role of Bernice Plumpton.

She stood and shook Gerald's hand firmly, then he grabbed a thick folder off his desk and led her out into the lobby. Before she left, he handed her the packet of information. She smiled and thanked him, then let out a huge sigh of relief as the door closed behind her and she was on the sidewalk outside the firm.

CHAPTER 42

*S*he hurried to her car and whipped off the high heels as soon as she slid behind the wheel. Bill had told her a thousand times when they were teenagers that she shouldn't drive without shoes, but this time it couldn't be helped. Her feet would be nothing but bloody stumps by the time she reached Juniper Junction if she didn't take those cursed shoes off.

As she drove back to Juniper Junction a thousand questions ran through her head, but only one kept returning to the forefront. *What were the "personal reasons" Gerald took his money out of Tranquilitea?*

The two men must have had an argument. Over what? What could have caused such a rift between them that Gerald wouldn't continue to invest his money in the new tearoom? Surely he had to know that withholding his money might mean that the tearoom would have to close until Ted could find another source of funding.

I wonder if Michelle had a will when she died. I wonder if Ted got any money from her. Lilly made a mental note to ask Gretchen to check the court records next time she had a few spare minutes. Surely there must be a way to learn the contents of a deceased person's will.

As soon as she got back to Juniper Junction Lilly went straight to the shop. Harry had opened and was helping a customer pick out a ring for her husband. He did a double take when he saw Lilly, probably startled by the amount of makeup she was wearing. She tugged off her coat and headed to the employee restroom to change into more comfortable clothes and remove some of the face paint. She had learned early on in the jewelry business that customers were less intimidated when she didn't wear a high-power outfit and lots of makeup, and that suited her just fine.

She slipped into her everyday low-heeled pumps and called Bill.

"What's up?" he asked.

She dispensed with any preamble. "I've done a little digging and I think that Gerald McIntosh has something to do with Michelle Conover's murder."

"You're kidding. What do you mean by 'a little digging'? I swear, Lilly, you're going to cost me my job one of these days if you don't knock it off. How many times do I have to tell you to let the police handle the murder investigations?"

"And how many times do I have to tell you not to talk to me like that?"

"Do you want me to come down there and cuff you?"

"You wouldn't dare. I'll tell Mom."

"Mom would be on my side and you know it."

"She always is."

"All right, that's enough. Are you going to stop interfering with police business or am I going to have to arrest you?"

"You can't arrest me. I'll tell Noley that you're going to pop the question."

"You're killing me, Lilly."

"Anyway, you're welcome. I have figured out a key piece of this whole puzzle. Trust me—it's Gerald McIntosh. He pulled his money out of Ted's tearoom just recently."

"Thank you. I'll pass this along to the appropriate person. I have to run. Have you talked to Noley?"

"Not since yesterday. I wouldn't wait if I were you, Bill. Ask her today."

"Don't tell me what to do. But okay, I will."

They hung up. Lilly tried to remember their conversation word for word. She didn't recall actually promising to stay out of the police investigation, nor did she recall promising not to interfere. *Interfere.* It was such a judgmental word.

* * *

She had packed a lunch for work so Harry wouldn't have to mind the shop alone again that day. It was after closing time before she could finally run over to the jail to visit Hassan.

"Any news?" he asked when he saw her and the guard had departed.

"I found out that Gerald McIntosh has pulled his money from Tranquilitea. Something must have happened between him and Ted to cause a pretty big rift. I mean, to ruin Ted's livelihood like that, it must have been huge."

"Just don't get hurt trying to figure it all out."

"I won't."

She told Hassan about Bev's brokenelbow, then about all the drama with Bill and Noley.

"Tell your mom I hope she feels better soon," Hassan said. "And tell Bill to quit being stupid."

"I've been telling him that for decades. He doesn't listen." Lilly laughed.

When visiting time was up, Lilly hugged Hassan and whispered to him, "I feel like we're getting close. I think Gerald McIntosh is the key to everything."

"Just be careful."

He squeezed her hand and she left. Next stop: Bev's house. Nikki answered the door when she arrived. "How's Mom?" she asked.

"She's in a miserable mood. I doubt you're going to want to stay too long."

"Oh, dear." Lilly led the way into the living room, where she found Bev sitting on the sofa. "Hi, Mom!" She used her cheeriest voice.

Bev gave her a death stare. "What do you want?"

"I just came by to see how you're doing. How is your arm?"

"It hurts. What did you expect?"

Lilly glanced at Nikki, who raised her eyebrows as if to say *See? I told you so.*

"I hoped it would be a little better by tonight."

"It hurts more at night."

"Oh. I'm sorry to hear that."

"It's normal," Nikki said. "Like a lot of other things, the pain tends to be worse at night because she's been up and moving around all day long."

"Oh? What did you do today, Mom?"

"You're looking at it. I just sat here."

"I don't mean she was out shopping or playing tennis," Nikki explained. "I just mean that she's been awake all day, using her arm without even realizing it. Like picking up and setting down the television remote and shifting to situate herself more comfortably. She doesn't have to move around a lot for her arm to get tired."

"Is it any better than yesterday?" Lilly asked Bev.

"Not a bit."

"Is there anything I can do for you? Want me to stop at the grocery store?"

"Nikki went this morning, didn't you?" Bev asked the nurse. Nikki nodded, shooting Lilly an apologetic look. "You're about twelve hours too late, Lilly."

"Sorry about that," Lilly mumbled. This new personality of her mother's was wearing her down. She sighed.

"Now what?" Bev asked.

"Nothing. Say, I'm going to be bringing Laurel home on Sunday. I'm sure she's eager to see you."

"You're making a mistake, mark my words. But it will be good to see her. I hope she hasn't gotten fat like so many girls do when they go away to college."

Lilly stared at her mother in disbelief. She couldn't keep her mouth shut any longer. She ignored the pleading gestures she could see Nikki making in her peripheral vision.

"Mom, I don't know what's gotten into you, but I hope it gets out of you pretty soon. You haven't had a pleasant word to say to me in days. And now to say that about Laurel, it's just plain mean. For your information, she's lost weight because she's so unhappy there. But even if she'd gained two hundred pounds, she'd still be your granddaughter and I would expect you to keep your mouth shut about it." Lilly spun around to face Nikki. "I'm sorry, Nikki. I just couldn't let this go another minute. If I want to listen to abuse like this, I'll go somewhere besides my own mother's house."

Nikki tilted her head and smiled sadly at Lilly while Bev watched, her eyes wide. Then, to Lilly's surprise, Bev's face crumpled and she started to cry softly.

"I can't seem to help it, Lilly. I'm sorry. You know I would never say anything to Laurel and I love her no matter what. I love you, too."

Lilly swallowed. She glared at the television screen because she was going to cry, too, if she looked at her mother.

"This is part of Bev's disease," Nikki said in a soft voice. "Bev knows that, but it doesn't make it any easier, does it, Bev?"

Bev shook her head and sniffled loudly.

Despite her best intentions, a tear rolled down Lilly's cheek. "I'm sorry, Mom. I shouldn't have lashed out like that. This is hard for me." Her throat was hurting from keeping the tears in, and all she wanted was to go home.

"It's hard for everyone," Nikki said. "Bev, how about a snack?"

Bev nodded, still sniffling.

"I need to go home," Lilly said. She leaned close to Bev and kissed her cheek. "I'm sorry, Mom. Can we try a do-over tomorrow?"

Bev answered by giving Lilly a confused look.

"I mean, let's start fresh tomorrow. I'll do better, I promise."

Bev nodded.

"Let me go lock the door behind Lilly and I'll be right back," Nikki said. "You stay right where you are, Bev."

Lilly didn't want Nikki to leave Bev alone for more than a few seconds, so she hurried to the front door. She had to admit she felt a surge of relief at leaving Bev's house, too. Nikki accompanied her and whispered, "Starting fresh tomorrow is a good idea. I think the pain in her arm is bothering her and she's upset and angry about it. That's why she's been unpleasant. Don't let it get you down, because you haven't done anything wrong. Personality changes are common and it seems that's what we're seeing here."

"Thanks for everything, Nikki. You'd better get back in there with her. I'll call tomorrow." Lilly could hear the door lock behind her as she descended the front steps to the sidewalk. What she needed was a glass of wine and a good book.

But Fate had a better idea.

CHAPTER 43

$\mathcal{L}$illy had just sat down on the sofa in her living room with a rather large glass of pinot noir when there was a knock at the front door. Barney launched himself off the couch and barked as though the thing that knocked was coming to kill both of them.

It was Noley.

Tears streaked down her face and she gave Lilly a tremulous smile when Lilly opened the door.

Mouth agape, Lilly pulled Noley into the house and glanced up and down the street. "What happened? What's wrong?" She couldn't keep the alarm from her voice. "And where's your car?"

"I walked over. Do you have any tissues?"

Lilly closed the door behind Noley and hurried into the powder room to grab a box of tissues. She returned to the living room and held the box out to Noley, who was standing in the middle of the room, looking pitiful.

"What's going on? Sit down," Lilly directed. Noley did as she was told.

"I just can't take it anymore," Noley said, taking a deep, shaky breath. Lilly waited, knowing Noley would continue. "I just don't think I can compete with Bill's job anymore. I don't want to break up with him, but I can't continue like this, either."

Lilly was glad Noley couldn't see her blood beginning to boil. If Bill didn't do something soon, she was going to let him have it. She grasped Noley's hand in her own. "Noley, Bill wants—"

There was another knock at the door. Barney, barely able to handle the excitement of a second evening visitor, flew to the door, barking as though the sound alone might magically open it.

Bill stood outside, raking his hands through his hair. "I can't find Noley. Her car is in her driveway, but she's not answering the door or her phone. I'm worried about her. Has she called you?" His words tumbled out in a rush.

Lilly held the door open and gestured for him to enter. The small foyer wasn't visible from where Noley sat in the living room, so Lilly leaned over to hiss to Bill, "She's here, dummy. You should have listened to me!"

He looked at her with a mixture of confusion and horror. "What's wrong? Is she okay?" He craned his neck to see into the living room.

"Lilly, is everything okay?" Noley appeared in the foyer. Her eyes widened when she saw Bill, and she immediately clenched her jaw and turned away.

Lilly glared at Bill and nodded toward the living room. He took a tentative step in that direction, then turned to her. "Why is she here? Why didn't she drive? What's wrong?"

"Ask her yourself."

He stepped into the living room, where Noley was now

standing with her arms crossed over her chest, facing away from Bill and Lilly.

"Noley? Are you all right? I stopped over at your house and I was worried when you didn't answer the door. What's wrong, Nol?"

Noley turned to look at Bill. Her eyes, which had been glittering with anger, softened just a bit. She looked at the floor.

"Noley? Is everything okay?"

Noley just shook her head. Bill gave Lilly a helpless look. Lilly had to get them to talk to each other somehow.

"I'm going to get two more glasses of wine. While I'm in the kitchen, I want you two to sit next to each other on the sofa. Don't even think about sitting anywhere else. And for Pete's sake, say something to each other." She left the room without a backward glance, hoping they would do as she instructed.

When she returned to the living room, they were seated on opposite ends of the couch. They both looked miserable. Bill slumped back and looked at the floor while Noley blinked back tears, looking everywhere but in Bill's direction.

Lilly set two glasses of wine on the coffee table in front of the sofa. "You were supposed to sit next to each other." She took her own wine from the table and moved over to the armchair. Barney sat in the middle of the floor, looking from one human to the next, probably wondering what had happened to disturb his peaceful evening.

Everyone sat in silence for what seemed to Lilly like hours. Finally she spoke. "You two have some talking to do. You've both been talking to me, and as flattering as that is, it's not getting you anywhere. I'm going to take Barney outside and when I come back in, I want you talking to each other. Come on, Barn." Lilly stood up and gestured to Barney. He cocked his head and looked for a moment like he would rather keep an eye on things in the living room, but eventually the thrill of going outside won out and he followed Lilly through the kitchen and down the back steps.

Lilly checked her watch about a hundred times over the next ten minutes. She was ready to go back inside and Barney, having done his business and snuffled through the bushes in the backyard, was waiting for her at the back door. Clearly he was ready to go back inside, too. He wagged his tail when she finally stood up and joined him. She closed the door quietly behind her in the kitchen and tiptoed to the doorway to the living room. She gasped.

Bill was down on one knee in front of Noley. He withdrew the blue velvet box from his pocket and opened it, holding it up so Noley could see the ring nestled inside.

"Noley, you mean more to me than any job ever could. You know that. The overtime was only to be able to buy you the ring you deserve, and it will never happen like that again. I just need you to give me the chance to prove it. Noley, will you marry me?"

Both Noley and Lilly were crying. Lilly wanted to run into the living room and have a big group hug, but she figured it was bad enough that she had spied on her brother's marriage proposal to her best friend. She couldn't turn away and give them any privacy, though, until she heard Noley's answer. She slunk back further against the kitchen wall.

Noley sniffled loudly, then she and Bill laughed. "I didn't really want to break up with you," she said, sobbing now. "I just thought your overtime would be our whole life if we stayed together."

"No. No way. I promise."

"Then yes, I'll marry you. I love you, Bill." She was openly bawling.

Lilly waved her arms back and forth in front of her with excitement. Barney was sitting next to her, and he looked up and gazed at her with his big brown eyes. She reached down and tousled the fur on his head. "Okay, Barn. We've given them enough time. Let's go," she whispered.

Barney raced into the living room, followed closely by Lilly, whose tears were flowing freely, too. She took one look at Bill and his tears, and wept with happiness.

The three of them stood there crying, then started to laugh. Noley leaned into Bill, who put his arm around her and kissed the top of her head. "Did you know about this?" she asked Lilly through her tears. She held up her hand so she could admire the gorgeous ring, then turned it so Lilly could see it.

Lilly nodded. "The proposal or the ring? I knew about both. He bought the ring at my shop. He wanted to plan something really special, but once I knew how sad you were, I told him he had to bag that idea and just ask you in a hurry."

"And I hadn't planned on doing it tonight, here, at Lilly's house, but the timing just seemed right," Bill said. He looked at Lilly. "Were you watching?"

"Only the important parts." She could feel her face redden. "I know I shouldn't have, but I just couldn't tear myself away."

Noley laughed. "That's okay. I'm so happy that you're here to share this with us!" She moved out of Bill's arms to embrace Lilly, then Bill put his arms around both of them.

"Thanks for everything, Lil," he said. Noley smiled and nodded her agreement, gulping and wiping away more tears.

"What are you two doing, standing around here?" Lilly asked, wiping her own eyes with her sleeve. "Go out somewhere and celebrate!"

"Should we?" Bill asked Noley.

"Do you have to work?" she asked him in a teasing voice.

"No way. Let's go tell Mom, then over to the tapas bar off Main Street. No police there, I promise."

She grinned and they left after thanking Lilly again for all her help.

The evening hadn't turned out so bad, after all. She got to watch two of her favorite people get engaged and it had happened right in her living room. She couldn't wait to tell Laurel all about it.

CHAPTER 44

*L*illy had a spring in her step when she visited Hassan the next day. "Guess what happened," she said in a singsong voice when she saw him.

He smiled, crinkling up the corners of his eyes. "It's good to see you smile," he said. "What happened?"

"Bill and Noley got engaged lastnight *in my living room.*"

"That's terrific! And you were there?" He looked confused.

"Well, I was watching from the kitchen. I shouldn't have, I know, but I couldn't help myself. It was the sweetest thing. He hadn't planned on asking her at my house, but they were both there and it just happened. He must have been carrying that ring around with him everywhere."

Hassan wore a wide smile. "When I get out of here, let's take them out to dinner to celebrate."

"First, *I'm* taking *you* out to dinner to celebrate getting out of this stinking place. Then we'll celebrate their engagement. And it's good to see you smile, too."

"My cheeks were hurting from frowning all the time," he said.

"We'll have you smiling again soon." They chatted, trying to keep things light, until it was time for Lilly to leave. The shop was busy that day, so she barely had any time to think until she closed up that evening. She went straight home for a long, hot bath.

It was mid-morning the next day when Lilly phoned Nikki. "How's Mom today?"

"She's doing really well. Last night Bill and Noley came by and told her the news, so she's over the moon this morning."

Lilly smiled to herself. *This would probably be a good time to go see Mom,* she thought. She glanced at the clock on the dashboard. She didn't have time to visit her mom and still open the shop on time, so she promised Nikki she would be by the house after work. "I can't be there long because I need a good night's sleep tonight. Beau and I are leaving early to pick up Laurel tomorrow."

"Beau is excited for Laurel to come back to Juniper Junction," Nikki said. "He misses having her around."

Why didn't he miss her for the fifteen years he was gone? Lilly chided herself. *No bitterness allowed.* They needed to present a united front to Laurel when it came to her responsibilities after leaving college, so she didn't want to entertain negative thoughts about Beau.

The day passed quickly. Noley came in to have her ring sized and they talked about wedding dates and colors. Bill and Noley were wasting no time on the preparations, though they hadn't chosen a firm date yet. They were partial to an August wedding, which only gave them nine months to pull everything together. Lilly promised to help everywhere she could.

That evening Lilly drove over to Bev's house right after she closed the shop. Bev had apparently forgotten about the wedding over the course of the day, because she was in a foul mood from the minute Lilly walked through her front door.

"Nice of you to come by," Bev said.

"I was here just last night, Mom."

"Who said you weren't?"

Lilly tried smiling brightly through clenched teeth. It hurt her cheeks. "Want to play cards?"

"No."

"Want to watch television?"

"That's what I was doing when you came in."

"Do you mind if I join you?"

Bev waved her hand toward the television set. "Suit yourself."

Lilly suppressed a sigh and sat down on the sofa.

Nikki, probably sensing the tension oozing from Lilly, piped up from the other end of the sofa. "Bev, why don't you tell Lilly about your visit from Bill and Noley?"

Bev broke into a wide smile. "They're getting married! I thought they already were married, but I guess not. Isn't that wonderful news, Lilly?"

It was like her mother had turned into a different person. Lilly smiled with relief, glad that Bev's mood had changed. "That's great news, Mom. I'm so happy for them."

"I can't wait to have more grandchildren."

Don't hold your breath, Mom.

"Do you think they'll buy a new house together before they get married?" Bev asked.

"I doubt it. Planning the wedding will take up a lot of time, and they're both still working full time, so I don't think they'll have time to put both of their houses on the market and buy one together. But maybe after they get married they'll find a house they both like."

"Oh, I hope they don't move out of Juniper Junction," Bev fretted.

"I wouldn't worry about that, Mom. They both love Juniper Junction."

"Well, even if they did move away I would still have you nearby, Lilly. That's important."

Lilly smiled, suddenly unable to speak. A lump grew in the back of her throat. There were times she wondered if her mother had a sentimental bone in her body. Then there were times like this, when Bev was more expressive about her feelings toward Lilly. Bev had never been a demonstrative mother, but lately Lilly had been feeling like nothing she said or did made Bev happy. Now she was reminded that wasn't the case.

"Nikki, I think I would like to go to bed now. Lilly, dear, thank you for coming over. I'm sorry if I was rude. You know that your visits are very important to me."

Lilly stood up and stepped over to Bev, who had lifted her cheek for a kiss. Lilly stooped down and kissed her mother's cheek, then leaned in and hugged her shoulders. "I don't know if I'll be by tomorrow, Mom, because I have to go pick up Laurel in the morning. We might be all day."

"That's all right, dear. Just come by whenever you can."

Nikki stood behind Bev, beaming. She must have known how happy Lilly would be to get even a slight measure of approval from her mother.

Lilly went home and practically fell into bed. She had a lot on her mind, but uppermost was her happiness that her mother had shown her a tiny glimpse of her old self that evening.

CHAPTER 45

*B*eau was only five minutes late when he pulled up in front of Lilly's house the next morning. Lilly had prepared two travel mugs of coffee, figuring he would be running late. She didn't want to have to make a stop for coffee once they were on the road. She handed him the coffee through the open window of his car.

"I'll follow you," he said. "You know where you're going, right?"

Lilly fought the urge to roll her eyes. "Yes. I'll try to park right in front of her dorm so it's easier to load up the cars."

Beau nodded and Lilly got into her own car. Noley had promised to let Barney out a couple times during the day, so Lilly was glad she didn't have to take him up to school. It would be chaotic enough without adding a dog to the mix.

She drove quickly, willing herself not to look into the rear view mirror lest she see Beau flashing his lights at her to stop at the next rest area. It would be just like him to insist on stopping somewhere for a greasy breakfast.

She pulled onto campus and slowed down immediately,

since the speed limit on campus was ten miles per hour. Beau almost hit her from behind, having apparently missed the speed limit sign. She shook her head.

Laurel was waiting for them in front of her dorm, practically hopping from one foot to the other with glee.

Lilly got out of the car and Laurel ran to hug her. "Thanks, Mom. A million times, thanks. I can't wait to get out of here."

Beau walked up to them and Laurel hugged him, too. "Thanks for coming, Dad. Can we go get my stuff now?"

The three of them trooped up to Laurel's room, where all her belongings were stacked a bit haphazardly on her side of the large, sunny room.

"You're sure about this, Laurel?" Lilly asked.

"More sure than anything."

"All right, then. Let's get everything packed into the cars. We'll try to get most of it into my car. That way it's easier for your father to unload his car right into our house before he goes home."

"Okay." They decided that Laurel would ride back to Juniper Junction in Beau's car so that more stuff could go with Lilly.

After about a dozen trips down to the cars and back up to Laurel's room for more first semester detritus, they were almost done. Lilly and Beau were sweating from exertion despite the chill in the air. They sat on Laurel's stripped, standard-issue bed while they waited for her to finish packing up the little things she had used over the past day or so, then they went down to move the cars while Laurel said goodbye to the friends who lived on her floor.

It was well past noon when Laurel was finally ready to go.

Lilly started her car in the parking lot and Beau, who was parked next to her, beeped his horn and rolled down the passenger-side window. He leaned across Laurel, who was in the passenger seat. "Hey, you made me miss breakfast with your insistence on coming right up here this morning. What do you say we all go out to lunch? My treat." Laurel's face lit up.

"That's fine with me. Where to?" Lilly directed the question to Laurel.

"There's a great bagel shop just off campus. Why don't we go there?" Laurel suggested.

"I'll eat anything. I'm starving," Beau said. He rolled up the window and he led the way with Laurel giving him directions. Lilly followed in her car.

It took about a half hour to find two parking spots. Lilly was ready to scream. Beau was smiling when they all got out of the cars. "That wasn't too bad, was it?"

Lilly didn't answer him. "Lead on, Laurel." Laurel walked ahead of her parents to the bagel shop, which was closer than Lilly had expected. In all the driving around to find a place to park, she hadn't realized what a small distance they had actually covered.

The bagel place was charming and as soon as she sniffed the carbohydrates in the air inside the warm restaurant, Lilly realized how hungry she was, too. Beau stood back so she and Laurel could order first. Laurel and Lilly both ordered thick bagel sandwiches with ham and cheese, then Beau stepped forward and ordered The Rocky Monster, a bagel sandwich with three kinds of meat, three kinds of cheese, and all the fixings.

"Dad, that's kind of gross."

"I'm hungry, Laurel. I wouldn't have had to order that if your mother had let me stop for breakfast."

"You could have eaten breakfast at home, you know," Lilly said.

They made their way to a table for three in the middle of

the restaurant, where people were sitting in very tight quarters. Lilly had to keep her handbag on her lap so it wouldn't trip other people or so no one would walk into it hanging from the back of her chair. When the sandwiches came, Lilly and Beau agreed that Laurel had chosen a great spot for her last lunch in Rocky Gulch.

Laurel and Lilly ate their own lunches, then watched in amazement as Beau somehow consumed his entire sandwich. "It makes me sick just looking at that," Lilly said. Laurel nodded, her nose wrinkled.

"I didn't gain the Freshman Fifteen. Refusing to eat sandwiches like that is the way I did it," Laurel said. Lilly chuckled. Of course, Laurel had only been at school for two months of her freshman year, but Lilly didn't mention that. What she really wanted to mention was how Laurel would be expected to get a job and/or attend community college classes once she was at home, but she figured this wasn't the time or the place for such a discussion.

When Beau finally finished his meal, Lilly stood up first. "I'm going to run to the ladies' room. I'll meet you out front."

Laurel and Beau took up their jackets and made their way to the front door while Lilly found herself in a long hallway waiting for the restroom. A wide staircase ran along one wall and Lilly was surprised to see another little dining room tucked under the stairs and extending toward the back of the building several feet. It held only a few tables and Lilly wondered how the owners had ever been able to carve more dining space out of the tiny restaurant. It was an architectural wonder.

When Lilly came out of the ladies' room she couldn't resist a peek into the tiny dining room under the stairs. It was adorable, with four tiny tables for two crammed into the space. A few wall sconces lent ambience while the wooden floor gave the room a sense of warmth and comfort. She was turning around to leave when she did a double take.

Gerald McIntosh was seated at one of the tables.

And he was holding hands with the man seated across from him.

CHAPTER 46

*L*illy was quite sure Gerald hadn't seen her. He was concentrating all his attention on his companion. His face had the look of a man in love.

But he's married. To a woman. What is going on here?

Lilly ducked out of sight quickly so she wouldn't attract Gerald's attention. She almost walked into a server coming into the room. Speaking with her hand over her mouth to muffle her voice, she apologized for her clumsiness and left the restaurant in a hurry.

Outside Beau was listening as Laurel pointed out some places of interest nearby.

"Sorry it took me so long. There was a line," Lilly said. She walked briskly away from the bagel place. "Ready to go?" she asked over her shoulder.

Lilly drove back to Juniper Junction lost in thought. She would have plenty of time to talk to Laurel later, so she was glad Laurel had decided to ride with Beau.

So Gerald McIntosh is gay. What does that mean and how does that change anything?

She thought back through all the things she knew about Gerald: community-minded, philanthropic, family man.

Family man. *I wonder if his wife knows he's gay. I wonder who else knows.*

I wonder if Ted knows.

She remembered the watch Ted was buying for a "special someone." It was a unisex watch, so it could have been for a man or a woman. She had just assumed it was for a woman. Then she remembered how Gerald had suddenly yanked his funding for Ted's tearoom.

Was it possible Ted and Gerald had been romantically involved? If they had been, it appeared they weren't anymore

Now she *had* to know why Ted and Michelle had gotten divorced. Who might know the answer to that?

Gretchen.

Gretchen might be able to obtain a copy of the transcript of the divorce proceedings, Lilly thought. *I might be able to figure out from the court documents if Ted and Michelle divorced because Ted is gay.*

She was almost back in Juniper Junction, so she decided to wait and call Gretchen once the cars were unpacked and Laurel was settling in at home.

It took a couple hours to unpack the cars, get everything lugged up to Laurel's room, and send Beau on his way. Lilly had just picked up the phone to call Gretchen when Laurel came bounding down the stairs into the kitchen.

"What's for dinner?"

"Oh, honey, I haven't even gotten that far. How about takeout?"

"Why don't I make something? I haven't cooked since I went to school."

"If you want to cook, I'm all for it. See what we have in the fridge. You might be disappointed."

"I'll be able to do something, don't worry."

Lilly smiled and picked up her phone again. She was scrolling through her contacts for Gretchen's number when the phone rang in her hand. Bill.

"Hi. What's up?"

"Nikki just called. She knew you were away picking up Laurel today."

Lilly's pulse started thumping. "What's wrong? Did something happen to Mom?"

"She got so angry about something that she broke a glass. In her hand. Nikki's taking her to get stitches. I guess it's pretty bad."

"Oh, no. Are you going to meet them at the hospital?"

"Noley and I are going."

"I'll meet you there. Bill, I'm worried about her. She hasn't been herself."

"I know. She's been short-tempered and mean. I don't know what set her off, but I'm sure she or Nikki will tell us when we get to the hospital. I'll see you in a few minutes."

"Okay, bye." Lilly hung up and called to Laurel. "Laurel! Gran cut her hand and needs some stitches. I'm going over to the hospital to see her."

"Can I go?"

"Yes, but it'll be boring. We'll probably just sit and wait."

"That's okay. I haven't seen Gran in a long time."

"Okay, let's put dinner on hold. We'll grab something later. I'll let Barney out for a minute or two, then we'll head out."

Barney could barely contain himself now that Laurel was back in the house. He had been jumping around, prancing in circles, and barking almost continuously since she had walked through the door. And he wouldn't leave the kitchen to go out back unless Laurel went with him.

Lilly looked at her watch while she waited for Barney to do

his business. He was so excited that it was several long minutes before he and Laurel came back inside.

"If we're just going to sit and wait when we get there, why are you in such a hurry?" Laurel asked a few minutes later as they were driving across town. "Is she hurt worse than you told me?"

"No, it's not that. It's just that ... well, Gran hasn't really been herself lately. She's been in sort of a bad mood almost all the time. I don't want to lollygag getting there and have to listen to her tear me up and down for not caring about her."

"She wouldn't do that."

Lilly's lips were set in a grim line. "I'm afraid she would. And she has. I wouldn't have mentioned it, except I think you need to be prepared for it. It's like she's a different person."

Laurel was very quiet for the rest of the drive to the hospital. Lilly remembered the crack Bev had made about the Freshman Fifteen and cringed. She hoped her mom wouldn't have anything negative to say in front of Laurel.

When they arrived at the hospital, Bill and Noley had just gotten there. Nikki had a worried look in her eyes and Noley was talking quietly to her. Bev was nowhere to be seen.

"Where's Mom?" Lilly asked.

"Getting an X-ray," Nikki said.

"What for? Wasn't it just a cut?"

"The doctor thinks there might still be glass in her hand, so he ordered an X-ray just in case."

Bill and Noley were thrilled to see Laurel, who wore a broad smile and looked happier than Lilly had seen her at any visit to the college. Bringing her back to Juniper Junction had been the right decision.

Nikki smiled at Laurel. "It's good to see you, Laurel. Your grandmother has missed you."

"Has she really?" Laurel glanced at her mother.

"Of course she has." Nikki had caught the look. "Did your mom tell you she's not been herself lately? It's true, but she still loves you."

Laurel smiled and looked at her feet. Lilly hoped she wasn't getting teary-eyed. She didn't want Laurel to cry on her first night back at home.

But then Laurel looked up and smiled again. "I missed her, too. I can't wait to see her."

A nurse came into the waiting room a few minutes later to talk to Nikki, and Nikki introduced Bill and Lilly to her.

"Your mom does have a few small shards of glass embedded in her hand, so we're going to need to get those out. I'm afraid you're going to be here a little longer than we originally thought."

"That's no problem," Lilly said. "Can we see her?"

"She's resting, but I think a couple people can go in at a time. She's much calmer than she was when she came in."

Lilly gave Nikki a questioning look that was echoed by Bill.

"It was pretty bad," Nikki said. "She was in pain and I think she wasn't even aware that she was yelling at everyone."

Lilly could feel herself blush. That wasn't like Bev. She had never been the type of person who would go screaming into an emergency room, no matter how much pain she was in. She was always stoic, never obnoxious. This different Bev was concerning to Lilly.

CHAPTER 47

"*D*o you want to go in first?" Lilly asked Bill.

"Why don't you and I go in together? Noley and Laurel and Nikki can wait here while we go see her. Then they can go in." He turned to the other three. "Is that all right with all of you?"

They all nodded and Bill and Lilly followed the nurse to Bev's bed. Lilly stood on one side and Bill on the other; the nurse left so they had some privacy. Bev's eyes were closed, but she was wincing, so they knew she wasn't asleep.

"Hi, Mom," Lilly said. She didn't want to startle Bev, so she didn't touch her. Bev's eyes opened slowly and glanced from Lilly to Bill and back again.

"Lilly and Billy. What are you two doing here?" Bev sounded groggy.

"Nikki called to tell us you hurt your hand. We wanted to make sure you're okay," Bill said.

"That was nice of you. You didn't have to come, though. I know how busy you are, Billy."

Lilly glared at Bill. It wasn't his fault that Bev always

mentioned the importance of his career, but she couldn't help it. It wasn't like she was a layabout who asked for handouts, but that was how she always felt when Bev harped on Bill's job.

She took a deep breath and tried to let it go. "Mom, how does your hand feel?"

Bev looked at her hand as if it weren't part of her body. "It hurts, I suppose. But as long as I don't move it, it's all right."

"The nurse said the doctor is going to get the shards of glass out of there and I think you should be able to go home after that," Bill said.

"That's good." Bev was still staring at her hand.

Lilly thought she almost preferred the miserable Bev to the automaton lying in front of her.

"Mom, is there anything we can do to make you more comfortable?" she asked.

"I don't think so, Lilly. Thank you for asking, though."

"How about another visitor?" Bill asked. "There's someone in the waiting room who would love to see you."

"Who? Nikki? I've seen her."

"Not Nikki, though she's out there. Someone else."

"Who?" Bev gave him a suspicious look.

"We'll go out and send her in. You'll see." Bill smiled.

Bev narrowed her eyes. "Is it someone I don't like? Is it that Edna LaForge?"

She was referring, of course, to Lilly's next-door neighbor. The two older women were not friends. Lilly was surprised Bev had remembered Edna's name.

"No, Mom." Bill chuckled. "It's someone you like. Just a minute." He ducked through the curtain surrounding the bed and Lilly could hear him walking toward the waiting room.

"Who on earth is here? I don't want to see anyone," Bev

grumped. Now she sounded more like her recent self. Lilly was relieved.

"Don't worry, Mom. This is a nice surprise."

A couple minutes later Bill returned. He held the curtain so Laurel could peek in. Bev's eyes lit up.

"Laurel!" Bev looked at Lilly as if for confirmation. Lilly smiled. "You came here to see me?" Bev's face crumpled and she started to cry.

One look at her gran crying and Laurel started to cry, too. *So much for Laurel not crying on her first night back in Juniper Junction,* Lilly thought.

Laurel moved toward the bed and wrapped her arms around Bev as best she could. Noley had followed her into the room and she placed her hand on Bev's good arm but didn't say anything. She was blinking back tears, too, as were Lilly and Bill.

Finally Laurel stepped back. "Did you know I was coming home, Gran?"

Bev nodded. "I think someone told me. But I didn't know you were here already. When did you get back?"

"Just a few hours ago," Laurel said. "It's good to be home."

"I'm so glad you're here." Bev gripped Laurel's hand with her good hand and they stayed like that until it was time to clear out and let the doctor get to work.

"Mom, we'll be in the waiting room." Lilly leaned down to kiss her mom's forehead. Bev was still smiling.

"Thank you for bringing Laurel to see me," she said. "That was just what I needed."

Lilly returned to the waiting room, where Nikki was pacing.

"So, Nikki, what made Mom mad enough to crush a glass in her hand?" Bill asked.

Nikki stopped pacing. "She missed a minute or two of her favorite game show because she was in the bathroom."

"That's it?" Lilly couldn't help staring at Nikki with her mouth hanging open.

Nikki nodded. "I'm afraid so."

"So Gran actually crushed a glass in her hand? Like a drinking glass?"

"Yeah. She's changed a bit since you last saw her, Laurel," Nikki said.

"A bit?" Lilly almost snorted. "She's a completely different person."

Nikki nodded again. "She is. That's part of the disease, Laurel. It's not unusual for people with this type of dementia to suffer from a shift in personality. People who used to be carefree and happy become angry and withdrawn. That's what has happened with your grandmother. She can't help it. She doesn't like the person she's become, but she can't help it."

"It's really sad," Laurel said.

"It is. But we just keep loving her." Lilly put her arm around Laurel's shoulder. "When we remember how much we love her, it's easier to deal with her new personality."

Laurel nodded, but didn't say anything.

Bill took Noley's hand and cleared his throat. "We've been talking about wedding dates. We were thinking an August wedding would be nice, but we've agreed that because of the changes taking place with Mom, it'll be better to move up the timeline." Noley nodded and squeezed his hand.

"So what have you decided?" Lilly asked. She realized with a pang that she'd barely spoken to Noley about the nuptials. She had so much on her mind that the wedding had fallen to the bottom of the list.

"Spring." Noley looked up at Bill and he nodded. "Late April, early May."

"Wow. That doesn't give you much time to plan. But I think it's a good idea to have the wedding sooner rather than later. We don't know what Mom's going to be like by spring."

"That's what we thought." Bill gave Noley a look that made Lilly feel like crying. It was so warm and full of love that Lilly wanted nothing more than to see Hassan right that minute. But she stood up straighter and squared her shoulders.

"Laurel, it's a good thing you came home when you did. Noley and Bill are going to need all the help they can get to pull offa wedding in just a few months." Laurel grinned for the first time since laying eyes on Bev.

"You mean I can help?"

"Of course you're helping," Noley said. "How else are we going to do this?"

Laurel immediately began ticking off ideas while Noley listened. Lilly was content just knowing Laurel had something to keep her mind off Bev, at least temporarily.

It seemed like hours before the doctor came into the waiting room. "Your mom's all set," he said to Lilly and Bill. "I don't think we need to keep her overnight, so someone can take her home. But you have to make sure the dressing is changed twice a day."

Lilly introduced Nikki to the doctor. "Nikki stays with Mom during the day, and there's another nurse who comes at night." Nikki assured the doctor she would change the dressing regularly.

"Your mom is quite a character," said the doctor with a smile.

"Yeah, we know."

Lilly, Bill, Noley, and Laurel said their goodbyes to Bev at the hospital and Nikki drove Bev home. She was going to talk to Meredith to update her, and Lilly had promised to stop by the next day.

"Where to for dinner?" she asked Laurel as they drove out of the hospital parking lot.

"I can make us something," Laurel offered.

"Are you sure you want to do that?"

"Yup."

"Okay, sounds good."

When they got home Laurel rummaged through the refrigerator and found leftover roasted vegetables, some deli ham, and part of a log of goat cheese. Lilly watched in amazement as Laurel whisked several eggs, chopped the vegetables, threw in the meat, and combined everything in a frittata on top of the stove. She sprinkled the cheese on top and slipped the entire skillet into the oven. A short time later Laurel pulled out a golden masterpiece that tasted as good as it looked.

"Laurel, where did you learn to do this? It's delicious!"

Laurel shrugged. "Watching Noley, I guess."

"This takes a lot of skill. I'm really impressed."

"I've made meals before, Mom."

"I know. I guess I had forgotten. You can make dinner every night from now on."

Laurel smiled. "Cool."

CHAPTER 48

After dinner Lilly helped clear a path to Laurel's bed through all the boxes, bins, and bags on the floor of her bedroom. They were both exhausted and Lilly had decided that everything else, including calling Gretchen, would have to wait until the next day.

But at work the next morning, the first thing Lilly did was phone the lawyer.

"Can you do me a favor?" she asked.

"What is it?"

"I need you to look up the documents from a divorce proceeding for me."

"Your divorce?"

"No. The divorce of Ted and Michelle Conover."

"The same Michelle Conover whose death has caused endless problems for Hassan?"

"The same one."

"I might be able to do that. Can I ask why?"

"I want to know if the divorce was because Ted was seeing someone else."

"I doubt that information would be in the documents, Lilly."

"Can you just try? Please? I'll pay you, obviously."

Gretchen sighed. "All right. I'll do it, but only because it might help Hassan if there's evidence in the documents that could send the police looking for another suspect and create reasonable doubt for a jury."

Lilly's ribcage tightened. She didn't even want to think of Hassan's case getting as far as needing a jury. "Thanks. Just send me the bill."

"No need to pay me. I'll be at the courthouse later today and I can just look into it while I'm there."

"Thanks, Gretchen. Call my cell as soon as you find anything."

Lilly hung up and opened her laptop. She typed Ted's name into the search bar and waited to see what would come up.

Most of the articles were about Tranquilitea: it's opening, the story behind Ted's decision to open it, things like that. Human interest stories. But on the second page of search results, Lilly found something interesting.

It was a mention in a police blotter from Lupine.

Lilly clicked on the article, which was really just a short sentence. It noted that one Ted Conover had been detained briefly in Lupine for disturbing the peace.

Hmm. I wonder what he did to disturb the peace. Lilly knew just the person to ask. Her fingers flew over the keys on her phone as she dialed Bill's number.

"Hi. What's going on?" he asked.

"I need you to do something for me."

"What?" His voice took on a wary tone.

"I need you to find out why Ted Conover was detained in Lupine for disturbing the peace."

"I already know why. It's because he was disturbing the peace."

"You know what I mean. I want to know exactly what he did."

"Okay, but first tell me why you're asking."

"Because I have a theory and I want to see if it's right."

"What's your theory?"

"My theory is that Gerald McIntosh and Ted Conover were having an affair."

"What?"

"You heard me. Gerald McIntosh is gay and something happened between him and Ted. He suddenly pulled his money out of Ted's business. And Ted was in my store recently buying a unisex watch for a 'special someone.' I think it may have been Gerald."

"Okay. And then what? You think that Gerald or Ted killed Michelle?"

"I think Gerald killed her. I think he and Ted may have been seeing each other during Ted's marriage and that Michelle found out. Gerald, who is married, is well known in Lupine as a family man and maybe he thought Michelle would let it slip that he's gay and an adulterer. That might make things difficult for him. Or maybe Michelle even threatened to outright spill the beans. That sounds like something she would have done."

Bill was silent for a moment. "You know, you might have something there."

"Told you."

"Okay. The reason Ted's name is in the police blotter is because a neighbor of Gerald McIntosh called the police on him."

"Why?"

"Because he was in Gerald's front yard, shouting obsceni-
ties at Mrs. McIntosh."

"Why was he doing that?"

"He wouldn't say, the wife wouldn't say, and the neighbor
couldn't make out the words, only the really bad words and
Ted's tone of voice. Gerald apparently wasn't home."

"How do you know all this?"

"Remember the day I stopped in the store and told you I
had been at the tearoom to talk to Ted about something that
took place outside Juniper Junction?"

"Yes."

"The Lupine PD called and asked that someone go talk to
Ted about the incident. I volunteered."

"I'm glad you did. Hmm. I wonder if Ted went to Gerald's
house to harass the wife because he was having an affair with
Gerald. Like a stalkery kind of thing."

"It's possible, but we don't want to get ahead of ourselves.
It's also possible they're just good friends, Lilly. Maybe Ted was
there to stick up for his buddy because the wife was
haranguing Gerald. Don't get carried away. Since Ted stopped
yelling and left the neighborhood after talking to police, no
one ever knew what exactly he was yelling about."

"Okay. Thanks for checking. Any more news about Ted? Or
about Ivy's murder?"

"Nothing that I know of."

"Okay, thanks again. Talk to you later."

This new information gave Lilly more food for thought.
There was definitely some kind of relationship between Ted
and Gerald. The more she contemplated it, the more she was
convinced that the relationship was romantic, or had been, and
that Michelle had threatened to expose Gerald, the man
known all over Lupine as a family man. Man of the Year, for
heaven's sake. When Michelle threatened to tell everyone that

he wasn't the family man everyone thought he was, Gerald killed her.

It made perfect sense. But where did Ivy's death fit into the puzzle?

It was late afternoon when Gretchen called.

"I've been in court all day, so I didn't get a chance to call before now," she said.

"That's fine. Did you find anything?"

"Yes. The main reason given for the divorce was adultery by Ted."

"I knew it. Any details?"

"No details about the adultery, if that's what you mean. The only details were financial. Michelle made a lot more than Ted."

"That's interesting. I wonder who got Michelle's money when she died. If there was any."

"I can check the probate records another day."

"That's okay. It doesn't really matter, since we know that Ted needed at least two investors for his tearoom. Whether Michelle left him money or not, there obviously wasn't enough to keep his business afloat. Maybe she was a silent investor before they divorced. Or even after."

"Next time I'm in probate court, I'll check for you."

"Thanks, Gretchen. You've been a big help."

So Ted had committed adultery during the marriage. That sealed it. He must have been having an affair with another married man and Michelle was angry and hurt and lashed out at Gerald by threatening to expose him.

So Gerald killed her.

CHAPTER 49

*A*fter work she raced over to the jail to see Hassan before she went to her mother's house. She had so much to tell him.

As soon as they were seated across from each other and the guard had taken up his post on the other side of the metal door, Lilly launched into the story of everything that had happened since picking up Laurel the prior day. Had it only been one day ago?

Hassan's eyes widened when she got to the part about seeing Gerald holding hands with another man at the bagel bistro, but he said nothing, waiting instead until Lilly finished her story.

"You've been busy," he finally said.

She grimaced. "But not in a good way. Between you being in here and my mother being sick and having to pick up Laurel from school and trying to figure out who killed Michelle and Ivy, I've barely had time to think about anything else. But I feel like we're getting closer to springing you from this hole and Laurel seems happier than I've seen her since the day before she left for school in August, so those are both good things. I'm afraid there's not much I can do about my mom, but we just keep hoping she has more good days than bad."

"I feel terrible about your mom. I wish I could visit her."

"And I would bring her here to see you, but she really doesn't like to leave the house. As it is, she's been to the hospital twice in the past week. Not only that, but I haven't told her you're in here. I haven't wanted to upset her." What she didn't tell Hassan was that Bev couldn't remember who he was the last time she had mentioned him, so she had decided to avoid mentioning him to her again, at least until he was released.

"That's probably for the best. I miss my own parents, too."

"Well, I'm sure they'll visit the minute you get out. They must be dying to see you. I'd love to see them, too." Lilly was very fond of Hassan's parents and the feeling was mutual.

"They want to spend Thanksgiving here, so hopefully I'll be out by then."

"I know you will. I told you, I'm going to figure out who killed Michelle and Ivy and you'll be out of here in no time."

"Well, I'd like to get out of here in no time, but not at the expense of you being in any kind of danger. So don't do anything heroic, okay? Promise me?"

"I promise."

A few minutes later the burly jailer barked that time was up and Lilly stood up to leave.

"All right, okay," Lilly muttered. The guard shot her a dirty look.

She couldn't wait to get him in trouble.

The next day brought a number of customers into the shop, and in particular one who seemed to be in a very bad mood. Lilly had just returned from lunch to find Harry busy with a customer. Or rather, he was listening to a customer rant loudly about the prices in the shop. Lilly swiftly assessed the situation and rescued Harry.

"Madam, I am the owner of the shop. Can I be of assistance?" She could see out of the corner of her eye that Harry had relaxed his shoulders with relief.

"How do you expect visitors and tourists to afford the pieces in this place?" the woman asked, waving her arms to take in the whole shop.

"Madam, I would be happy to show you some of our lower-priced pieces, and if those don't suit you I'm certainly able to provide you with the names of other shops nearby that sell jewelry at lower prices." *And lower quality.*

"I've already seen what those other stores have to offer." The woman waved her hand dismissively. "You have much nicer things in here."

Lilly inclined her head to acknowledge the compliment. "The prices in this shop reflect the quality of the craftsmanship and the quality of the gems, the stones, and the metals we sell. I'm afraid that with high quality comes higher prices."

"This is ridiculous. I'd love to see the house you live in and the car you drive." The woman pointed her finger at Lilly.

Lilly was not about to stoop to the stranger's level by talking about her personal income. "Ma'am, I suggest that you leave now and find another place to buy souvenirs."

Just then her cell phone rang. Normally she wouldn't look at it while she was interacting with a customer, but she didn't care about this particular woman in the least, so she glanced at her phone. It was Nikki.

"Excuse me, ma'am, I do need to take this call." She hovered her finger over the *talk* button while she waited for the woman to leave.

The woman finally walked off in a huff. If she could have

slammed the door behind her, Lilly was sure she would have. She rolled her eyes at Harry and he grinned.

"I'm glad that's over," he muttered.

Lilly answered Nikki's call. "Hi, Nikki. Anything wrong?"

"Your mother is asking for you," Nikki said. She added in a whisper, "She's crying, but don't worry. I think she's okay. She's just having a bad day."

Lilly felt a pang of sadness. "Can you put her on?"

"Sure. Hold on a sec." Lilly could hear Nikki murmuring soothing words to Bev, then Bev came on the line.

"Hello, Lilly?" Bev sniffled loudly.

"Hi, Mom. How are you doing?"

"I'm so upset, Lilly, and I don't know why. I just can't stop crying."

"Can you think of anything you'd like to do that would make you happy? How about going out for ice cream? Or visiting Mildred?"

"No. I don't want to go anywhere or see anyone. I just want to sit in my living room."

"And you don't know what's made you upset?"

There was silence from Bev, then another loud sniffle. Then a quiet voice. "I can't remember what your father looks like."

Lilly inhaled sharply as her stomach twisted. *She and Dad were married for decades. And she can't remember what he looks like? How long until she doesn't know what I look like or what Bill looks like?*

"Mom, there are lots of pictures of Dad in the house. There are even a few right in the living room. Can you set one next to you?"

"Yes, but I can't remember what he looks like when I close my eyes." Bev was openly weeping now.

Lilly spoke gently, trying to keep the tears and sadness

from her own voice. "Mom, do you remember how much he loved you?"

"Of course."

"Then that's the important thing. It's not what he looked like, but how he made you feel. And if you can remember that, you have everything you need."

She could hear Bev swallowing a sound in her throat. "He used to say he loved me as much as spring loves sunshine."

That sounded like something her dad would have said. How lucky that Bev could remember it.

"See? Those are the important things to remember. But I'll still ask Nikki to set up one of his photos on the table right next to your favorite chair."

"Thank you, Lilly."

"Are you feeling any better now?"

"Yes. I feel better." Lilly knew her mom was telling the truth, because she could hear the smile in Bev's voice.

When Bev had passed the phone back to Nikki, Lilly asked her to place a photo of Bev and Daniel on the table where Bev could reach it easily. "I'll look for other photos of Dad and bring them over. Thanks, Nikki."

When Lilly hung up she took a deep breath, feeling a crushing weight on her shoulders. She must have had a forlorn look on her face, too, because Harry looked at her with concern.

"Is everything okay, boss?"

Lilly sighed. "Dementia sucks, Harry."

He tilted his head and blinked. "I'm really sorry, Lilly."

"Me, too."

CHAPTER 50

*L*illy looked around the store, lost in thought. Finally she spoke to Harry. "Have you had lunch?"

"No. Why?"

"I was thinking of going for a walk. I need to clear my head. First an uppity—and cheap—potential customer, then a phone call that ruins my day. I'm going to close the shop for a little while. I don't want to leave you in charge because it's not fair of me to keep doing that to you, so I'll take my walk while you're having lunch and then we'll reconvene in an hour or so and get through the afternoon. Does that sound okay?"

"Sure. I just wish I could help somehow."

"Thanks, Harry. But there's nothing that can be done. We'll get through it."

"Okay." He reached for his jacket. "Can I bring anything back for you?"

"No, thanks. I don't feel like eating."

Harry left and Lilly grabbed a piece of paper from the counter. She wrote "Be back in an hour" and noted the time, then taped it to the door and locked it behind her.

It was a chilly day, so she set out at a brisk clip. She walked along Main Street as far as the town square, then turned and took one of the side streets and kept walking. After several blocks, Lilly looked at her watch and decided to head back to the shop. A half hour had passed and it would take her about that same amount of time to return to Juniper Junction Jewels. She turned down another block that would take her back to Main Street.

As she walked, she could feel her headache melting away and the fears about her mom fading into a melancholy acceptance. She and Bill would simply have to deal with Bev's declining health and try to do it with brave faces.

The wind had picked up and she could smell the barest hint of snow in the air. A little frisson of excitement raced through her. As much as she loved fall, she also loved the changeover to winter and the days of hushed snowfall, warm beverages, heavy sweaters, and crackling fireplaces.

She was almost to the corner, smiling to herself, thinking about snow and wintertime and all things cozy when a car passed her at a pace that was far too fast for the residential neighborhood. It never even slowed for the stop sign. She frowned at the driver, though he or she couldn't possibly have seen her.

When she got to the corner to turn toward Main Street, she noticed the car careening into the alley behind the shops that were across the street from Juniper Junction Jewels. Assuming it was a shop employee, since generally only shop owners and employees parked in the alleys, she followed the car, intending to ask the driver to slow down next time.

She was surprised when she reached the end of the alley and saw Ted emerge from the offending car. He knew better than that. Lilly frowned again and quickened her pace toward Ted.

As she walked closer, though, she could see that Ted was crying. It wasn't often one saw an adult crying in public, and her frustration turned to concern when she saw him.

"Ted!" she called. She didn't stop to think that she didn't care for the way he had treated Hassan or whether he would want anyone to see him in this vulnerable state—she simply saw someone in pain and knew she needed to offer her help.

He whirled around and gave a half wave, obviously embarrassed that someone had seen him in such a state.

"Ted, is everything okay?" Lilly was jogging now to catch up to him.

"Hi, Lilly. Yes, I'm okay. I'm sorry you had to see me like this."

She waved her hand at him. "Please. It's already forgotten. Is there anything I can do to help?"

He seemed to think about it for a moment. "Actually, could you carry this bag for me?" He reached into the passenger side of the car and withdrew a large paper shopping bag. He handed it to her and then picked up what looked like a very heavy box from the same seat. "Let me just unlock the back door of the shop," he said, his keys dangling from one finger under the box.

He was not having an easy time juggling the box while trying to unlock the tearoom door, so Lilly offered her free hand to hold the bottom of the box.

"Thank you, Lilly." He finally pushed the door open and walked into the darkened back room of the store. Lilly followed him closely, carrying the bag.

He turned around and took it from her, then she turned to leave. She didn't want to force herself upon him, asking nosy questions when he was still probably upset.

"Wait, Lilly. There's something I'd like to talk to you about."

"Sure, Ted. What is it?"

He flipped on the light and motioned for her to sit in the chair opposite his at his desk. She sat down on the edge of the seat, glancing at her watch. She only had a few minutes to get back to the jewelry shop, so she hoped this would be quick. Maybe she shouldn't have been so hasty to scold him about his driving.

"I know why you're here. It's because I was driving unforgivably fast down that street."

"Well, you *were* going pretty fast. I was just worried in case there were children around who might dart into the street."

"I'm sorry about that. I wasn't thinking. It won't happen again."

"And you won't run a stop sign again?" Lilly asked with a smile.

"No. Definitely not. That was foolish of me."

"Not to worry, Ted. We all make mistakes." Lilly stood up to leave.

"Sit down, Lilly."

She almost rolled her eyes, but remembered that he was upset about something and she didn't want to appear too rushed to talk to him.

"What are you doing out during business hours?" he asked.

"I needed to clear my head, take a walk. I closed the shop for an hour. That was about an hour ago." She hoped he would take the hint and make this quick.

"Oh. Well, listen. I've been meaning to talk to you."

"About what?"

He walked around the side of the desk and came to stand next to her. Looking up at him, she realized suddenly how big and tall he was. She started to stand up, too, but he put his hand on her shoulder and held her in place.

"About Gerald."

Immediately Lilly was on her guard. How did Ted know that she knew about Gerald?

"Of course he recognized you in Rocky Gulch. And he knows you saw him there with his new boyfriend." Ted sneered and that last word came out with an ugly sound. "He called and told me about it."

"Oh, was he there? I didn't notice him. I was there to pick up my daughter." Something in the tone of Ted's voice warned her not to let on that she had seen Gerald.

Ted gave her a mock-surprised look. "Oh, no?"

Lilly shook her head.

"That's BS. What is your fascination with Gerald, huh? He told me you visited him at his place of business, too, but you looked different. He didn't let on that he knew you. So spill it. What is it with Gerald?"

"I don't know what you're talking about, Ted. But I need to get back to the shop."

She was mildly surprised when he stood back so she could stand up. She walked to the back door of the tearoom, her legs quaking slightly from the danger she had sensed, and reached for the doorknob.

Just then a knifelike pain cut through her shoulder as Ted grabbed her arm and twisted it hard behind her back.

CHAPTER 51

"*L*et go of me, Ted! What are you thinking?"

"I'm thinking I shouldn't let you go until you tell me what's going on with Gerald!" His face was just a couple inches from hers, spittle flying from the corners of his mouth onto her cheeks. She winced in disgust. He shook her hard enough to rattle her teeth.

"Stop it!" She glared at him in defiance. What was this man's problem?

"Tell me everything you know about Gerald!"

"Ted, I barely know him at all. I know he works at the same financial firm where Michelle worked in Lupine, and I know that he's a community-minded family man. And, since you told me just a minute ago, I assume he's gay."

"Why were you at his office?" Ted asked, this time a little more calmly.

"It's none of your business." She was stalling for time as her mind raced, trying to think of a good, plausible lie to tell him. Obviously this man was deranged and it wouldn't do to admit she was really scoping out Gerald's place of work.

"It just became my business. Tell me, Lilly."

"I was inquiring about finding a broker for my investments," she lied.

"Again, BS." He twisted her arm tighter behind her back.

"Ted, I'm telling you the truth. What's wrong with you?"

Lilly was shocked when Ted let go of her arm and broke down in wracking sobs. He covered his face with his hands and sank to his knees. She took the opportunity while he wasn't looking to dash off a text to Bill:

911. Tearoom. Hurry.

Luckily Ted didn't seem to hear the soft sound of the text as it sent. Lilly closed her eyes for a second and prayed that Bill would arrive soon.

Every ounce of sense she had screamed at her to leave the tearoom, but her heart wasn't listening. This was clearly a man in a great deal of pain, and she wanted to do what she could to help. She tried to forget the throbbing in her shoulder while she bent down to get closer to Ted's weeping form.

"Ted, is there something I can do to help? Someone I can call?"

Without warning, Ted banged both fists on the concrete floor. It had to have hurt. He looked up at her with red-rimmed, blazing eyes. "And who are you going to call? My dear, departed ex-wife? My old hag of an aunt? My ex, Lupine's Man of the Year?" He let out a harsh, barking laugh. "I don't have anyone left to call, Lilly! No one!"

Alarm bells finally started to go off in Lilly's head. Something was beginning to click in her mind and she quietly took a step toward the door. Ted continued to cry, loudly, so she was able to take another step, then another...

"That old bat wouldn't talk to me anyway, even if she was

alive," he said, looking up at Lilly again. She knew he was referring to Ivy. She glanced toward the door, willing Bill to bust in.

But he didn't, and she knew she was going to have to handle this situation until he got there.

Ted had noticed her darting look. "You know, don't you, Lilly? You know I killed Ivy."

And her mind made the last *click*.

"Ivy withdrew her investment in the tearoom, didn't she?" Lilly asked.

Ted scoffed.

"She took it back when she realized you were having an affair with a man."

Ted glared at her. "What makes you think that?"

Lilly almost shrugged, but managed to keep still. "I don't know. I guess I just...." Her voice trailed off.

"She took the money back when she realized I bought that watch for Gerald to try and get him back, which I never should have done. She reasoned that if I had enough money to buy Gerald an expensive watch, I had enough money to keep my tearoom afloat. And it's all your fault because *you* told her about the watch! *And* Gerald kept the watch!" Ted was in a fury now.

"That woman practically raised me after my father died when I was a teenager! How could she do that?"

"I thought your father died on September eleventh."

"He did. September eleventh, 1985."

"So not *the* September eleventh?"

"No. And what business is it of yours, anyway? You are so damn nosy!" *So Ivy had just said September eleventh to raise Hassan's hackles. What a witch.* He had been speaking almost calmly, but his fury returned. He stood up unsteadily and swung his arm toward Lilly in an attempt to—to what? Lilly wondered. To grab her? To knock her down?

She ducked away from his grasp and reached for the door handle just as it flung open with a splintering noise and a burst of movement. Bill stepped into the back room, having kicked the door in. Another officer quickly entered behind him. Lilly stumbled into Bill's arms.

"Thank God you're here." She turned and pointed at Ted. "He killed Ivy Leachman. He told me he did it."

Ted hung his head, not even attempting to disavow Lilly's words. He let out a loud sigh and moved toward his desk. "Let me just...," he began.

Lilly instinctively moved away from Bill, who had immediately stiffened. The other officer put his hand on the holster around his waist. She just had time to take in those details when Ted reached for a pair of open scissors on his desk and threw them at Lilly with a shocking amount of force.

"Get back!" Bill yelled. Lilly tried to duck as the scissors went flying past her head. She could feel a warm wetness on her temple.

What happened next was a little fuzzy. Without having to draw their weapons, Bill and the other officer wrestled Ted to the ground. When they stood up, Bill's partner clapped handcuffs on Ted's wrists and Bill strode over to where Lilly lay on the ground, stunned.

"It looks like the scissors grazed your head. Let me call an ambulance and we'll get you fixed right up. No, don't try to get up. Just stay where you are."

His partner led Ted out the back door of the tearoom while Bill radioed for an ambulance. He told the dispatcher to make sure the ambulance came to the alley behind the tearoom.

Bill knelt next to Lilly while they waited for the ambulance to arrive. It wasn't long before Harry appeared in the doorway behind the tearoom.

"Lilly! What happened? Are you all right?" He rushed forward and Bill held up his hand.

"Don't come any closer, Harry. We've got a crime scene here and we don't want you to mess it up."

"Oh, okay, sure." Harry took several steps backward until he was standing just outside the back door in the alley.

"I'm okay, Harry. But I may need you to watch the store for the rest of the day."

CHAPTER 52

$\mathcal{L}$illy refused to go to the hospital after the paramedics had bandaged her head. They asked her to visit her own doctor, at the very least, to be checked out more thoroughly, and she promised them she would.

She wouldn't have time for that for a while, though.

Bill made her go home and asked Noley to stay with her for the rest of the day and overnight to make sure she was okay. Lilly wished she could stop over at her mother's house, but Noley put her foot down. Laurel called Bev and made apologies for Lilly, saying she had a bad headache. Noley and Laurel slept in Lilly's room that night, one on an air mattress and the other on a chaise lounge in the corner.

"I thought a sleepover would be fun, but this isn't what I had in mind," Lilly said before falling asleep. "I wanted to have a wedding-planning sleepover with just us girls."

"We'll have that kind of sleepover, I promise." Noley made sure Lilly's pillow was propped under her shoulder as Laurel kissed her mom's cheek.

The next morning Lilly was sore and bruised—in fact, her

arm and shoulder hurt as much as the side of her head—but she insisted on driving to the jail so she could be there the minute the doors opened to visitors. She had some good news to share with Hassan.

"Ted confessed to killing Ivy! Can you believe it?"

"What happened to you?"

"Oh, don't worry. I just got into a scrape with Ted and my head was grazed a bit. Nothing to fret about."

"What? Grazed with what?"

"Scissors. But listen, that's not what's important here. What's important is that you're no longer a suspect in Ivy's murder! You're one huge step closer to going home!" She was beaming.

Hassan's stern countenance broke into a smile. "You're amazing, you know that? What would I do without you? Are you sure you're okay? I want to hear the whole story."

"You would perish without me and I'm sure I'm okay. So here's what happened."

She proceeded to tell him everything about her encounter with Ted. He shook his head, his eyes wide. "I can't believe this. I will never be able to thank you enough, love."

"You'll find a way, I'm sure," she said with a wink.

"Do you think he killed Michelle, too?" Hassan asked.

"I've been thinking about that. I have no idea. We'll have to see if he confesses. He rolled over pretty easily when he talked to me about Ivy."

She glanced up and saw the guard approaching. She lowered her voice. "Looks like my time is up. I'll be back tomorrow. I'm so excited!" She let out a soft squeal and Hassan squeezed her hand.

"Lilly, would you mind doing one more thing for me?"

"Of course not. What is it?"

"There should be two checks in the mail at my house.

Would you mind picking them up and depositing them in the bank? My account information is in my desk. I wouldn't ask you to do this, but this is a guy who is notoriously short on funds and if I can't cash the checks I won't be able to pay other vendors."

"Got it. I'll pick up the checks tonight after dinner and deposit them tomorrow morning."

"Thanks. And Lilly, take someone with you. I don't want you going over there by yourself."

"I will."

She stopped at Bev's house, where Bev was grumpy and Nikki had had a very long day.

"Nikki keeps touching my hand," Bev tattled.

Nikki smiled grimly. "To change her dressing. Once. That's the only time I've touched her hand."

"Mom, she has to change the dressing so the wound can heal."

"I can do it myself."

Lilly smiled at Nikki over Bev's head. "Mom, please let her change the dressing. It only lasts a minute and it's her job. She has to do it."

"Well, all right." Bev's tone was grudging and gruff.

Thanks, Nikki mouthed to Lilly.

"Mom, I've got to run. I'm starving and I want to see what Laurel has been up to today. I'll be back tomorrow." Lilly kissed Bev's cheek and left.

When she got home, she was surprised to find that Laurel had made dinner. And not just any dinner, but a fabulous meal of grilled flatbread pizzas with roasted butternut squash, portobello mushrooms, and Gorgonzola.

"Laurel, this is delicious. What made you think of combining these things and putting them on a pizza?"

"Just an inspiration, I guess."

"Well, it's superb."

"Thanks. Mom, I've been thinking about what I'm going to do now that I'm not at school anymore. I'd like to take cooking classes at the community college. Isn't that what Noley did? I think I would love a job like hers."

Lilly sat back and looked thoughtfully at Laurel. "You know, that's a great idea. You should definitely look into that. You should talk to Noley about it, too. She didn't go to the college here in Juniper Junction, but she did go to culinary school."

"Maybe you can talk to her?"

"No way. This is your idea, it's up to you to talk to her. Trust me, being able to talk to people is a life skill."

"Ugh. All right. Maybe tomorrow."

"Definitely tomorrow. The longer you put things off, the harder they are to do."

"Nick called me today. He heard that I was back in town."

Lilly's head jerked toward Laurel, but Laurel was looking into a cupboard, not at her mom. "What did he want?" Nick had dumped Laurel without preamble during her senior year of high school. He was the last person Lilly wanted Laurel to be hanging around with.

"Just to talk," Laurel replied lightly. She shrugged. "He thought maybe we could get together tonight for a little while."

"And what did you tell him?" Lilly had to be careful here. She didn't want to suggest that seeing Nick was a bad idea, because she feared Laurel's response would be to see him as soon as possible. On the other hand, she didn't want to suggest that seeing Nick was a good idea, either.

"I told him we could meet over on the square for a little while, but that I've got stuff to do. I won't stay long. And don't worry, Mom, we're not getting back together."

Lilly wanted to heave a sigh of relief, but she knew better. She would wait until after the rendezvous to gauge Laurel's feelings.

"Tonight?"

"Yeah."

"Okay. I have to run over to Hassan's for a few minutes to pick up the mail. I assume you won't be out late?"

"I won't be too long. I want to finish setting up my room."

"Okay."

Laurel left a few minutes later. Lilly was glad to see that she hadn't put on makeup or fixed her hair or changed out of the comfy clothes she had been wearing.

She picked up the phone and dialed Noley's number, but there was no answer. She called Bill next. Also no answer.

"All right, Barney. It looks like you're the lucky one who gets to go to Hassan's house with me tonight."

CHAPTER 53

*W*hen they arrived at Hassan's house, she held tight to Barney's leash—she didn't want him getting away in the dark. Her hands began to sweat a little bit as she approached the front door. She had determined to check out every room, just to make sure things were okay, but she wasn't looking forward to it. She slipped her key into the lock and it turned quietly.

She swung the front door open and glanced down at the floor, where the mail was sitting in a messy pile, having come through the mail slot in the door.

She stepped over the pile and peered cautiously into the living room. All clear. Dining room, clear. Kitchen, clear. Hassan's office, clear. Lilly heaved a sigh of relief. It was time to check upstairs.

"Come on, Barney," she said. She was whispering, and she chuckled at herself. There was no reason to be nervous.

She walked quietly and a bit reluctantly up the stairs, and she was glad that Barney was equally quiet behind her on the leash. He seemed to have absorbed some of her anxiety.

She took a deep breath and looked inside Hassan's room. It was in good shape, as were all the other rooms upstairs.

"Just one more place to check, Barn," she said. The last place she wanted to go was Hassan's backyard, but she knew she wouldn't relax when she got home if she didn't check it to make sure no one had been back there.

She had reached the bottom of the stairs and was walking to the kitchen and the back door when the doorbell rang. She froze and Barney set up a cacophony of barking and whining.

"Okay, Barn. Relax. We'll just see who it is." Barney either couldn't hear her or chose to ignore her and raced to the front door, dragging his leash behind him on the floor.

Lilly walked up to the door and pressed her ear against it. "Who's there?" She was trying to sound assertive and strong, but her words came out sounding harsh and mean.

"It's Oliver, from across the street." The sound from the pounding of Lilly's heart was almost too loud to hear Oliver, but she forced herself to calm down and take a deep breath. Barney didn't—he kept barking and leaping at the door as if the grim reaper were on the other side.

"It's okay, Barney. It's Oliver." Lilly opened the door and smiled. "Hi, Oliver. Is anything wrong?"

"Hi, Lilly. Nothing's wrong. I just came over because I saw lights going on and off in Hassan's house and I was worried someone had broken in."

"Thanks, Oliver. That was me. I was just checking the rooms, making sure everything is okay." Barney continued to bark, forcing Lilly to raise her voice so Oliver could hear her. "Barney! Stop it!"

Oliver smacked his arm and stepped inside, closing the door behind him. "Mosquitos are thick tonight. Do you want me to stay while you finish checking things out?"

"We just have to check the backyard, so we'll be fine." Then she thought for a moment about how scared she had been the last time she saw Larry in the backyard. "Actually, Oliver, would you mind? I'll only be a minute."

"No problem at all." Lilly led the way through the kitchen, with Barney still in full voice. "Hush, Barn." She clicked on the patio floodlights and opened the door to the backyard. She and Barney stepped outside, where Barney stood quietly for a moment. Lilly unclipped his leash and then, apparently hearing something that was out of Lilly's audible range, Barney took off running. Pretty soon he was in darkness. Lilly shivered. She didn't know what was out there. She called for him and when he didn't return, she turned around to look into Hassan's kitchen. Oliver was leaning with his rear end against the kitchen counter.

"Barney, come!"

Barney continued to bark, so Lilly figured he was probably hot on the trail of a rabbit or other small creature. She went back inside knowing he would return in a minute or two, once the little critter escaped under the fence. Hassan's backyard held endless amusements for the pooch.

"What's new, Oliver?"

"Nothing much."

"Are you still working at the feed store?"

He nodded. "Yeah." As he spoke, Oliver moved around the end of the kitchen counter and locked the door to the backyard.

"What are you doing?" Lilly asked.

"I don't want the dog in here."

"Oliver, he's—"

"Go in the living room. Now." Oliver jerked his head toward the living room and Lilly felt a chill sweep up her arms.

"What for? I'm going to let Barney in."

Oliver placed himself between her and the back door so she couldn't unlock it. By now Barney had returned to the back door and was barking more insistently.

"I said go in the living room *now*."

"Okay. Fine. What's the matter with you, Oliver?"

The young man didn't answer.

"I think you'd better leave now."

He let out a harsh laugh. "I'm not leaving. Not until we've had a talk."

"A talk about what?" Lilly was moving toward the living room, watching Oliver over her shoulder.

"About my parents."

"What about your parents?"

"Don't pretend you don't know about my parents. For God's sake, the whole neighborhood knows."

"Knows what? That they had a fight? So what? Lots of people fight." They were both standing in the living room now.

Oliver sneered at Lilly and pushed her down onto the sofa. He paced back and forth across the floor, just feet from where she sat.

"Do you know what they were fighting about? Huh?"

"No. It's none of my business."

"They're fighting because my father is in love with Michelle. Was in love with Michelle. That's why!" His voice had risen. He stopped pacing and smashed his fist against the wall near the entrance to the foyer. Lilly jumped.

"I'm sorry, Oliver. I really am. But that has nothing to do with me, so I think this is something you need to discuss with them. It's time for you to leave now." She could hear Barney hurling himself at the back door. Hearing him frantically trying to get in reminded her of the night she and Hassan had been walking Barney and he had barked so furiously at Oliver. Lilly had assumed he was just excited, but had he been trying to communicate something to her? Something she ignored?

"But you keep sticking your nose in other people's business, trying to find out who killed Michelle. So it does have something to do with you, I'm afraid."

He's gone around the bend. He can't mean what I think he means.

Lilly cast a nervous look toward the back door. She wished she could see Barney. She hoped he wasn't hurting himself by slamming his body repeatedly into the door.

Oliver ran his hands through his hair, making it stand up on end. It gave him a crazed, maniacal look. "Why do you think my father didn't want to go away for Christmas? He didn't want to leave Michelle! How do you think I felt when he wouldn't stick up for me when Michelle called the cops on me because of my muffler? How do you think my mother felt about all this? How else was I supposed to save my mother's dignity? Michelle was nothing but a lowlife pig who deserved exactly what she got." His nostrils were flaring and he was becoming more and more agitated. Lilly tried to calculate whether she could make it to the front door without him catching her, but he broke into her frantic thoughts.

"I know what you're thinking, Lilly, but it won't work." He shook his head in mock sadness. "If only you had minded your own business and if only that terrorist boyfriend of yours hadn't made Michelle so angry. It's a perfect set-up, see? He's on the hook for killing Michelle and you won't be able to pin anything on me." Oliver advanced slowly toward Lilly, his hammy fists clenching and unclenching.

Despite her fear, Lilly saw red when Oliver mocked Hassan like that. She swallowed hard and willed herself to shut up and not say anything that would make her situation worse.

But that wasn't like her.

"Oliver, you're the only lowlife pig I see. You racist thug."
She gave him her best defiant stare.

When he lunged at her, she leapt up from the sofa and tried
to run around the end table next to it. He flung himself in her
direction, grabbing her ankle. She went down hard, but she
managed to kick him in the arm with her other foot.

He let out a grunt of pain as he let go of her ankle. "I'll kill
you, too!" he hissed. She scrambled to her feet and tried
kicking him again, but he was too fast. He rose, too, with a
speed that surprised Lilly. She ran behind the sofa; he was
standing in front of it now.

Without breaking eye contact with her, he swept the coffee
table out of the way with one swift kick and threw himself
toward her, using the sofa cushion as catapult.

When they both landed on the floor behind the sofa in a
tangle, Lilly spied the cord from the floor lamp that stood just
a few feet away. She yanked on the cord, plunging the room
into near darkness and causing the lamp to topple over. She
reflexively protected her head with her arms when the glass
lampshade shattered, sending glass flying everywhere.

She held out a brief hope that the lamp had hit Oliver, or
that he had at least been cut by some of the flying glass, but her
heart sank when she saw that he had raced toward the
entrance to the living room. It was the only way in or out of
the room, so he clearly wasn't about to let her go.

She looked around frantically, wishing that she had paid
more attention to Barney when he tried to warn her about
Oliver. The light was very poor, since the only illumination
came from a wall sconce in the foyer, but her eyes alit on the
end table, where there was a geode that a client had given
Hassan as a gift many years ago. She wondered if Oliver had
seen it.

"The only way you're leaving this house is in a body bag."

Oliver's voice was chilling. With the light behind him, Lilly figured she could see him better than he could see her. She inched toward the end table, hoping he couldn't see her well enough to know what she was doing.

He advanced into the room, his arms reaching along the walls for a light switch. In a second or two, Lilly knew he was going to find the switch and he would see that she was trying to get to the geode.

As her fingers closed around the rock, the room was suddenly flooded with light. Oliver squeezed his eyes shut for just a moment when the light came on, and she knew she couldn't wait another second. She hurled the rock at Oliver's head, simultaneously letting out a scream.

There was a terrible crash of breaking glass as Oliver let out a shriek of pain. But he was still on his feet, obviously still conscious, and clearly enraged. Blood seeped profusely from a gash on the side of his head.

Lilly barely had time to notice that the barking had finally stopped.

"Who's in here?" a voice yelled.

CHAPTER 54

$\mathcal{L}$illy recognized the voice. "Larry! I'm in here! Help!"

Still keeping her gaze trained on Oliver, who appeared stunned from the blow to his head, she could see a streak of movement out of her peripheral vision.

"Keep Barney out! There's glass everywhere!"

Larry raced into the room and stopped short when he took in the scene before him.

"Help me, Larry," Oliver said. "This nut tried to kill me."

"No, Larry! He's lying! He killed Michelle!"

Larry looked from Lilly to Oliver and back again. He had been trying to hold Barney back, but a big dog hyped up on adrenaline was too much for him to handle. Barney flew into Oliver, knocking the young man off his feet. He gripped Oliver's arm with his teeth, not hard enough to break the skin, but hard enough to suggest to Oliver that he'd better sit still. A low growl issued from his throat.

"That's all I need to see," Larry said. "Dogs can sense things. I'm calling the police."

He stood in the doorway to the living room while he dialed

his cell phone. "They're on their way. Lilly, are you all right?" Larry advanced toward Lilly, but she waved him off.

"Larry, stay where you are. I don't want to take a chance that Oliver can get away." Larry nodded and maintained his guard. Lilly stood up gingerly and limped toward the front door. She unlocked it and left it ajar before returning to the living room.

Barney never let up his grip on Oliver's arm until two of the responding police officers had handcuffed Oliver and jerked him to his feet.

"Good boy," a third officer said, rubbing Barney's head. He turned to Lilly. "We're going to need you to answer some questions, but as soon as we're done I think you're going to need to get this pup's paws checked out by a vet."

Lilly looked down and was dismayed to see that several thin trails of blood followed Barney's footsteps. She hoped the questioning wouldn't take long. There was a knock at the front door, which was still ajar, and a fourth officer walked in. He was quickly advised of the circumstances and he offered to take Larry's statement.

Lilly led the way into the kitchen so Barney wouldn't step on any more glass, but she saw that Larry had thrown a patio chair through one of the French doors to get into the house. Glass littered the kitchen floor, too. She cleared the glass from a space with her foot as Barney limped into the room behind her. He plopped onto his belly in the spot she had cleared once Lilly and the officer had seated themselves at the table.

The officer asked Lilly to describe everything that had happened that evening beginning with her arrival at Hassan's house. She told him everything, from being afraid to look around to thinking it was kind of Oliver to offer to stay in the house while she checked the backyard.

When she had answered all the officer's questions, he told

her the police would very likely be in touch with her again. Larry had already left, having finished talking to the officer in the living room, but he returned with a large piece of plywood and a hammer and nails. He set to work boarding up the French door and was done very quickly.

After she saw the officers to the front door, she knelt down in front of her dog. "Come on, Barney. Let's get you fixed up."

She led a hobbling Barney to the car and helped him into the back seat. She had finally calmed down enough to dial a number on her cell phone without trembling and she couldn't wait to talk to the first person on her list. She dialed the number, then started the car and backed out of Hassan's driveway.

"Hi, Gretchen. I figured you should be among the first to know that someone has confessed to killing Michelle Conover."

"You're kidding. Who was it? What happened?"

Lilly related the entire story to Hassan's lawyer while she drove to the emergency veterinarian's office in Lupine.

"This is wonderful news, Lilly. I'll be at the courthouse first thing in the morning and get things moving so Hassan can go home. He's a very lucky man."

"I'm so happy, Gretchen."

Her next call was to Bill, who had already heard about the incident at Hassan's house and had tried calling Lilly four times while she was talking to Gretchen.

"What happened?" He didn't waste any time on niceties. "Are you all right?"

For the third time that night, she told the story of what had happened.

"You seem to attract violence, you know that? You should have asked me to go with you," he scolded.

"I tried, but neither you nor Noley picked up. I don't even want to know what you two were doing, but just know that you were my first choice. As it is, I'm on the way to the emergency vet with Barney right now."

"What happened to Barney?"

She explained that the poor dog had stepped on a lot of broken glass.

"I'll pick up a big treat for him and bring it to your house tomorrow."

"Thanks. Listen, I'm pulling into the vet right now and I need to call Laurel. I'll talk to you tomorrow."

Laurel was shocked to learn what had happened while she was out with Nick. She let out a little sob when Lilly told her that Barney had been hurt.

"Is he going to be okay?"

"Totally okay, I'm sure of it."

Once Lilly had reassured Laurel that she and Barney were not badly hurt, she had one quick question for Laurel.

"You and Nick aren't getting back together, are you?"

"Not a chance. I don't know what I ever saw in him."

Lilly breathed a silent sigh of relief. Once upon a time Nick had been a great help to her, but things had changed since then and her concern now was for Laurel's future. And after the way Nick had treated her, it probably wasn't a good idea for him to be part of that future.

They hung up and Lilly took Barney inside. He whimpered a little bit, but he was pretty brave, considering there was no place on earth he hated more than the vet's office. And the vet and her staff worked quickly to patch him up.

When Barney was ready to go home, three of his paws were heavily bandaged and he was having a hard time walking. Not so much from the pain, the vet had said, but from the strange sensation of the bandages. Lilly promised to do her best to keep him quiet and still until the paws had healed, but she and the vet both knew that was a pipe dream.

By now it was the middle of the night, and Laurel had waited up to greet Lilly and Barney when they got home. She hugged Lilly and immediately sat on the floor to kiss Barney's head and offer sympathy, love, and a treat that Lilly saw her slip into Barney's mouth.

CHAPTER 55

The next morning the news was all over town that someone had confessed to the murder of Michelle Conover. Lilly was taking the day off because of the injuries she had sustained over the past two days, so she was at the jail when visiting hours began. Even Hassan was aware of what had happened.

"Thank God you're okay," he greeted her.

"I'm fine. Barely a scratch."

Hassan shook his head. "What am I going to do with you?"

"Love me even more."

He grinned. "You got it. I'm so sorry, Lilly. I never should have asked you to go over there. I truly thought that everything would be okay."

"There was no reason to think it wouldn't be okay."

"I'm just glad you're all right and that I'm getting out of here."

Lilly couldn't stop smiling.

Hassan was going home.

Lilly promised to pick him up and take him to his house as soon as the formalities of his release had taken place.

She went home to rest while she waited, and found Noley and Laurel in the kitchen, cooking up a storm.

"What's this?" she asked.

"Tonight's dinner," Laurel said with a smile. "I talked to Noley and I'm going to be her new intern." Lilly looked at Noley and found her best friend smiling broadly.

"This will be so much fun," Noley said. "I've never had an intern before, so I'm really excited about it. Laurel is going to make a great chef."

"We're making a celebration dinner for Hassan. You can bring him here to eat before you take him to his house."

"That's so nice of you two."

They worked in the kitchen while Lilly slept in the living room. The doorbell and Barney's subsequent barking frenzy woke her up. It was Bill.

"I've gotten the whole scoop," he said, sitting down across from Lilly in the living room. "Oliver not only killed Michelle, but he was one of the idiots who forced themselves into Hassan's foyer on Halloween night and later vandalized the place. He did it after you and Hassan left the house for the block party and then he joined his mother there. He recruited some idiot friend of his to go with him, and we've already arrested that kid, too. Turns out Oliver's as bigoted as he is stupid. He didn't even think about it at the time, apparently, but his actions set up Hassan to look like Michelle's killer.

"It also seems that Eugene really did have a serious crush on Michelle. I guess it was pretty obvious, so Sally knew about it. And Oliver is a total mama's boy. So he did what he thought was necessary to help his mom."

"Why did he pull her off Eugene when she attacked him?"

"So she wouldn't get in any legal trouble. He certainly didn't do it out of love for his father."

"What a waste of a young life." Lilly made a sound of disgust. "I was sure Gerald had killed Michelle. I was way off."

"A couple guys went to get a statement from Gerald regarding his involvement in the tearoom. It seems he would have liked to kill Michelle himself, but he's smarter than that. She did, in fact, threaten to expose him as an adulterer and a gay man because he and Ted were having an affair. He had intended to come clean about everything, but he wanted to do it on his own timeline, not Michelle's. His wife figured it out after Ted showed up at their house, ranting and raving."

"Thanks for clearing up my questions."

"You're welcome. It smells good in here. What's cooking?"

"Go ask Noley and Laurel. They're whipping up dinner. I'm going to pick up Hassan and we're all having dinner here. Want to join us?"

"Definitely."

Lilly cried when she saw Hassan walk out of the jail later that afternoon. She could have sworn she saw tears in his eyes, too. She took him back to her house and Hassan was delighted to have a home-cooked meal for the first time since the night he was taken to jail.

The Water Wheel reservation could wait—the dinner Laurel and Noley made was as good as anything a five-star restaurant could dish up. And the mood was light and gleeful as they all celebrated the end of Hassan's ordeal.

Lilly took Hassan home after dinner, after she could pull Barney away from him, that is, and waited on the sofa in the living room while he checked out the rest of the house and took a long, hot shower in his own luxurious bathroom.

He finally came down and sat next to Lilly, put his arm

around her shoulders—very gently—and pulled her close. He kissed her as she deserved to be kissed and afterward kissed her again. And again. She felt safe and warm and stayed as late as she could, until her head and shoulder were throbbing.

"Tomorrow I'm planning to go into the shop, but after work do you want to come over to Mom's house with me? I know she'd love to see you."

Hassan grinned. "I'd love to see her, too. Do you think she'll recognize me?"

Lilly sighed. "I hope so. We'll find out. I'm learning that I can't change what's happening with her, so I'm just trying to accept things as they are and move forward. There will probably come a day when she won't recognize any of us."

"I love you, Lilly." He kissed her one last time before she left.

"I love you, too, Hassan."

The next day she made a point of calling the jail and lodging a complaint about the racist guard. She felt better after that, and she and Harry were busy all day with customers who were gearing up for the Christmas season.

She picked up Hassan after work and they drove to her mom's house.

"Don't worry about her not recognizing you," she assured him as they got out. "If she does, great. If she doesn't, that's okay, too. We just keep on loving her no matter what."

Nikki opened the door to them, a wide smile on her face.

"Good to see you, Nikki," Hassan said.

"Same to you, Hassan. Glad you're out of that awful place."

"You seem especially happy tonight, Nikki. Did Mom have a good day?"

"She did. But that's not why I'm smiling."

"Oh? Why are you smiling?"

Nikki held up her left hand. On the third finger there was a diamond, sparkling in the light from the foyer lamp. She wriggled her fingers and Lilly felt something fall in her stomach.

"Beau asked me to marry him!"

THE END

LAUREL'S FRIGHTFULLY GOOD FRITTATA

2 T. butter
1 large onion, sliced in half and then thinly sliced
¾ t. salt, divided
Pepper
8 large eggs
¼ c. milk (Laurel uses 2%, but you don't have to)
½ - 1 c. chopped deli ham (can also use any leftover ham, chopped)
½ - 1 c. chopped roasted vegetables of your choice (use whatever leftovers you have in the fridge. You can also use jarred red peppers, patted dry)
1 handful of chopped fresh herbs of your choice (Laurel uses basil, thyme, and oregano)
1 small log goat cheese, crumbled

Position a rack in the oven to approximately 8" below the broiler. Preheat the broiler.

In a skillet over medium heat, melt the butter. Add the onions, ½ t. salt, and some pepper to taste. Cook, stirring occasionally, until the onions are very soft. This should take about 15 minutes. When onions are done, remove them from the skillet and set aside. Set the skillet aside, but do not wipe it out because you're going to use it again.

In a medium bowl, whisk the eggs and the milk with the remaining salt and more pepper to taste.

Place, eggs, ham, vegetables, herbs, and cheese into the skillet. Stir gently.

Place skillet over medium heat and stir gently for a couple minutes. After that, let the egg mixture sit for about 5 minutes, without stirring, until the bottom is browned and set.

Transfer the skillet to the broiler and cook for about 5 more minutes, until the eggs are lightly browned. Remove skillet from oven and cover; let sit for 5 more minutes.

Invert frittata onto a serving plate. You can serve it at room temperature, but Laurel likes to serve it piping hot with salsa.

LARRY'S BONE-CHILLING CHILI

(Larry's chili would not go over well in Texas because it has beans, but the neighbors seem to like it)

1 lb. ground round, browned and drained
1 8-oz. can tomato sauce
1 15-oz. can kidney beans, undrained
1 15-oz. can chili or pinto beans, undrained
1 lg. can tomatoes and chiles
1 onion, chopped
1 small green pepper, chopped
1 small red pepper, chopped
Dash Tabasco sauce
Crushed red pepper, optional

Combine all ingredients in a Dutch oven. Cook over low heat, stirring frequently, until bubbly. Serve with grated cheddar cheese. Larry also likes to serve cornbread and honey butter with his chili.

TED'S BLOODCURDLING BROWNIES

For the Brownies:
1 ¼ c. flour
1 t. salt
½ c. cocoa powder
2 c. chocolate chips, divided
2 sticks butter (1 c.), chilled and cut into pieces
1 ½ c. sugar
½ c. light brown sugar, packed
5 eggs, room temperature (leave them out for about an hour before baking)
2 t. vanilla

For the Frosting:
2 c. powdered sugar
4 T. butter
2 T. light cream
½ t. mint extract

For the Glaze:

1 oz. unsweetened baking chocolate, chopped
1 T. butter

Preheat oven to 350 degrees. Grease a 13x9" baking dish. You can line the dish with parchment paper, if you like. That's what Ted does.

In a medium bowl, whisk together flour, salt, and cocoa powder.

Fill a medium saucepan with about 2-3" water. Bring the water to a simmer over low heat. In a large heat-proof bowl, place 1 ½ c. of the chocolate chips and the pieces of chilled butter. Heat the chocolate and butter, stirring constantly, until the chocolate is melted and smooth. Remove bowl from heat; add sugars and stir until well-blended.

Add eggs, one at a time, to chocolate mixture, stirring well after each addition. Stir in vanilla.

Add flour mixture to chocolate mixture. Using a spatula, fold gently just until combined. Fold in remaining chocolate chips.

Pour batter into prepared baking dish. Bake until toothpick inserted into middle comes out almost clean. This may take up to 45 minutes or more, but start checking at about 30 minutes, just in case. These are very fudgy brownies.

Cool completely on wire rack.

Make the frosting once the brownies are cool. Combine all frosting ingredients in a large bowl. Beat well until you have reached spreading consistency. Spread over brownies and chill until set.

Make the glaze. In a microwave-safe bowl, melt the unsweetened chocolate with the butter in 15-second increments, stirring each time, until chocolate is smooth. Drizzle spoonfuls of glaze over the brownies from a regular spoon (a soup spoon works well) held several inches above the pan. This gives the brownies an artsy, sophisticated look perfect for a tearoom.

*V*alentine's Day was Lilly Carlsen's least favorite day of the year, followed closely by the day the clocks spring forward. Both days left her tired, grumpy, and in need of chocolate. In the case of Spring Forward, she usually settled for strong coffee. In the case of Valentine's Day, though, nothing but chocolate would do.

She had been forced to buy her own chocolate beginning the year she married Beau. He wasn't much of a romantic and didn't like chocolate, anyway. And from the time he had left her and their two toddlers fifteen years previously, she hadn't had a boyfriend who would buy her chocolate for Valentine's Day.

Until now.

Lilly had been dating Hassan Ashraf for over a year. This would be their second Valentine's Day together, but the first one didn't really count because Hassan had been on a gem hunting trip in Sri Lanka and hadn't even been able to get in touch with her via telephone. He had given her a box of chocolates, a bouquet of roses, and an apology when he returned from his trip.

But this year was going to be different. This year he would be in Juniper Junction and they already had reservations at their favorite restaurant, The Water Wheel. He knew how much Lilly loved chocolate, so she was pretty sure she could look forward to a gorgeous box of gourmet treats from her favorite chocolatier.

Her only dilemma was what to give Hassan for Valentine's Day. He didn't need jewelry, so a watch was not an option. He didn't usually wear ties, so that wasn't a good idea, either. She had been browsing online to find leather-bound travel journals, but she wasn't sure he would use one of those.

Valentine's Day was fast approaching and she needed to make a decision.

The weeks leading up to Valentine's Day were among the busiest of the year at Juniper Junction Jewels, Lilly's shop on Main Street in the small Rocky Mountain town. It usually started getting busy midway through January with romantics looking for the perfect gifts for their Valentines. Lilly had always thought it interesting that women tended to do their shopping early—men tended to wait until the last minute.

Her favorite days in the shop were when men came in looking for engagement rings. Though some of them had ideas for precisely the ring they wanted, the majority of them were unsure of themselves and needed some gentle guidance through the process of buying such an important piece of jewelry.

That was where Harry, Lilly's shop assistant, came in handy. Harry wasn't just a darling man—he was also a natural when it came to knowledge of different gems and stones, and many of the men who came into the shop in search of an engagement ring seemed to relax under his capable attention.

It was early February and Juniper Junction Jewels had been bedecked in pink, red, and white gauze, cupids, and hearts since mid-January. Lilly hated the sickly sweet look, but it was necessary.

Toward the end of the day, Harry and Lilly were taking the pieces of jewelry from their light pink velvet displays and placing them in the vault until the next morning. Harry lingered over the rings, paying special attention to one with a pale pink sapphire in a white gold setting.

"Isn't that a gorgeous ring?" Lilly asked, noticing that Harry had slowed his pace in dismantling the displays.

"Mm-hmm," he answered, staring at the bauble.

"Say, how's Alice these days?" Lilly asked. Harry had been dating Alice for many months, and the young woman was every bit as sweet as Harry. The two were a perfect match.

Harry's head snapped up and he gave Lilly a suspicious look.

"Why do you ask?"

Lilly smiled. "I just happened to think of her when I saw you mooning over the pink engagement ring. If I remember correctly, Alice's favorite color is pink."

Harry blushed four shades darker than the ring.

"She's fine. Just studying hard. Midterms will be here before she knows it," he said, sidestepping the elephant in the room—was he was looking at the pink ring with the intent of buying it for Alice?

Lilly grinned and dropped the issue. It was obviously making Harry uncomfortable.

"Let's get these pieces put away and go home. It's been a long day," she said. Harry turned his attention away from the dazzling ring and picked up several bracelets to take to the vault.

"Have you heard the forecast?" he asked over his shoulder. "It's supposed to storm tonight."

Lilly glanced outside the big plate glass windows in the front of the shop. It had already been dark for almost an hour.

"I heard that. The clouds rolled in this afternoon."

"I can't wait for spring," Harry said. Lilly smiled, but didn't answer. She loved winter, with its moods and its snowfall and its cold temperatures. Fall was her favorite season, but winter was a close second.

When they had locked the vault and triple-checked it, they both left. Snowflakes were already falling thickly.

"Be careful getting home," Harry said, then drove off.

Lilly stood looking at the sky for a moment before getting into her own car. She loved watching the snow fall through the darkness. She shivered just a little and followed Harry out of the alley behind the shop and onto Main Street.

* * *

Barney, the Carlsen family's soft-coated wheaten terrier, greeted Lilly, as usual, with a frenzy of barking and tail-wagging when Lilly walked into the kitchen through the back door.

"Hi, Barn!" she said, laughing. The big lug of a dog jumped up and placed his paws on her coat, trying to lick her face. She bent closer to him to accept his kisses.

"Hi, Mom," Laurel said as she came down the stairs and into the kitchen.

"Hi, honey. How was school?" Lilly was finally getting used to having only one child at home. Tighe had been away at college since the previous August, and though Lilly had been sure she would never adjust to the situation, she was getting accustomed to it. She brushed away the thought that Laurel, a senior in high school, would be following her brother out of the nest in another six months.

"It was good." Laurel opened the refrigerator door. "What's for dinner?"

"Leftovers," Lilly said. "Can you grab the jar of soup in there?" Laurel handed her mother a large jar of *zuppa Toscana* they had made over the weekend and Lilly emptied it into a pan on the stove. While the soup warmed she cut slices of Italian bread and placed them on the table with olive oil for dipping.

"Can I go over to Nick's tonight?" Laurel asked as they sat down for dinner.

"I don't think you should. There's a storm coming and I don't want you out driving in it," Lilly warned.

"All right. I'll just call him and tell him I can't come."

Lilly looked at her daughter. She had expected a barrage of whining and eye rolling, but there was nothing. Lilly wondered what was going on.

She got her answer a couple minutes later.

Laurel toyed with her bread, breaking it into tiny pieces and arranging them in a circle on her plate. "Vanessa is going shopping for her prom dress this weekend."

"Oh?" Lilly suspected Laurel would want to accompany her best friend.

"I think I'm going to go with her," Laurel said.

"That sounds fun," Lilly said. "Isn't it early to be shopping for a prom dress?"

"Not really. Lots of girls have their dresses already."

Lilly had a hunch about where this conversation was headed.

"Maybe I'll look for a dress while I'm out with Vanessa," Laurel suggested.

"Has Nick asked you to prom?" Lilly grinned.

"Not yet. But it can't hurt to have a dress picked out, right?" Laurel's grin matched her mom's.

"No, it can't hurt."

"Depending on the price, do you think you could help me pay for it?" Laurel asked.

Well, that escalated quickly, Lilly thought. *So that's why she didn't give me a hard time about staying home tonight.*

"I suppose I could chip in some," Lilly said. "Um, how much are you thinking of spending on a dress?"

Laurel shrugged. "Five hundred dollars, maybe."

Lilly almost choked on her bread. "Five hundred dollars?" she wheezed. "For a prom dress?"

Laurel must have sensed her mother's disbelief. Anyone with a pulse would have sensed it.

"I'm just throwing a number out there," she hastened to explain. "I have no idea how much the dress will cost."

"I don't mind helping to pay for a dress, but for heaven's sake, Laurel, my wedding dress didn't even cost five hundred dollars."

"That was ages ago, Mom. I'll look for something cheaper than that, obviously," Laurel said, her tone taking on just a hint of snippiness.

"Good." Lilly unclenched her jaw. "Where are you going to look for dresses?"

"Ruby Red's," Laurel said. Lilly glanced at her daughter out of the corner of her eye. Ruby Red's was the most fashionable dress shop in town. Also the most expensive.

"I doubt you'll find a prom dress under five hundred dollars at Ruby's."

"We'll look at other places, too." Laurel hurriedly pushed the rest of dinner into her mouth. "I have a lot of homework to do. I'll come down and do the dishes in a little while."

I raised a smart girl, thought Lilly. *She knows how to make a quick exit and she knows that by mentioning the word "homework" I won't give her grief. Well played, Laurel. Well played.*

PREVIEW OF CAPE MENACE: A CAPE MAY HISTORICAL MYSTERY

08 January 1711

I was afraid of wolves even before I journeyed to America. Stories of the creatures abounded in England, where no wolf had trod for two hundred years. Stories of their vicious appetites, of their stealth and speed, of their nighttime prowling through forests and dales.

Just stories, but I believed them, nonetheless.

So when I saw my first wolf in the woods near our new home in New Jersey, I was given quite a fright. It was getting dark and my mother and I were hurrying through the woods to get home from delivering a packet of herbs to a family nearby. The husband had cut his leg and was suffering greatly from the pain.

I stopped short when we came upon the wolf. I knew straightaway what it was, for I had seen the pictures that accompanied all the stories I had been told. Mamma told me in a low voice to remain still and it would go away, but she did not remain still. She moved toward me ever so slowly until she was standing directly in front of me. The wolf watched us with its haunting eyes, its huge paws motionless in the snow and its nostrils widening and narrowing as it sniffed the air.

I did not realize I had been holding my breath until the wolf turned away and padded farther into the woods. Mamma unclenched her fists, which she had been holding tight against her legs, and turned to me.

"We shall not come through the woods again at dusk. We must respect the animals that hunt in the nighttime. We are the intruders."

Even then, she had known how dangerous wolves could be.

CAPE MENACE CHAPTER 2

04 DECEMBER 1712

*T*he day Mamma disappeared she had been feeling unwell. After harvesting the remainder of the root vegetables from the garden before the ground was frozen solid for the winter, we wrote a letter to Grandmamma, Mamma's mother, in England. We told her of the rapidly-approaching winter weather, but I forgot long ago what else was in the letter.

Mamma asked me to go to the tavern in Town, where letters from people in the village were held for mailing. She would have gone with me, but she was needed in the apothecary since Pappa was busy preparing the fields for the winter fallow. Mamma had heard that Captain Winslow was in the village, en route to Philadelphia from his home further south, and that he would be crossing to England soon. He had been the captain of our ship when we sailed from England to Philadelphia, and he had been the one who told Pappa about the fertile farmland farther to the south in New Jersey. He and Pappa had become good friends during the crossing. Since that time, he had taken our letters back to England for us and returned with letters from Grandmamma and others. We always waited anxiously for news of his return to Town.

Going into Town was exciting because there were always people about, but more than that, it was exciting because it was so close to the water. Looking down over the bay from the twenty-foot-tall bank at the end of the main street of Town, I could often see fishing boats, whaling boats, and vessels from the north and the south laden with goods like sugar, soap, and tea. I loved the smell drifting up from the harbor, too—the tangy scent of the salt water mingled with the smell of fish and the scent of wet ropes coiled on the sand. When a whale had been killed, the odor wafting from the beach was never pleasant, but there was no such odor that particular day.

Down the road, at the house closest to mine, I stopped to ask my friend Patience if she would go with me to the village. She agreed to go with me not only because she was my best friend, but also because it gave her some time away from her own heavy responsibilities at home. With four younger sisters, she was often called upon to help with the cooking, the cleaning, and even some of the farm work.

Upon arriving in Town, we watched the activity among the fishermen and sailors for a bit. I was happy to see Captain Winslow down among the other men. He was standing on the ground not far from where his boat, the *Hope*, was moored. He was gesturing toward *Hope*'s hull and talking to one of his crew nearby. Patience and I clambered down the embankment and ran over to where he stood. When he saw us, his face broke into a broad smile. He was so dapper in his uniform of the trading company. He wore a dark blue waistcoat with shiny gold buttons and a dandy pair of white breeches. They were true white, too, not the dingy white of our homespun and wool. He told us of his upcoming trip to England and talked to us, just as if we were grown women, of some of the work that had to be done before he could leave.

"I'm glad you've brought this letter today, Sarah," he told me. "We are hoping to leave by tomorrow or the next day. The voyage promises to be a long one. I'll put your letter with the others you've given me. What special thing would you like me to bring back for you this time?" He winked then because my answer was always the same.

I didn't hesitate. "I would love a bit of tea," I told him with a smile.

"I knew it," he chuckled. "You miss your tea, don't you? Well, you shall have tea upon my return."

"Thank you, Captain." We took our leave after wishing him and his crew safe travels.

Patience and I climbed back up the steep slope and wandered a bit along the main street, but since it was cold outside and Patience hated the cold, we left and parted ways at her house.

When I arrived back at our house Mamma wasn't there. I didn't worry at the time because there were many reasons she could have been gone: often she would leave to attend a sick neighbor, or help Widow Beall with her chores. Goodman Beall, a fisherman, had recently been lost at sea, leaving his poor wife with eight children and few means. Or Mamma could have gone out to pick herbs, which she often did. Though Pappa was the apothecary, Mamma was a skilled herbalist in her own right and she spent a great deal of her time preparing remedies and tinctures for those who needed medicines.

I set about preparing the dinner we usually had at midday. Pappa would be in soon and would be very hungry. I was surprised that Mamma hadn't prepared the potatoes in the hearth ashes before she had left the house.

Mamma still wasn't home when Pappa came in a short time later. He had to get back to work, he said, so he couldn't wait for her to eat his meal. I decided to wait for Mamma to return before eating. After Pappa left, I cleared off the table and stacked his trencher away. I sat down to begin the mending in the basket near the hearth. I worked for several hours, as the light outside began to wane and shadows shifted inside the house. Still no word from Mamma. I was hungry.

But I wasn't worried yet.

Early in the evening, after darkness had fallen, Pappa came back into the house. I had fixed supper and we ate together. It would be the first of countless meals we would eat without Mamma. But we didn't know that yet.

"I'm not worried," Pappa assured me, but his eyes belied his words. Mamma had never simply gone away and not told Pappa or me where she was going. And she certainly had never stayed away after dark.

Pappa pushed himself away from the table after our silent, listless meal and took his hat and cloak from the hook near the door. "I'm going to Widow Beall's to see if Mamma is there."

I nodded, turning away from him so he couldn't see the fear in my eyes, couldn't hear my breathing becoming shallower, faster. I didn't want him to think I was being silly.

After an hour, Pappa came home. He opened the door slowly. I looked up from where I sat by the fire, expecting to see Mamma follow him through the door, but he was alone. He looked at me solemnly, his eyes strained and worried. "She hasn't been at Widow Beall's at all today."

"Do you think she went into Town for some reason?"

Pappa stroked his beard. "Not without telling one of us." He was silent for a few moments, then seemed to come to a decision.

"I'm going to see Daniel Ames. He'll help me look for her."

Patience's father was a kind man, always willing to help a neighbor. "We'll gather a few more men and spread out."

"What should I do?" I didn't want to be idle while Pappa was out looking.

He looked around searchingly, as if Mamma would appear at any moment from behind the bedchamber curtain. He closed his eyes and rubbed his beard again. "Wait for her here. I don't want her to find us both gone when she comes back."

I didn't know what to do while I waited, so I sat, staring at the flames, straining my ears for the sound of a footfall outside. But I heard nothing except faraway shouts, shouts I knew were from the men helping Pappa look for my mother.

"Ruth! Ruth!" they called over and over. I finally put my hands over my ears. I couldn't bear the thought of Mamma lying somewhere, hurt or sick, unable to answer their cries.

Where had she gone? My stomach was twisted into knots. I stood and paced the room, peering uselessly into the darkness each time I passed the window, hoping I would see her running lightly up the path to the door, her cloak billowing behind her, a lantern swinging gently in her hand.

But I saw nothing. Nothing but darkness.

It was hours before Pappa came home again. This time Goodwife Ames came with him. I raised my eyebrows in question.

"Eliza Ames is going to stay with you tonight, Sarah. I'm going back out with Daniel and some of the other men from the village and we're going to keep looking for your mother. You need to get some sleep." He took another lantern and two candles from the shelf above the fireplace and was out the door again before I could ask any questions. I looked at Goodwife Ames, not knowing what to say.

She obviously didn't know what to say, either, but she tried.

"I'm sure Ruth just became lost looking for herbs. They're bound to find her."

I didn't tell her what I was thinking: Mamma never got lost. She knew her way around the forest with her eyes closed.

"Or maybe she's helping a neighbor," Goody Ames suggested feebly. She knew as well as I that my mother could have heard the men shouting for her from any of the neighbors' houses.

There was only one explanation: she was gone.

Suddenly I was struggling to take a breath. Everything faded into a brief darkness as a buzzing sound grew louder in my ears. I tried to catch my own fall, but ended up in a heap on the floor. Goody Ames let out a cry and rushed to my side. She knelt and cradled my head in her lap, smoothing my hair as it tumbled in an unruly mass from my cap.

"There, there," she cooed. "The men'll find your mother, do not worry." Everything went black again and the last thing I remember is seeing Goody Ames's face, her concerned eyes searching the room wildly for something that would help me.

When I woke up I was alone in the bedchamber, covered to my chin with a counterpane. I was simultaneously perspiring and freezing. As it all came rushing back to me, I thrust back the counterpane and ran out into the main room, my feet cold on the wooden floor. Goody Ames sat in the chair next to the fire, and another woman stood by the window with her back to me, peering out into the darkness as I had done.

"How long have I been sleeping?" I asked in a tremulous voice.

Goody Ames's head came up with a jerk. Perhaps she had been sleeping, too. She stood quickly and crossed the room to me, her hands held out. "You were in a fit, so once your breathing became normal again I let you sleep." She motioned to the other woman, who was still looking out the window.

"The pastor's wife came over to see if we needed anything. She helped me get you into the bed."

Mistress Reeves turned around from her post at the window, her long face solemn. "It's the middle of the night, Sarah. I came to see if you and your father needed anything and I decided to stay and keep Goodwife Ames company while we wait for the men to return."

I looked from one woman to the other, trying to read their thoughts on their faces. "Where's Pappa?"

"He's still out looking for your mother, my dear," Goody Ames replied.

"I'm going to help them," I declared suddenly. Goody Ames looked at me with something akin to horror in her eyes.

"You cannot go out there alone!" she cried. "We don't know what happened to your mother. It's not safe for you to be out there alone. What about the wolves?" She had apparently forgotten her earlier assurances that my mother was simply delayed with a neighbor or had become lost searching for herbs.

"I am going," I told her quietly. Mistress Reeves watched us with wide eyes.

"I agree with Goodwife Ames," she said firmly. "The forest is not a safe place for a young lady to be alone, especially in the middle of the night."

"I won't be alone. There are lots of men out there looking for Mamma. I want to help. I can't stay inside any longer and do nothing. Surely you can understand that?" I asked them in a pleading voice.

They looked at each other. Neither woman suggested going with me. Patience's mother was afraid of the dark, so I knew what she was thinking. She was weighing the terror she would feel going into the forest in the middle of the night against the responsibility she felt for me. Exasperated, I gave her an excuse to stay in the house.

"Goodwife Ames, would you please stay here in case Mamma returns? I know Pappa doesn't want her to come back to an empty house."

I could see the relief on her face, even in the flickering firelight.

"Of course I will, dear."

"And Mistress Reeves, could you perhaps get some cider ready for the men to have when they come in from their search? I'm sure they'll want for drink."

She nodded. I suspected she didn't want to be in the woods at night, either.

Before the two women could think of any more protests, I pulled on my shoes and cloak and hurried outside, shutting the door firmly behind me. I headed northwest, directly into the forest where Mamma often looked for herbs and plants. She *had* to be in the forest. She hadn't said anything about going out to pick herbs that morning, but there was no other explanation.

There were animals in the forest, wild animals, and I hoped she hadn't run into any of them. There were coyotes. There were raccoons and bears.

There were wolves.

If she had stumbled upon a hungry animal … I couldn't stand to think about it. I tried to focus on finding her favorite spots in the near-darkness, with just a feeble lantern to guide my steps. I walked slowly, since the light from the candle only illuminated a few feet in front of me. I had to step carefully to avoid running into a tree or a rock.

I called for Mamma many times, until my throat became hoarse and it was hard to speak. I called even though I was afraid for myself. But there was no reply. My breath quickening, my mind conjured up images of Mamma lying on the cold, unforgiving ground. Was it possible she had become too ill to get home? After several paralyzing moments I was able to force myself to be calm and move forward through the trees. The lantern swung gently in my hand, the light from the candle dipping and swaying as I moved. Then I stopped.

Straight ahead of me were two small, bright circles, reflecting the candlelight from my lantern.

"Mamma?" I asked breathlessly. There was no answer.

"Mamma, are you all right? It's me." I took a cautious step toward the circles. A low, guttural growl greeted me as realization dawned. It wasn't Mamma. It was an animal, and I was in its home, its hunting space. I took a slow step backward, then another, keeping the lantern as still as possible. The bright circles grew larger as the animal approached.

I was terrified. The possibilities sped through my mind as I considered what to do next. I couldn't remember what Mamma had told me the time we saw the wolf in the forest. Should I turn around and run toward home? Should I try to climb the nearest tree? Should I dash past the animal, whatever it was, and run farther into the woods? But fear rooted me to the spot where I stood. Another menacing growl escaped the throat of the beast, this time much closer. I closed my eyes, wondering in a flood of panic if this was how my mother went missing. Then, in an instant, I made my decision. I couldn't stand here and wait to be attacked by the animal, so I spun around and ran.

But the animal was more nimble than I. It set off after me as I crashed through the thick forest, its long howl splitting the air. And I knew with sudden clarity that the monster behind me was a wolf. I could practically see its teeth, its foaming mouth, its hungry eyes, the hairs on its strong back standing in a long, straight line.

I dashed headlong through the trees, the lantern swinging wildly, the wolf panting behind me. I ran straight into a tree, banging my head hard and falling to the ground. A searing pain shot through my ankle. I was dizzy and sick to my stomach, but I picked myself up and continued hobbling along as fast as I could. The wolf did not slow its pursuit.

It seemed I had been running for miles, though I suspect the chase only lasted a few minutes. My lungs were burning, my legs had become jelly, and my head and ankle screamed for relief. As I raced through the dark maze of trees, I spied two spots of uneven light just a bit farther ahead. I recognized the light as lanterns, likely held by men from the village looking for Mamma. I tried yelling, but my throat was closed from fear and exertion. A choked sob escaped my lips and I heard raised voices coming from the direction of the lights.

"Ruth? Is that you?" a man's voice shouted.

I didn't know the voice, but I could have cried in relief when the wolf, apparently sensing danger from the voices ahead, stopped abruptly and turned, running away in the direction from which we had come. I stumbled to a stop, falling on the ground, my chest heaving and my ankle and head throbbing.

Footsteps rushed toward me as I struggled to sit up. "Ruth?"

"No, it's Sarah," I answered hoarsely.

"Sarah! What are you doing out here?" One of the men held a lantern close to his face so I could see him. It was Pastor Reeves. Without waiting for an answer, he asked, "Have you seen your mother?"

"I came out here looking for her, but I surprised a wolf and it's been chasing me," I explained in a rush. "I wasn't able to find her." My feeble voice trailed off.

Pastor Reeves bent down so the lantern was close to me. "Are you hurt, my child?"

"I've hit my head and turned my ankle." Pastor Reeves and the man with him bent over me and decided between themselves that the other man would hold all three lanterns while Pastor Reeves helped me walk home. I wanted to curse myself for taking them away from the desperate search for Mamma.

When I limped slowly through the door, Goody Ames roused herself again from the chair next to the dwindling fire and Mistress Reeves hurried forward to help me into the room, where I sat down at the table. The men didn't stay long, explaining that they were still searching for my mother, and left after I thanked them several times for being in the forest just when I needed them. I shuddered to think what would have become of me if that wolf hadn't been scared off.

I prayed Mamma hadn't met with a similar fate.

Goody Ames found some clean linens in Pappa's shed and worked quickly to bandage my swollen, purple ankle. The pain was overwhelming. There was little to do for my head, where a large bump had formed. Mistress Reeves looked on as Patience's mother worked.

"It was the will of God that you were hurt," Mistress told me severely. "He did not want you to go looking for Ruth because young women should not be in the forest at night. Goodwife Ames and I told you as much."

Goody Ames looked up at her and I could see the surprise and dismay on her face. I remained silent. Though Mistress Reeves surely knew God's ways better than I, I didn't think God wanted to punish me—after all, hadn't He put the men in the forest to help find me?

"I know there are tonics in the apothecary," Goody Ames told me. "I'm going to find something to relieve some of your pain."

I listened to tinkling glass as she rummaged through Pappa's carefully arranged bottles and jars in the apothecary shop. Eventually she returned with a brown bottle. I recognized it as one we had brought with us from England.

"I found the birch bark tonic," Goody Ames said. "You just need a good sip of it and the pain in your ankle shan't be as bad."

I grimaced and took a swig from the bottle. I swallowed the foul liquid and squirmed uncomfortably. I was thankful Goody Ames didn't know about the bottle of laudanum Mamma always kept under her bed or I would have been drinking that, I was sure. Mamma had brought it from England, too, but seldom had occasion to use it.

Goody Ames helped me to my feet and led me over to the chair next to the hearth. "Sit here," she insisted, turning to stoke the fire. "You can't go out looking for your mother again in this condition. We shall have to wait for news from the men. I found lavender in the shop. I am going to make you a lavender tisane to ease the pain in your head."

I sipped the hot tea Goody made for me and the three of us sat in the darkened room, the only light and sound coming from the low, crackling fire.

Before daybreak several men from the village trudged through the front door. I only needed to look at their faces to know they had not found Mamma. Pappa was not among their number. They were tired, hungry, and thirsty. Goody Ames and Mistress Reeves bustled about, ladling cider for the men and serving them the porridge that had been hanging in a kettle over the fire. Most of these men would spend the entire day working or helping Pappa search before being able to return to their beds for sleep.

There was little talk among the people in the house. The men chewed their food silently and quickly before heading back out again to continue searching until the break of day.

None of them met my eyes before leaving. I couldn't blame them.

Pappa came home much later, long after sunrise. Goody Ames had returned home to rouse her family and Mistress Reeves had left, too, after stoking the fire for me and milking both cows. Thankful for her help, I sent her home with a measure of molasses for the pastor's morning meal.

When Pappa came into the house, I hastened to fix him a hearty meal, despite the pain in my ankle. He sat at the table, alternately staring straight ahead and cradling his head in his hands, his fingers raking through his hair. I longed to assure him that Mamma would come home to us, but the words wouldn't come.

I put the porridge in front of him and he looked at it blankly. He lifted the spoon to his mouth and put it down again without touching the food.

"Pappa, you must eat," I said gently.

He pushed himself back from the table. "I can't."

"Would you like some salt pork?"

He shook his head. "I don't want anything to eat."

"Please? You must eat something."

He sighed. "All right, Sarah. If it will make you happy I will eat a bit of salt pork. I will not be going into the fields today. I'm going out again to look for her. If anyone comes needing any remedies from the apothecary, will you help them?"

"Of course."

He left shortly and came back again after nightfall. Some of the men from nearby farms were able to help him search during the day since they didn't have as many chores to do now that winter was coming. None of the men saw so much as a single sign of her.

Pappa looked at me with arched eyebrows when I served him supper. "Are you limping?"

I nodded. "It's nothing. I turned my ankle." Because of my skirts, he couldn't see the bandage still wrapped tightly around the lower part of my leg. I was glad—I didn't want him worrying about me, too.

That night, under the counterpanes Mamma and Grand-mamma had made, I tried to sleep but tossed and turned most of the night. I could hear Pappa moving around the main room, too. I stayed as silent as I could, listening for Mamma's step, but it never came.

Over the next several days, Pappa searched for Mamma from before dawn until after dark. Men from Town and other farms helped every day, but their numbers dwindled as the time dragged by. Goody Ames and Mistress Reeves, along with other women from the village, visited me every day. I didn't want them there. They thought I needed help with chores, but I wanted to do the work by myself.

Finally one evening Pappa sat down heavily in his chair after a long, cold day spent searching outdoors in vain.

"Sarah, she's not coming home."

We never found a trace of Mamma's body, and Pappa and I were convinced that she had been killed by a wolf, perhaps by the very same one that had chased me that first night she went missing.

I've hated wolves ever since.

GET EXCLUSIVE NEWS FROM AMY M. READE

Please visit https://www.amymreade.com/newsletter to sign up to receive monthly news, updates, promotions, contests, and recipes.

ABOUT THE AUTHOR

Amy M. Reade is a cook, chauffeur, household CEO, doctor, laundress, maid, psychiatrist, warden, seer, teacher, and pet whisperer. In other words, a wife, mother, community volunteer, and recovering attorney.

She's also the *USA Today* and *Wall Street Journal* bestselling author of the Juniper Junction Holiday Mystery series, The Libraries of the World Mystery Series, The Malice Series, and three standalone books. She lives in southern New Jersey, but loves to travel. Her favorite places to visit are Scotland and Hawaii and when she can't travel she loves to read books set in far-flung locations. She wishes she had a green thumb.

Made in the USA
Coppell, TX
30 January 2022

72658270R00204